Everything you ~~could want to know~~
—and more—
about

WORLD'S MOST ELIGIBLE BACHELOR

Symon Cope

Occupation: "Well, I'm a rancher with a heck of a spread in Montana. But I like to think of myself as an adventurer."

Most Frustrating Experience: "Being stuck on my ranch with tempting Miss Brooks. That hot-tempered, sweet-looking little lady is enough to make this billionaire cowboy forget he's a gentleman."

Most Exciting Moment: "The day I discovered the only way to win an argument with that gal was to kiss her..."

Marriage Vow: "A spirited bride is what a man like me needs. Kind of like Pamela Brooks. Not that I'm in the market for a wife. But if I was, I know that feisty beauty and I would have some kind of wedding night!"

Dear Reader,

We are thrilled to bring you another original love story in the WORLD'S MOST ELIGIBLE BACHELORS series. Each of these twelve brand-new novels centers around one of the most sought-after single men on the planet and the lone lady who snares the incredibly wealthy, world-class bachelor. Talk about winning the love lottery!

You're sure to be delighted by these sensual, heartwarming stories. These books capture the intimate lives of the larger-than-life men named each month by the fictitious *Prominence Magazine* as a World's Most Eligible Bachelor. And we've enlisted the genre's most gifted, highly acclaimed authors to tell their gripping stories.

An average, everyday, run-of-the-mill millionaire just wasn't man enough for supertalented author Jackie Merritt. She had to create *Big Sky Billionaire* playboy Symon Cope, a rich adventure seeker used to indulging his every whim. Then Sy gets stuck on his family's gigantic cattle ranch with a no-nonsense lady. And his bachelorhood whims turn to wishes of...matrimony.

Don't miss next month's exotic hero in beloved author Tracy Sinclair's *The Seductive Sheik*. This tall, dark and deeply passionate male shares his palace bed with an American beauty. Will he offer her a permanent place on his throne?

Until next month, here's to romance wishes and bachelor kisses!

The Editors

Please address questions and book requests to:
Silhouette Reader Service
U.S.: 3010 Walden Ave., P.O. Box 1325, Buffalo, NY 14269
Canadian: P.O. Box 609, Fort Erie, Ont. L2A 5X3

World's Most
Eligible Bachelors

Jackie
Merritt

Big Sky
Billionaire

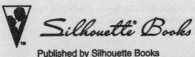

Silhouette Books

Published by Silhouette Books

America's Publisher of Contemporary Romance

If you purchased this book without a cover you should be aware that this book is stolen property. It was reported as "unsold and destroyed" to the publisher, and neither the author nor the publisher has received any payment for this "stripped book."

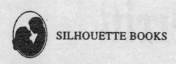

SILHOUETTE BOOKS

ISBN 0-373-65022-1

BIG SKY BILLIONAIRE

Copyright © 1998 by C.J. Books, Inc.

All rights reserved. Except for use in any review, the reproduction or utilization of this work in whole or in part in any form by any electronic, mechanical or other means, now known or hereafter invented, including xerography, photocopying and recording, or in any information storage or retrieval system, is forbidden without the written permission of the editorial office, Silhouette Books, 300 East 42nd Street, New York, NY 10017 U.S.A.

All characters in this book have no existence outside the imagination of the author and have no relation whatsoever to anyone bearing the same name or names. They are not even distantly inspired by any individual known or unknown to the author, and all incidents are pure invention.

This edition published by arrangement with Harlequin Books S.A.

® and TM are trademarks of Harlequin Books S.A., used under license. Trademarks indicated with ® are registered in the United States Patent and Trademark Office, the Canadian Trade Marks Office and in other countries.

Printed in U.S.A.

A Conversation with...
Top-selling author
JACKIE MERRITT

What hero have you created for WORLD'S MOST ELIGIBLE BACHELORS, and how has he earned the coveted title?

JM: Symon "Sy" Cope was named a World's Most Eligible Bachelor because of his desire to try everything at least once. He's flown airplanes—and jumped out of them—hang glided, climbed mountains, raced cars and boats. But an injury has this Big Sky billionaire in need of the heroine's tender, loving care.

What kind of heroine did you create to snag your WORLD'S MOST ELIGIBLE BACHELOR?

JM: Only a strong woman could deal with a man of Sy Cope's nature. Pamela Brooks, physical therapist, makes Sy well again in spite of himself. She is consistently upbeat regardless of his intermittent dark moods. Sy not only comes to admire Pam and her unflagging determination, but he falls in love with her.

What about WORLD'S MOST ELIGIBLE BACHELORS appealed to you? And what other recent titles do you have out?

JM: The series is appealing because only extremely interesting men would ever attain such a title. I was asked to write about a rancher, and Sy, of course, returns to his beautiful Montana ranch to recuperate after his accident.

THE BENNING LEGACY, a series about three sisters, was out in 1998. Titles include: *For the Love of Sam* (6/98 Silhouette Special Edition); *A Montana Man* (8/98 Silhouette Desire); and *The Secret Daughter* (12/98 Silhouette Special Edition).

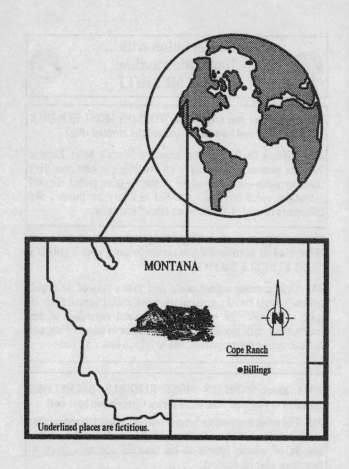

MONTANA

N

Cope Ranch

•Billings

Underlined places are fictitious.

Prologue

Dr. Charles Donnelly stood at the open door of his private office, located almost dead-center within the perimeters of his medical quarters. He was smiling warmly.

"Good morning, Mrs. Cope. Please come in."

The elderly lady smiled brightly as she entered the room. "Good morning, Doctor. Thank you for seeing me."

Dr. Donnelly shut the door. "You're very welcome. Please sit down."

Roberta Pierce Cope settled herself into a chair at the front of a large desk, and Dr. Donnelly took his own chair behind the desk. He was not Mrs. Cope's physician, but he had met with her several times in the past three months, due to his caring for her grandson, Symon Cope. She was here to discuss Symon, of course. He'd guessed that when he realized her name was on his appointment agenda for the day.

He spoke congenially. "Mrs. Cope, I assume some questions have arisen about Symon's progress?"

"Symon is uppermost in my mind these days, Doctor, but I'm not here to take up your time with a lot of questions for which I already know the answers. No, it's something else—an idea—that brought me here today. Before I get to it, however, I'm going to ask you to please start calling me Miss Bertie, as everyone else I know does."

There was a twinkle in the lady's bright blue eyes that

Dr. Donnelly admired. He couldn't help grinning. "Miss Bertie it is."

Miss Bertie smiled indulgently. "I realize it's a rather childish nickname, but that's because I was a very young child when my parents began using it. I grew up with it, Doctor, and when I married Jacob Cope over fifty years ago, he liked it and never called me anything else. So you see, childish or not, Miss Bertie is who I am."

"Yes, ma'am." Dr. Donnelly was in his forties and estimated, quite accurately, that Miss Bertie was past seventy. She was a little bit of a woman, beautifully dressed, her white hair perfectly coiffed, with an air of dignity that somehow melded with that merry twinkle in her eyes. He didn't doubt, even a little, that Miss Bertie Cope was above average in intelligence or that she possessed a marvelous— perhaps even a mischievous—sense of humor.

Bottom line: he liked her and was genuinely interested in the "idea" she was here to pass on to him. Obviously it had something to do with Symon, her only living relative. This was information that Symon had given him, not Miss Bertie. *The Cope family consists of only two members, Doctor, my grandmother and myself. My parents died two years apart when I was in my early twenties.*

Dr. Donnelly knew other things about the Cope family. Their roots were buried very deeply in a ten-thousand-acre cattle ranch about thirty miles from Billings, Montana, which was where he lived and practiced medicine. He'd heard that the ranch had been in the family for four generations, and that the Copes were very well-off financially.

Then there was that publicity about Symon a while back. *Prominence Magazine* had named him as one of the world's most eligible bachelors. The article had cited Symon's many athletic feats and now he was seriously disabled. Physical infirmity for a man of Symon's nature had to be even more difficult than it was for people who had always lived a quiet, passive existence.

Realizing that he was letting his thoughts wander, Dr. Donnelly leaned forward. "Tell me about your idea, Miss Bertie. I'm sure it has something to do with Symon."

"It has *everything* to do with Symon," she responded pertly. "Dr. Donnelly, are you satisfied with his progress?"

He could be nothing but honest with this straightforward little lady. "No, ma'am, I'm not. Symon should be much further along in his recovery than he is."

Miss Bertie nodded. "My opinion, exactly. He's depressed, despondent and feeling sorry for himself. He is never going to recover completely as long as he's in that frame of mind. Don't you agree?"

Dr. Donnelly hesitated. Miss Bertie's description of her grandson's state of mind was completely accurate, but did he agree with her prognosis? Besides, ethically speaking, he really shouldn't be discussing a patient with another party, even if it was that patient's concerned grandmother. He spoke slowly. "Let's talk about that idea of yours."

Miss Bertie nodded. "Yes, let's do that. It occurred to me the other evening that Symon lives entirely with men."

Dr. Donnelly blinked. "And?" he said, mystified as to where Miss Bertie might be leading him.

"I moved to town years ago, Doctor. Symon was rarely around, although between you, me and the fence post, the ranch was where he should have been instead of traipsing all over the world climbing mountains and racing cars." Miss Bertie pursed her lips for a moment. "I never approved of his life-style, you know. Do you realize that he was flying airplanes at fourteen years of age? Jumping out of them, too. His parents, my son and his wife, may they rest in peace, never once said no to any of Symon's whims. The more dangerous the sport, the more Symon seemed to love it. Oh, no, I never quite approved of the way Thomas and Corinne brought up their son, and I told them so on several occasions. Of course, they paid me very little mind. He was *their* son, after all, and they always seemed inordinately proud of his adventurous spirit.

"Where Symon got it from, I'll never know. His grandfather and father were as steady as they come, totally contented to stay home and work the ranch. What's strange, Doctor, is that now that Symon *can't* wander the globe or risk his neck doing all of those dangerous things he loved so much, I truly cannot bear his unhappiness." Miss Bertie sighed. "Sometimes I simply do not understand myself."

"*I* understand that you love your grandson, Miss Bertie," Dr. Donnelly said quietly. "His skiing accident and resulting injuries must have been hard on you."

"Doctor, I'm an old lady. It's not myself I'm worried about. I want to see Symon happy again."

"Miss Bertie, Symon's legs and back will probably never again be strong enough for him to do any mountain climbing. *Can* he be happy under those circumstances?"

Miss Bertie sat up straighter. "I believe he can. He would have to adjust to a calmer life-style, of course, and that's where my idea comes in. As I said before, Symon is living with men. Even the cook on the ranch is a man. There's a man keeping the house and another tending the grounds, and of course, all of the ranch hands are men. Doctor, his live-in physical therapist is a man."

Dr. Donnelly frowned slightly. "I seem to be missing your point, Miss Bertie."

"Well, goodness, it's perfectly obvious. Symon has always enjoyed female companionship, and since going home from the hospital, he hasn't even *seen* a female, other than me. Dr. Donnelly, you must be familiar with all the therapists in the area, and some of them must be women. What

I'd like you to do is to recall his current therapist and replace him with a woman. An attractive woman, Doctor. She has to be capable, of course—Symon does need the treatments. She should also be intelligent and strong-minded. Symon is not easy to deal with in his present state, and she should be the sort of woman to put him in his place whenever necessary.''

There was an almost shocked expression on Dr. Donnelly's face, and Miss Bertie laughed. "Goodness, Doctor, I'm not requesting a woman of low moral fiber. But I would bet the ranch that a pretty face would perk up Symon's spirit. I honestly can't think of anything else that might do it. It's at least worth a try, don't you think?''

Dr. Donnelly sat back in his chair to think it over. Symon wasn't making the progress he should be making. His present therapist was a well-trained, experienced man. In truth, Donnelly hadn't once considered sending a woman to the Cope ranch. He had always used male therapists for male patients, and female therapists for female patients. It was his opinion that people in need of therapy were more comfortable with members of their own sex, inasmuch as there was a great deal of intimacy involved in the treatments.

But in this case, Miss Bertie could be right. Symon was a young man, and it wasn't natural for a man his age to never even see a woman.

Miss Bertie sat quite still and watched Dr. Donnelly. It was obvious he was trying to align his thoughts with hers, and it pleased her that he would do that. At least he wasn't so set in his ways that he wouldn't consider an unusual form of treatment for a patient.

"I believe that emotional therapy is as important as physical," she said quietly. "I do not expect any great romance to develop or anything like that, Doctor, but I do believe, quite strongly, that just having an attractive woman on the place would alter Symon's attitude. Right now there is not one single reason for him to care about his appearance. Sometimes when I drive out and visit him, he hasn't even shaved. Knowing my grandson as I do, I am positive the presence of a pretty woman would, at the very least, remind him that he's a man. You do get my drift, don't you?''

Dr. Donnelly cleared his throat. ''Yes, I think I do. There is one young woman I could talk to about this. She's an excellent therapist and highly intelligent. Now, whether or not she would be interested in this job, I couldn't say. I would have to be up-front and honest with her, of course.''

''Why?'' Miss Bertie asked bluntly. ''Why would she have to know more than Symon's medical record? Goodness, let her form her own opinions about Symon. If she's as intelligent as you say, she will figure out the situation in no time. Perhaps they would become friends, and I really do believe a female friend is exactly what Symon needs right now.''

''Surely he *has* female friends. Don't any of them visit him at the ranch?''

''Not that I know of. You see, Doctor, Symon has changed so much since the accident that I'm not sure he would even welcome a female visitor.''

''Then how do you think he would react to a female therapist?''

''Badly,'' Miss Bertie said in quick response. ''But I'm sure you could get around any objections he might raise.''

''What you're really suggesting is a conspiracy,'' Dr. Donnelly said with a frown.

Miss Bertie smiled. ''That's exactly what I'm suggesting. You see, Doctor, I would do almost anything to have Symon well and happy again. Will you help me?''

Still frowning, Dr. Donnelly tugged at his left ear. Miss Bertie could tell how hard he was thinking, undoubtedly attempting to balance personal ethics with his professional desire to bring Symon to full recovery.

She sat perfectly still and let him do his thinking. He got up, walked around the room, sat down again and doodled on a pad. Finally, he spoke.

"All right, we'll give it a try. Bear in mind, however, that Symon is my patient. You are expecting—or hoping for—a positive result from this idea. Should I see the opposite occurring, Miss Bertie, I will do what I think best without consulting you. Symon must come first."

"I couldn't agree more. I realize my idea might fall flat, but I do believe it's worth trying." Miss Bertie got to her feet. "Thank you for your time. Good day, Doctor."

She left the office wearing a beaming smile. Whether Dr. Donnelly knew it or not, *she* knew she was on the right track.

One

The Cope ranch house was delightfully reminiscent of another era. The main section had two stories comprised of bedrooms, sitting rooms and a library-den. A one-story wing contained the kitchen and dining rooms of various sizes and uses. The house sat on a rise and overlooked a branch of the Whitehorn River and miles of verdant fields. The entire valley was surrounded by distant mountains that changed colors as the sun moved from one horizon to the other throughout the day. There was not another ranch in sight; everything Symon Jacob Cope could see as he sat in the sunroom at the front of the house—ground level—was part of the Cope ranch.

This was his favorite room and where he spent most of his time these days. Walls of windows provided unobstructed views in three directions. During hot weather the windows were removed and stored, allowing a pleasant, cooling breeze to drift through the screens. Sy felt it now, on this Monday morning, as he awaited the return of Jerry O'Conner, the physical therapist who had been treating him since his release from the hospital. Jerry took weekends off, leaving on Friday evenings and returning on Monday mornings. He should be coming along any moment now.

Sy turned his gaze from the long, meandering driveway to the serene splendor of burbling river and open fields. Cattle grazed in their usual lazy manner, and farther out,

Sy spotted a small herd of antelope, which also availed themselves of the lush grass in the valley.

Sy was particularly despondent this morning. The weekend had dragged. Not that he and Jerry had become great friends, or that Sy enjoyed the therapy Jerry administered. But life had become a boring routine, and without Jerry around, there weren't even discomfiting treatments to take up the time. Sy knew he should work up some interest in the operation of the ranch, but the foreman, Hoke Brenner, was as efficient as they came, and Sy found the whole thing stifling. It wasn't because he disliked his home. He'd been born in this very house and had nothing but fond memories of growing up here. But the ranch had never been enough. From the time he could remember, he'd been all but consumed with inner fires to explore the rest of the world, to see places, people and things with his own eyes, to stretch his abilities to the limit and to try everything at least once. It was depressing to remember the almost constant excitement that had pounded through his veins and to realize that now he felt only ennui and frustration.

He heaved a woebegone sigh and glanced at the driveway again. From this room he could see nothing of the working portion of the ranch, other than those cattle in the fields across the river. The barns, sheds, corrals and such were behind the house, with a good half acre of lawn in between. It didn't amuse or entertain him to see men on horseback, anyhow, men with strong backs and legs, and this undoubtedly influenced his affection for the sunroom. If he was hiding in there, so be it; if anyone had a right to privacy, it was him. Besides, he really didn't give a damn what anyone might think of his behavior. After all, *he* was the one who could barely get around on crutches and often had to rely on an accursed wheelchair, not anyone else on the ranch. He was, in fact, sitting in the damned contraption now.

To his right was a low table upon which resided a pitcher of water, a carafe of orange juice, several clean glasses and a bottle of pain pills. Oh, yes, there was also a stack of the latest magazines and some newspapers. He had absolutely no desire to read anything, but Calvin Lowe, the man who kept the house in good order, couldn't seem to get that fact through his head, and wherever Sy found himself, reading material was always close at hand.

For a moment Sy eyed the bottle of pills. His legs and back were aching unmercifully, but he detested the woozy feeling the medication caused in his head, and he avoided taking anything unless the pain became unbearable.

He ran all ten fingers through his thick dark hair, pushing it back from his face. It hadn't been cut since the accident and was down to his shoulders, much too long and unruly, but it wasn't something he worried about. Rarely even thought about, to be factual. When he did, it was with a hostile attitude. So his hair was long. So what? So he didn't shave every day. Was *that* anyone's business? No way, he always answered himself with an embittered twist of his lips. No damned way. There was little doubt in his mind about the personality changes he'd undergone since his injuries, and he felt that every one of them was completely justified.

The sound of an approaching vehicle brought his head around. He winced. Sometimes the simplest movement caused pain to skitter up and down his spine. His lips thinned grimly as he watched for Jerry's green van to round the curve in the driveway that would bring it into his line of vision.

But it wasn't a green van he saw, it was a cherry red, four-wheel-drive pickup truck, its paint gleaming in the sunlight like a freshly polished mirror. Sy's first thought was that Jerry had bought a new truck over the weekend, but as it got closer he could tell that a much smaller person than Jerry, who was over six feet tall, was behind the wheel. In fact, he realized in the next few moments, the driver was a woman!

His eyes narrowed speculatively. Who was dropping in at this early hour? Damn! The last thing he wanted was company.

Pamela Brooks parked next to several ranch vehicles and turned off the ignition. The house had her gaping. "Beautiful," she murmured while admiring the graceful lines and white stone siding of the building. The roof was black slate, and there were black shutters at each of the many windows, along with white wrought-iron railings along the second-floor porch, which ran the entire length of that section of the house. Pam had heard that the Copes were well-off, but she had never before seen a house quite like this one on a ranch.

Her career was physical therapy, and while she worked mostly for the Billings Therapy Center, at times she was called upon to administer treatment in a patient's home. Dr. Donnelly's request that she concentrate solely on one patient and even go so far as to move into his home for an unknown length of time was a first. She had wavered on an answer to that request for several days, during which time she had studied Symon Cope's medical records. His was a challenging case. By reputation Jerry O'Conner was an excellent therapist, and yet Mr. Cope was not advancing as rapidly as he should be. Pam had found herself wondering why. Or rather, why not?

Then she had read Jerry's daily reports of treatments and results, and those records had gnawed at her. Jerry's methods differed from hers, and something had told her that she could better deal with Symon Cope's particular problems than Jerry had been doing. That feeling was not caused by vanity, she was positive, as she did not believe that her abilities superseded Jerry's. But physical therapy was not a definitive art; every therapist she knew had his or her own techniques and routines. Her honest feeling was that her techniques would benefit Mr. Cope better than Jerry's technique had.

Thus, she had told Dr. Donnelly she would take the case, and here she was.

She pulled down the visor to check herself in the mirror, looked into her own green eyes for a moment, then tucked straying strands of sun-streaked blond hair back behind her ears. She had straight, shoulder-length hair and preferred to wear it off her face when working. Her makeup was sparse—a touch of eye shadow, a bit of blusher and a lightly applied lip gloss.

Did she look all right? There was a sliver of anxiety connected to that question, which ordinarily would not have occurred to her before meeting a new patient. But she knew all about Symon Cope having been named one of the world's most eligible bachelors by *Prominence Magazine*. The whole area had buzzed about it for weeks about six months back, and her interest had been so piqued that she'd gone out and bought the magazine for herself. Pam had never met anyone who'd even been mentioned in an international publication, and she just couldn't help being curious about a man who would attain such an unusual status.

Still, Mr. Cope's private affairs were none of her business. Lifting her chin in a show of professional detachment and pushing the visor up, she reached for the leather pouch in which she always carried pertinent copies of her current patient's medical records. There were other bags in the cab—her personal luggage—but she would bring those in later. Her first order of business was to meet Symon Cope.

In the sunroom Sy was wondering, rather grouchily, what in hell was taking that woman, whoever she was, so long to get out of her shiny red truck and show herself. There, he thought, she's getting out now. He frowned, because she wasn't at all familiar. She was small—no more than five foot two—and dressed in plain white slacks and blouse. He couldn't tell if her hair was long or short from this distance, and he thought for a moment about preferring long hair on women, long, flowing manes that a man could get lost in, and colorful, dramatic clothing. Noticing the large leather bag in her hand, he rolled his eyes. A saleswoman.

Well, Cal would get rid of her. Salespeople rarely got past Cal, and it was an even rarer event when they got to see Sy. Turning his head, putting the strange saleswoman out of his mind, Sy filled a glass from the pitcher of water on the table and took a drink. Holding the glass, he stared broodingly at the broad vista of river and green fields. A picture formed in his mind. He was at the open door of a small plane, harnessed into a parachute, awaiting a signal that the plane had reached the altitude he'd requested for his jump. The adrenaline rush was incredible. Every cell in his body was alert, ready and eager for the thrill of a long free fall, and then the lurch and thrust when he opened the chute.

"Good morning, Mr. Cope," a female voice sang out brightly.

The image of himself preparing for a jump dissolved like dust in a whirlwind. Annoyed, Sy turned his face to the door of the room. It was her, the saleslady, and she hadn't waited for an invitation to come in, either. She was already in and making herself comfortable on a chair not far from him! She placed the bulging leather case at her feet and smiled. He didn't smile back, but his black countenance didn't seem to daunt her.

"I'm Pamela Brooks, your new therapist," she said cheerfully. "I prefer Pam, though, just as Cal told me that you prefer to be called Sy or S.J., with your permission, of course. Cal's a very congenial man, isn't he?"

Sy's expression had remained cold and forbidding throughout her little speech. "Cal!" he roared, startling Pam.

Cal, who was a smallish man of fifty-six years, appeared almost at once. "What is it, Sy?" he asked in his usual mild-mannered way. "Do you need something?"

"What's this woman doing in here?" Sy snapped.

"She's got the credentials, Sy, I checked them. She's taking Jerry's place as your therapist."

Sy glared at Pam, who merely sent him another bubbly smile. "Like hell she is," Sy said through gritted teeth. "Bring me the phone, Cal."

"If you're planning to call Dr. Donnelly, let me assure you that he will only verify what Cal and I just told you," Pam said. She already felt that Cal could easily become a friend. Sy Cope was another matter.

Cal brought a portable phone over to Sy. "Here you go," he commented, placing the instrument in Sy's hand.

"Besides," Pam continued, "it's early, and Dr. Donnelly always spends this time of day at the hospital."

"I know his routine—probably better than you do," Sy said sharply. He punched a series of numbers into the phone. "I'm calling for Dr. Donnelly," he said brusquely when the hospital receptionist answered. "This is Sy Cope, and I need to speak to him *now*. Tell him it's an emergency."

Pam's left eyebrow went up, and she had to swallow a

laugh. She was an "emergency" to Symon Cope? How droll.

Cal had vanished, so it was just she and Sy waiting for Dr. Donnelly to come on the line. Pam used the time to look around. Pleasant room, she thought. Incredible views and a nice breeze coming in. Comfortable furniture, oodles of green plants. Yes, definitely a pleasant room.

"Doctor, there's a woman here..." Sy looked at Pam and growled, "What'd you say your name was?"

"Pam Brooks."

"Her name is Pam Brooks, and she said that she's replacing Jerry as my therapist. I won't have it, Doctor. There's not another woman on this ranch, and I sure as hell don't want the one exception to be my physical therapist."

Pam could tell that her new patient was feeling frustrated and angry. Obviously Dr. Donnelly was doing quite a lot of talking, and however many "buts" Symon interjected, the good doctor kept *on* talking. Pam tried to appear uninterested in the conversation by looking everywhere but at Sy. She pretty much knew what he was hearing since Dr. Donnelly had warned her that Symon Cope would most likely object to her taking Jerry's place, but Donnelly had also told her that he would handle it. She wasn't the least bit concerned about the outcome of the phone call and, in fact, reached into her pouch for a clipboard of papers and a pen, preparing herself for when the call was over.

Then she heard Sy bark rather sarcastically, "Suppose you tell me why Jerry needed replacing?" She could no longer stop herself from studying Sy Cope. He wasn't paying her any mind, anyhow, and she really did want to get a good look at him.

His hair was brushing his shoulders, which she didn't find at all unattractive. He had marvelous hair, in fact, thick and dark, with a slight wave. It did look as though it needed combing, however, and there was at least a two-day growth of whiskers on his face. Quite a handsome face, actually, she thought. Maybe unusually handsome was a better description. Rugged, slightly uneven features. Strong features, she decided, noticing the faint cleft in his squared-off chin and his heavy dark eyebrows.

He didn't look ill, she realized, admiring his very broad shoulders, but then illness wasn't his problem: he was recovering, or trying to recover, from physical injuries. He was dressed in worn jeans, a red-and-blue plaid shirt and house slippers. She'd worked with many people who used wheelchairs, so Sy using one couldn't possibly throw her. But her heart had reached out to the infirm since childhood, which was undoubtedly the primary reason she'd chosen physical therapy as her profession. At any rate, she didn't like seeing Sy in that chair and made a vow to herself to get him out of it. Reputedly he'd been a vital, active man before his skiing accident and she was going to see to it that he was again. She was suddenly very glad that she had accepted this assignment.

"Well, I still don't like it!" Sy punched the button that disconnected the call and threw the phone across the room. It landed on the flagstone floor and shattered into a half-dozen pieces.

Pam stared at it for a few moments, then asked calmly, "Did smashing that telephone make you feel better?"

Sy's furious blue eyes jerked to her. "It's my phone and my house. I'll smash any damned thing I want to smash. Get it?"

"What I get, Sy, is that when something doesn't go your way, you blow up. Now, I really couldn't care less if you destroyed the entire house in a fit of anger." Pam's gaze moved around the room. "Although destroying anything so beautiful seems shameful to me," she added. "But, as you

said, it's your house and you can do with it what you want.
However, it seems to me that channeling all of that angry
energy into a passion for getting well would be far more
beneficial than bringing down the roof, so to speak." She
smiled sweetly. "Would it be imposing too much on what
little good nature you have left if I asked what Dr. Donnelly
told you about my being here?"

"You know damned well what he told me." Sy's expression was so sour it could have curdled milk.

"Did he say I was the only live-in therapist available at
the present?"

"That was his story, which I find pretty damned hard to
believe. And he never did give me a straight answer about
what happened to Jerry." Sy eyed her suspiciously. "Do
you know?"

Pam shrugged. "I would imagine he's been assigned to
another case, but I'm only guessing. Dr. Donnelly didn't
discuss Jerry when he talked to me about coming out here."

"Well, why would he pull Jerry off *my* case and assign
him to another?"

"I wouldn't know." It was the truth; she honestly didn't
know why Jerry was out and she was in. Actually, she
hadn't been curious about it and still wasn't. Jerry could
have requested reassignment so he could stay in town, or
he simply could have asked for some time off. The possi-
bilities were endless and of no interest to her. She could
tell that she had her work cut out for her with Symon Cope,
and she wanted to get started. "Let's forget Jerry for the
time being. I have some questions for you." She poised
her pen to write on the top sheet of paper in her clipboard.

"What kind of questions?" Sy snarled.

"An eight-year-old could answer them. I'm sure you'll
manage."

"Let's get something straight right now. I don't want

you here and you're not going to get one ounce of cooperation out of me. It's for damned sure that I'm not going to answer a bunch of stupid questions that I've probably answered fifteen times before. Have I made myself clear?''

Pam had run into angry patients before. Some people simply could not accept disability of any kind and struck out at anyone within earshot. Obviously Symon Cope was in that category, and she had learned through the years that permitting a patient to get and hold the upper hand was a bad mistake. She had to immediately establish her position with this man, to convey the fact that she would not be trod upon by bad humor and temper tantrums.

She spoke evenly. "When you get really mad, do you throw yourself on the floor and kick your feet?"

Sy flushed. "Very funny."

Pam remained cool and unruffled. "I'm not trying to be funny. There's only one reason I'm here, to help you regain strength in your back and legs. I'm a very good therapist. I went to an excellent school and have five years' experience on the job. I've worked with people of all ages, and I'm proud of my success rate. I hope you're not objecting to my replacing Jerry because I'm a woman. No, you couldn't possibly be that petty. Not in this day and age. Why don't you explain why you *do* object to my taking Jerry's place?''

Sy stared at her while trying to come up with an answer that she hadn't already shot down. That was the moment he realized how pretty she was. He'd always enjoyed women, being with them, talking to them, making them laugh, and, of course, there'd been some that he'd found especially attractive. But he didn't have that particular feeling about Pamela Brooks, however pretty she was. What he felt was animosity toward her, anger. Her gall was astounding, and had she no pride? No sense of intrusion?

"If Donnelly won't get me another male therapist, I could always change doctors," he said gruffly.

"Yes, I suppose you could," Pam replied. "But are you sure you want to do that? Donnelly's the best doctor in the area for your type of injuries, and it isn't him you're objecting to, it's me. Look, if you really can't deal with a female therapist, I'll leave." It was a bluff and she was extremely interested in how he would react to it.

"Did I say I couldn't deal with a female therapist?" Sy growled.

Although she was relieved that he hadn't immediately told her to leave, Pam thought he sounded childishly petulant. "No, you didn't," she said. "But what else should I assume?"

Ignoring that question, he turned his head so he wouldn't be looking at her and muttered, "I can't imagine a woman your size doing what Jerry did."

"I don't intend to do what Jerry did. Oh, some of our methods overlap, don't misunderstand. But I have an entirely different program planned out for you."

Sy brought a frowning gaze back to her. "What do you mean by that? What kind of program?"

"Before we discuss specifics, am I staying or leaving?" Pam said bluntly. "Why waste your time and mine if the conclusion to this conversation is going to be my being booted out the door?"

Sy drawled wryly, "If I remember correctly, the last time we booted someone out the door around here was at least a year ago."

Pam laughed. "Then perhaps you're due?"

Sy knew his initial anger over Pamela's arrival had dissipated a great deal, which could be, he thought, due to her lively personality and ready smile. Obviously she knew how to deal with disgruntled patients, which oddly irritated

him. Her bubbly personality irritated him. Her pretty face
irritated him, and the idea of her administering therapy to
him gave him cold chills. Hell, he'd been half-naked during
Jerry's treatments. Would she expect the same?

He cleared his throat, realized he was still holding the
glass of water and took a swallow. Then he set the glass
on the table and looked at Pam.

"There's a hell of a lot of intimacy involved with physical therapy," he growled, and then proved that the topic
embarrassed him by flushing.

"Some, yes," Pam agreed. She looked directly into his
vivid blue eyes and grinned. "I guess you'll have to trust
me on this, because there's no way of proving it before-
hand. But believe me, Sy, there is nothing personal or sexual in my interest in your body. Your virtue will not be
under siege, I guarantee it."

His flush became almost fluorescent. "You don't beat
around the bush, do you?"

"I do believe we're beginning to understand each
other." Pam picked up her pen again. "Let's get these
questions out of the way, okay? Oh, I guess you haven't
said whether I'm staying or leaving, have you? Which is
it, Sy?"

Complete silence was all there was for several long moments. Pam sat perfectly still and kept her gaze on Sy,
awaiting his deliberation. His lips thinned, a muscle jerked
spasmodically in his jaw, his hands clenched the arms of
the wheelchair, and finally he spoke.

"You can stay on a trial basis. If it doesn't work out,
and I'll be the one to make that decision, I'll expect you
to leave without a long debate."

"Agreed," she said quickly, before he could change his
mind. "Now, question number one is…"

Two

Cal introduced Pam to Joe Pickett, the cook, then showed
her through the rooms on the first floor. No one had told
her the house had an elevator, and she supposed Cal used
it so that she would know how Sy was moving from floor
to floor. It was a nice surprise, because while inspecting
the first floor and realizing that all of the bedrooms had to
be on the second, she had wondered how Sy was managing
to ascend and descend the high, curving staircase in the
large, marble-floored foyer.

"It's a hydraulic lift, ma'am," Cal told her as they entered the elevator. "It was put in when Sy's mother became
ill. That was seven or eight years ago." The small man
looked thoughtful. "Or was it nine or ten years? Let me
see now. Mrs. Cope passed away first—she had cancer—
then about two years later, Mr. Cope was struck down with
heart failure."

The elevator moved at a snail's pace, but it was large
enough to accommodate a wheelchair, which, apparently,
had been its primary purpose. Probably no one in the Cope
family had ever imagined Sy needing it.

Cal seemed to have no qualms in relating information,
so Pam didn't hesitate to ask for some. "Does Sy have any
brothers or sisters?"

"No, ma'am. There's only one other Cope and that's
Miss Bertie. She's Sy's paternal grandmother. Getting up
there in years, she is, but still spry as a spring chicken.

You'll be meeting her, I'm sure. She drives out here about once a week. Real nice lady, she is. Never forgets Joe's or my birthday. Anyhow, it's just Miss Bertie and Sy now. Been that way for seven or eight years.'' Cal frowned. ''Or was it nine or ten years?''

Pam smiled at the amiable little man, and his countenance cleared. The elevator came to a halt and Cal opened the door. ''Here we are. There are six bedrooms up here, and each one of 'em has a private bathroom. Sy's using one bedroom, of course, one was converted into a therapy room, and the one Jerry was using needs fresh linen and things. You can take your pick of the other three.''

''Thank you, Cal.''

''I'm going to bring in your luggage while you look around and decide.''

''That's very nice of you. Thank you.'' Something occurred to her. ''Cal, where do you and Joe stay?''

''We each have a room in the bunkhouse. Sandy, too.''

''Sandy?''

''He's the yardman.''

''I see. And, of course, there are ranch hands.''

''About a dozen, ma'am. The ones who stay on the ranch full-time have rooms in the bunkhouse.''

''Cal, please call me Pam. I have a question. From what you've told me, everyone sleeps in the bunkhouse, and since Jerry was gone every weekend, should I assume that Sy has been alone in the house on those nights?''

Cal looked a bit sheepish. ''He thinks he was, Pam, but I just couldn't leave him alone. I've been sleeping on the sofa in the library on weekends. He had a nurse when he first got home from the hospital, but he fired her before the week was up. Said he couldn't stand her hovering over him and watching every move he made.''

Pam already knew about the nurse problem, and that Sy

had taken a stubborn stand on that issue. She touched Cal's hand. "It looks to me as though Sy has a very good friend in you, Cal Lowe," she said softly.

An endearing pink color appeared in the older man's cheeks. "I been with the Copes for a long time, miss," Cal said earnestly. "Watched Sy grow up, in fact. Me and the missus both."

"Oh?"

"Lost my sweet little wife four years ago," Cal said with misty eyes. "Angela—that was her name—was the housekeeper for a good long spell. I did the yard work then and helped Angela with the heavy stuff—the windows and things, you know? Anyway, when she passed on, I decided that no one knew this house any better than me, so I talked to Miss Bertie about my taking Angela's job. Miss Bertie was real happy with the idea, so we took on Sandy as the yardman, and it all worked out real well."

"So Miss Bertie does the hiring for the ranch?"

"Well, you see, Sy wasn't around at the time," Cal mumbled, averting his eyes.

Pam could see that this particular subject made Cal uncomfortable, so she didn't pursue it. But it made her wonder who, exactly, was running the ranch, Miss Bertie or Sy.

She shaped a warm smile. "I'll look around up here, Cal. Thank you for the tour of the first floor."

Cal brightened. "I'll be bringing in your luggage now." He stepped back into the elevator and closed the door.

Pam began peering into bedrooms until she came to the one that had been transformed into a therapy room. There was a long, white-enameled table, an exercise floor mat, an exercise machine with pulleys and weights and a cupboard full of white cotton sheets, blankets and towels. There were also several pillows on a shelf. Another white-enameled table held several bottles and jars. Pam picked them up and read what they were, then dropped them into the wastebasket. She had her own oils and creams for massage; she would not be using those.

She deliberately chose the bedroom next to Sy's. In her opinion he should be sleeping within calling distance, should he need help in the night. As he became stronger, and she knew he would with the proper treatment, he would be able to attend to any need that might arise himself. But for the time being she wanted to be close at hand. Cal, bless his kindly heart, had realized without a dram of medical training that someone should be nearby at night; Jerry *should* have known. Her opinion of Jerry's methods were definitely changing, and not for the better.

Like all of the bedrooms, her room was spacious, high-ceilinged with crown molding, nicely furnished and bright with natural light coming in through two large windows. One thing struck her as delightful—the bedrooms on this side of the house each had a door that opened on to the second-floor porch. She assigned exploration of the porch to a future pleasure.

Instead, she sat on the bed, bounced a bit and found it wonderfully comfortable. Her private bathroom had a shower *and* a tub, oak cabinetry and strikingly beautiful ceramic tiles on the floor and halfway up the walls. She had never stayed in a hotel as nice as this, and once again she was struck with the beauty of this marvelous old house.

Cal came in with her suitcases and set them on the floor. "Here you are, Pam."

"Thank you, Cal. As I told Sy, I'm going to unpack, settle myself a little and then get to work with him."

"I sure hope you can help him, Pam."

"So do I, Cal. Believe me, I'm going to do everything humanly possible to get him well. At least everything within the realm of my training and experience."

* * *

Downstairs Sy sipped orange juice and stared unseeingly at the view. He was still in the sunroom, still in the wheelchair, and he wasn't at all happy. Pam Brooks had invaded the ranch like a little storm trooper, and for some reason that he couldn't quite put his finger on, he felt as though he were being railroaded. It was an undefined suspicion, but something was going on that no one would talk about, not Dr. Donnelly, not Pam. Sy suddenly realized that if he could talk to Jerry, he might learn what it was.

Eyeing the broken telephone on the floor, he grimaced. Throwing the phone had been a childish show of defiance. Pamela Brooks probably had a very low opinion of him, and why wouldn't she?

But was his opinion of her much better? Barging in here, acting as though she knew it all, asking him those ludicrous questions. What in hell difference did it make if he'd ever been injured before the skiing accident? What did a broken collarbone and a couple of broken arms in his youth have to do with his current condition?

Then she'd had the nerve to get personal. He was still embarrassed about some of the questions she'd dared to ask. Nosy damned woman. His bodily functions and ability to perform sexually were none of her business, and he'd told her so in no uncertain terms. Her placid smile over *that* butting of heads still rubbed him wrong. And what was it she'd so busily written down regarding his refusal to answer those particular questions?

Actually, it didn't matter. He was more ticked off at Dr. Donnelly than Pam, anyhow. It *was* possible to look at her coming out here as just doing her job. It was Donnelly who had assumed he would meekly accept a female therapist and sent her to the ranch, after all. Every time Sy thought of the doctor's unmitigated gall, he gritted his teeth.

Cal came in. "Are you hungry, Sy? I could have Joe fix

up a nice little snack to tide you over until lunch." Cal spotted the broken telephone on the flagstones and went over and picked up the pieces. "What happened to this?"

"I threw it."

"Oh. Well, do you want me to bring in another one?"

"Yes, and find Jerry's home phone number and bring it, too."

"All right. Do you want something to eat?"

"Yeah, something sweet. A piece of that chocolate cake Joe made yesterday."

"I'll be right back." Cal walked out with the shattered telephone. He and Pam arrived at the kitchen doorway at the same time, and she laughed. She had a pleasant laugh that sounded almost musical, Cal thought. He also thought it was kind of nice having a pretty young woman in the house.

"What happened to that phone?" Joe asked as Cal dropped the pieces into the trash compactor.

Pam was impressed with the size and convenient layout of the kitchen, and also the way it was equipped with the very best in appliances. She had merely glanced at it when meeting Joe earlier, so she took her time looking around now. Joe's question made her smile to herself, and she waited to see how Cal would answer it.

"It got broke," was all he said, making Pam wonder if he knew any more about it, or if he was one of those rare people who didn't carry tales.

"All by itself, I suppose," Joe said with some sarcasm.

Cal shrugged, as though the subject weren't worthy of conversation. "Sy would like a piece of cake. Should I get it, or do you want to?"

"You know I don't like anyone messing up my kitchen. I'll get it," Joe said grumpily.

Pam broke in, "Just a moment, Joe. Sy's diet is the reason I came in here. Has he been eating a lot of sweets?"

Cal and Joe looked at each other, and Pam could tell that they both thought she was overstepping her authority. In plain words, what business was it of hers what Sy ate?

Well, it *was* her business, she felt very strongly, and she might as well make her position on that point clear right now.

"Sy's diet is an essential part of my therapy program," she said. "I want him on a low-fat, high-fiber diet. Very few sweets, no more than one a day, whether that be a slice of cake or a small candy bar. Joe, what did he eat for breakfast?"

Joe frowned and looked reluctant to speak. Because of Pam's determined and unyielding expression, he finally mumbled, "Ham and eggs, and a couple of jelly doughnuts."

"I see." She pulled some folded papers from the pocket of her white pants. "I don't mean to cause you extra work, Joe, but I want Sy on this diet." She unfolded the papers and held them out to the cook. He took them, again displaying reluctance. "Let me summarize the most important data for you," she said. "One serving of meat a day. Red meat three times a week, the rest of the time either chicken or fish. Avoid gravy and creamed sauces. Lots of fresh vegetables—preferably steamed—and fresh fruit. His between-meal snacks should always be fruit or raw vegetables. A little white cheese is acceptable, if he's really hungry, and a few crackers."

She took in their doubtful, uncertain faces. Sy was expecting chocolate cake, and it was obvious that neither of them wanted to deliver fruit or chopped carrots instead.

"Let me show you what I mean," she said, and went over to the basket of apples, oranges and bananas on one of the counters. From it she selected a large red apple, which she washed at the sink and dried with a paper towel. Smiling at Joe, she asked for a plate and a knife. "And some white cheese, if you have it."

Quartering and coring the apple, she placed it on the plate with two modest cubes of cheese and three whole wheat crackers. "There," she exclaimed to both men, who were gaping at her as though she were several pickles short of a full barrel.

She didn't let it bother her. "I'm going to see Sy now, so I'll take this with me. See you both later." Stopping at the doorway, she turned. "Joe, if you would like help with Sy's lunch and dinner, just let me know." She walked out with the plate.

"S.J.'s not gonna like this," Joe predicted gloomily.

"Nope, he ain't," Cal agreed.

Pam made her way to the sunroom and strode in as though she were delivering pure gold. "Here's your snack," she said, setting the plate on the table next to Sy.

He looked at it, then at her. "I didn't ask for that."

"No, you asked for cake. From now on, your between-meal snacks will be fruit or raw vegetables." Pam seated herself in the same chair she had previously used. Before he could express the fury she saw developing in his eyes, she started talking very fast and without a break, so he couldn't jump in, explaining in great detail the importance of a nutritional diet in the process of regaining muscle strength.

When she finally had to slow down for a breath, Sy took advantage of the moment and snarled, "What in hell makes you think you can tell me what to eat?"

"What makes *you* think I can't? How badly do you want to get well? Maybe that's where we should start." Laying her hands on her knees, she leaned forward. "Why don't you tell me what recovery means to you? Are you content with the status quo? Do you *want* to remain a semi-invalid for the rest of your life? You could, you know, very easily. Sy, you have men in this house who await your every command and then jump to obey. That's well and good, and you're very fortunate to have such loyal people around you. But blind loyalty can be a two-edged sword. Even if Cal and Joe knew something you asked for was bad for your health, they would never tell you so. I, on the other hand, will never have that trouble. You can always count on complete honesty from me.''

"I don't find that particularly consoling."

"Not today you don't, but you will."

Sy glowered at her. "Do you know what you are? A royal pain in the butt!''

"What I am is your savior, you jerk!'' Pam got up and drew a calming breath. She was letting Sy's anger and resentment get to her, which was a startling deviation from her normal relationship with patients. Just because Sy Cope was a total jerk didn't mean she had to tell him so. "I apologize for that remark. Now, eat your snack, then come up to the therapy room. And please don't ask Cal or Joe to help you. I know you can maneuver your wheelchair from this room into the elevator.'' Spinning, she marched out.

Sy stared at the vacant doorway for several minutes, then called for Cal to bring him another portable telephone and Jerry's number. Cal appeared with the two items almost at once, and Sy immediately placed the call. He got an answering machine; Jerry wasn't at home.

Upstairs, Pam paced the therapy room. She'd lost her temper, which was inexcusable. It was not going to happen again, she swore, no matter how irritating Sy might get. She could say anything that needed saying without resorting to name-calling. What on earth had possessed her to lambaste a patient like that?

In the sunroom, Sy eyed the snack plate with a malicious gleam in his eyes. If he had not had food for a week and knew in his soul that that apple was the only thing between life and a slow, painful death by starvation, he would not eat it.

And this was only the first battle he was going to win with Pamela Brooks. Perversely curious about what sort of torture she had planned for him in the therapy room, he wheeled the chair to the elevator.

Pam heard it coming and stepped into the adjoining bathroom to scrub her hands. When Sy came in she was at the cupboard, taking out a sheet and a blanket. Holding both, she looked at him.

"Do you need help to get dressed and undressed?"

"I've been managing. Why?"

"I'd like you to undress down to your underwear. If you're modest, use this blanket as a cover-up." She placed the blanket on his lap and then smoothed the sheet over the table. Because Sy hadn't made a move toward getting undressed, she added, "I'll wait in the hall. Please let me know when you're ready."

"Ready for what?"

The dark expression on his face would have cowed most women. All it did to Pam was increase her determination. She put on her own stubborn face. "I'm going to make an examination of your back and legs."

"It's been done, sweetheart," Sy said disgustedly. "Too many times to count, and I'm sure every exam has been duly recorded on my chart. You won't find anything that hasn't been found before. Why don't you just read the chart and save us both the embarrassment?"

A peculiar sensation streaked through Pam's system. He

hadn't spoken the word *sweetheart* in an affectionate or flirtatious way; in fact, he'd colored it with sarcasm. And yet it made her aware of him as a man—an unusually attractive man—and reminded her of her own femaleness. More flustered than she cared to admit—if only to herself—she concealed it by turning her back to Sy and smoothing the sheet on the table again.

Her normal composure was quickly recovered, and she turned to face him once more. "Sy, no matter how many technicians, doctors or therapists have conducted examinations, I have to explore your injuries for myself. Please understand that I cannot rely on other people's opinions. I've studied your postaccident medical records until I practically know them by heart, but until I make a hands-on examination, I will not have an opinion of my own."

"If you don't have an opinion of my condition, how'd you come up with that program for recovery you mentioned? And still haven't explained, if you'd care to remember."

"It may have to be adjusted, but I won't know that until I check your back and legs. Once I've done that, I will explain everything, if you wish." Pam walked to the door. "Please cooperate. Believe me, your cooperation is very necessary and definitely in your best interest. Call me when you're ready," she repeated, and went into the hall.

She pulled the door closed behind her, leaving it slightly ajar. Then, leaning against a wall, she heaved a rather shaky sigh. In her entire career she had not had to deal with anyone with Sy Cope's dark and forbidding personality. Apparently he was going to fight her every step of the way, or at least until he started seeing some positive results.

But that wasn't the reason she felt a bit unsteady. Sy exuded maleness, and *she* was responding to it! It was a startling revelation, to say the least, and one more thing she had never had to deal with before in her job. She thought of how much time she and Sy would be spending together, and of the intimacy of the treatments she had in mind. She could not, under any circumstances, let her emotions strain a relationship that was already difficult enough.

Through the crack in the door she could hear movement and some grunts and groans. She frowned. Had she asked him to do too much on his own? Had he lied about managing to dress and undress by himself? Worrying about it, she was on the verge of finding Cal to help Sy when she heard, "Yo, the hall. You can come in now."

Drawing a deep breath and putting on her most professional face, she pushed the door open. Wrapped in the blanket so that his arms and shoulders were bare, Sy was sitting on the edge of the table. His clothes were piled on the wheelchair.

"I expect this is where you want me to be," he said flatly, and scowled at her.

"Good guess," she said brightly. She was going to be cheerful and upbeat if it killed her. "I'm going to wash my hands. Be right back." Again she soaped and scrubbed her hands at the bathroom sink, this time taking a look at herself in the mirror. The lip gloss she had applied early this morning was gone, which she had expected. Her hair was in place, though.

Sighing, she dried her hands on a paper towel. Worrying about how she looked was silly. Sy Cope didn't like her and probably wouldn't if she was a beauty queen. He simply did not want a female therapist, and it was up to her to get past that outdated attitude.

Briskly returning to the therapy room, she approached Sy. "I need you to lie on your stomach." She couldn't decipher his expression, other than its unfriendliness. Without a word he began turning around so that he could lie facedown. Beads of perspiration popped out on his forehead and a white line encircled his thinly set lips.

"You're in pain!" Pam cried, and taking him by the shoulders, she brought him back to a sitting position. "Why didn't you say something? When did you last take your pain medication?" He had to be due, she reasoned. He was feeling far too much pain to have just taken his prescribed dose.

"Last night."

Her green eyes widened. "You've taken nothing at all today?"

"I hate those damned pills. I can't think when I take them. I only use 'em at night so I can sleep."

"Did Jerry know this? Does Dr. Donnelly know?"

Sy tried to shrug and winced from the effort. Pam felt a great weakness overcome her usual strength. She had a patient in pain who wouldn't take the medication that would relieve his distress. Her mind raced for a solution. She could call Dr. Donnelly and ask his advice, but she already knew what it would be: Sy *had* to take those pills, and on a regular basis, to boot.

But neither she nor anyone else could force them down his throat. She had to make him see reason. First, however, she had to learn his most comfortable position so he wouldn't be suffering while she talked to him.

"We have to talk," she said quietly. "Would you be more comfortable in the wheelchair while we do so?"

"If you think you're going to convince me to take those mind-clouding pills, don't waste your time," he said sharply.

Pam swallowed a caustic retort and folded her arms across her chest. "Sy, pain medication is not prescribed merely to dull physical discomfort. It permits mobility, of which right now you have very little. You have to be able

to move about. You're not even able to lie back so I can
conduct a simple examination. You have to take those pills.
Think of it like this. You have to take them now so you
won't have to take them later on. Doesn't that make sense?
The thing is, you're not going to get well if I can't administer treatment.''

Sy still looked stubborn, and she realized her arguments
had changed nothing. ''Okay, let's approach the problem
from another angle. How did Jerry deal with your refusal
to take pain medication?''

''He didn't nag me about it, that's for sure,'' Sy growled.

''I am not nagging you, I'm trying to explain the multiple
purposes of pain medication!'' Again she could feel anger
seeping through her veins, even to the roots of her hair. Sy
Cope was impossible.

They were at an impasse, she realized. He was not going
to take pain pills during the day, and yet he had to have
enough mobility to endure exercise and even ordinary
movements. That left her with one option.

Moving to the head of the table, she climbed up on it
and scooted down so that she was seated right behind Sy.

''What're you doing now?'' he asked, suspicion in every
syllable.

''I'm going to massage your back and relieve some of
your pain. Try to relax.'' Before she could touch him, he
slipped off the table to his feet and limped over to the
wheelchair.

''What is wrong with you?'' she called out in shock as
he pushed the chair from the room. Jumping off the table,
she ran after him. ''Sy, you at least owe me an explanation.''

He kept on pushing the chair. ''Massage never did anything except hurt like hell. If that's your miracle program,
you can forget it!''

She kept pace with him. "Sy, listen to me. Massage *shouldn't* hurt. It should ease pain, not cause it. In treating the neuromuscular skeletal system, massage is often used, but it has to be the right kind of massage."

"And I suppose you know the right kind," he said with heavy sarcasm.

"Yes, I most certainly do."

They had reached the door to his bedroom. "I'm going to lie down for a while." He and his wheelchair went in, and Sy closed the door in Pam's face.

"Sy, please!" Anxiously she knocked.

There was no response from within. Deeply troubled, she gave up and walked away with her head down.

In treating the neuromuscular skeletal system pressure is often tried and truer to be the right kind of massage.

"And I suppose you'd be the right kind," Sy said, with heavy sarcasm.

"Yes. I most certainly am—"

They had reached the door to his bedroom. "The son's...

Three

Pam stood at a window in her bedroom and found the forever view to be soothing to her frazzled nerves. Never before had she worked with a patient of Sy's temperament, but she was not yet frustrated enough to call Dr. Donnelly and admit defeat; there must be a way around the situation. An idea occurred to her, and she went into her leather bag and searched through its contents, praying that she had the pamphlet on specialized massage with her.

She found it and breathed a sigh of relief. It might help, it might not, but it was worth a try. Leaving her room, she slipped the pamphlet under Sy's door. She couldn't force him to read it, any more than she could force him to ingest pain pills that he despised. But if he did deign to read it, it might alter his attitude toward massage.

Returning to her room, she changed clothes. There was little point to her sitting around hoping Sy would suddenly become Mr. Nice Guy, and five minutes later, wearing fleecy shorts and top that permitted her skin to breathe, athletic walking shoes and a baseball cap, under which she had stuffed her hair, she skipped down the stairs and went outside through the front door. A small towel was tucked into the elasticized waist of her shorts.

As always before starting a long walk, she did some stretching exercises, preparing her leg muscles and tendons for the demands she would make on them. Deciding to use the driveway until she knew the ranch better, she set out.

She was beyond the house only a short distance when a piercing wolf whistle brought her head around. Near one of the corrals were two men, ranch hands, obviously, and they were grinning at her.

Smiling back at them, she lifted her hand in a friendly wave. They were probably wondering who she was, she thought, and picked up her pace. She was soon around the bend in the driveway and out of sight. It was at least a mile to the highway, which would add up to a nice little two-mile jaunt.

Pam was an avid believer in exercise. Walking, jogging, swimming, aerobics, they were all beneficial, and it was a rare day when she didn't spend at least an hour in some form of exercise. She was wonderfully healthy and determined to stay that way. Exercise and diet were key elements of good health, and she ate almost the exact same diet that she had ordered for Sy this morning.

Her mind wandered as she quick-stepped along the driveway. Sy was one of those people who resented disability so much that they made themselves miserable. Had he given Jerry as bad a time as he was giving her? She doubted it. The fact his new therapist was a woman infuriated Sy. Or—could this be true?—he was so modest that he couldn't deal with a female therapist. Was he really that old-fashioned? A man who had traveled the globe and lived for excitement? It seemed so unlikely, and yet what else should she think?

The tension Sy had felt from the moment of Pam's arrival had settled into his back. He was in agony. He couldn't move enough to get off the bed and he knew now that he shouldn't have lain down in the first place. Cal and Joe thought he was with Pam, so they weren't apt to come and check on him. He was as helpless as a turtle on its back, and so furious about it he felt as though he could explode.

Which, of course, increased his tension *and* the pain. He knew the problem: muscle spasms. Dr. Donnelly had told him that spasms could sometimes get so bad that the muscle actually bled. He had prescribed muscle relaxants, pain medication and physical therapy. None of it had really helped, as far as Sy was concerned. He wasn't much better off today than he'd been the day he'd come home from the hospital.

Against his will, his lips grim and pale, he reached for the bottle of pills on the bed stand. He couldn't bear the pain any longer, and he swallowed one of the pills without water. It began working in minutes. The pain subsided and his head got woozy. He cursed under his breath. How anyone could ever become addicted to drugs, he would never know. How could anyone actually *like* this feeling of disorientation?

And the pain wasn't really gone, it was merely disguised into something tolerable by what felt like layers of thick insulation. He hated it, he hated it all—the inability to do for himself, being stuck at the ranch, relying on pills to even get off the damned bed. And he hated the sympathy he saw in people's eyes. Friends had all but stopped coming to see him because he couldn't stand their platitudes, their lies, and one by one, he had told them so. He'd gotten so tired of hearing, "You'll be your old self in no time, S.J.," because he was never again going to be his old self. At least Dr. Donnelly had been honest about that. *With the proper treatment you'll be mobile, Sy, but don't count on climbing mountains and jumping out of planes again. Sorry, but that's how it is.*

Sy realized he was getting drowsy. If he lay there much longer, he would fall asleep, and he didn't want to sleep during the day. He could move now, and he cautiously turned to his side, let his legs dangle over the edge of the bed and pushed himself up with his hands and arms. It was the first thing he'd been taught in therapy in the hospital—how to lie down and get up without putting strain on his back and legs.

He got dressed, moving slowly and carefully, and pushed the wheelchair into the hall. Then he cautiously lowered himself into it and got settled as best he could. It was then that he noticed the pamphlet on the floor. Frowning, he moved the chair closer to the paper and leaned over and picked it up. It was an extensive article about massage therapy, which answered his question about where the pamphlet had come from. Pam, of course, had slid it under his door. She was nothing if not determined, he thought wryly. Well, he might read the article, he might not. He dropped it on the end of the bed, then wheeled himself from the room and to the elevator.

On the first floor he went directly to the sunroom. With his brain feeling as thick as cotton candy, he stared vacantly at the view.

Exhilarated from her walk, Pam approached the house. As she glanced into the screened sunroom, her eyes widened. Sy was in there! And he was dressed again.

Using the towel to wipe the perspiration from her face, she walked past the sunroom and to the front door. There was no way Sy could miss seeing her, she knew, but she acted as though she hadn't seen him. Once inside the house, however, she went directly to the sunroom door.

"Feeling better?" she asked. Sy's gaze moved to her and she could immediately tell from his glazed eyes that he'd taken a pain pill. Guilt and remorse hit her hard. He didn't like taking the medication and she had caused him such physical distress that he'd had to use it. Her heart sank with self-recrimination. So far she hadn't helped this man at all! Quite the opposite, in fact.

Noticing the yellowed apple sections still on the plate, she felt her spirit drop even lower. Maybe she *wasn't* the right therapist for Sy Cope.

But, dammit, neither had Jerry been the right therapist! she thought with renewed resolve. She was not giving up this soon!

Walking over to a chair, she sat down and pulled off the baseball cap, giving her head a shake to loosen her hair. Then, folding the towel into a small square, she said quietly, "You're not in pain now, are you?"

"I took a pill." Dull-witted as he felt, Sy still noticed the striking color of her hair and how pretty she looked with it framing her face.

Pam winced at the thickness of his voice, but at the very same moment a new argument for her therapy program occurred to her.

"I understand why you don't like them," she said.

"I doubt it." Sy slurred the three words but still managed to convey cynicism.

Pam maintained a steady gaze. "If you don't get well, you will need pain medication for the rest of your life," she stated calmly. "It's only simple logic, Sy."

He frowned as her "logic" slowly penetrated his foggy brain. A jagged, breath-stealing fear streaked through him. She was right and he was sickeningly, heart-wrenchingly wrong. What was he fighting against? Getting well? That idea was insane. He wanted to walk tall and straight again, he wanted to ride a horse again, he wanted to be *normal!* Resenting Pam because she was a woman was ridiculous. Was it because she was small and pretty and feminine, and her good looks and completely female smiles reminded him

a little too acutely of the forced celibacy he'd been endur-
ing since the accident?

He wondered if his hazy thoughts were making any
sense, but one of them required no debate at all: he did not
want to live on pain medication for the rest of his life!

And one other thought appeared: Jerry hadn't been doing
him a whole lot of good; maybe Pam—forget her gender—
could.

But what words should he use to explain his change of
heart? Backtracking and apologies had never been easy for
him. Until the accident, things had pretty much gone his
way.

He cleared his throat. "Maybe...maybe we should start
over."

Pam could see on his face how difficult it had been for
him to say that. Elation zinged through her because she had
finally gotten through to him, but she merely said, "I'm
willing." She got to her feet. "Give me ten minutes for a
shower, then come to the therapy room."

Just then Cal walked in with a tray. "Here's your lunch,
Sy." He looked at Pam. "Are you ready for lunch, Pam?"

She realized how hungry she was. "Yes, I am, Cal.
Thank you for asking."

"Would you like a tray so you can eat in here with Sy?"

"I'm going to shower first, Cal. I'll come to the kitchen
when I'm ready."

"Is there anything in particular you'd like for lunch?"
he inquired.

"I'll be eating exactly what Sy does."

Sy looked at her strangely. "You don't have to do that."
His lunch was a green salad and a large bowl of steamed
vegetables, and he couldn't imagine anyone preferring such
bland food over a hot roast beef sandwich, one example of
the kind of food Joe served the ranch hands at noon.

"It's the way I always eat, Sy," Pam explained. "I'm not doing it to keep you company."

"Well, it'll be ready in the kitchen when you are," Cal said, and left them alone.

"Make it twenty minutes instead of ten. We both need to eat," Pam said to Sy. "See you in the therapy room."

She walked out feeling as though she had finally accomplished something with Sy Cope. And from here on in, she was positive their relationship would only get better. She had her foot in the door, so to speak, and she was going to make sure she didn't do something to cause Sy to close that door again.

She was, in fact, going to make him strong and healthy. It was an exhilarating thought, and it elevated her mood to such a high plane that she took the stairs two at a time to the second floor.

Sy lay flat on his back on the table, with a large towel draped across his waist and hips.

"I'm going to raise your left leg," Pam told him. "Let your leg go limp so I can bend your knee." Her hand was cupping the sole of his bare foot. "What I'm going to do, Sy, is test the strength in each leg."

She could see the perspiration on his upper lip. Even with pain medication it was obvious that he was hurting. She was being very gentle with him, but causing someone to suffer was an awful feeling. Regardless, she had to know what, exactly, she would be working with. Testing his present strength was crucially necessary.

"Now," she said, "push your foot against my hand." She felt his feeble effort against her palm, said nothing and conducted the same test with his right leg. It was even weaker than the left, but then it had been more seriously injured, she knew from his medical records. Three breaks in the right leg, one in the left. The bones had healed, but he had been in a cast for a long time and his muscles had become lax. Pam was confident that exercise would remedy that condition.

What concerned her most was his back, which had taken a beating in a terrible head-over-heels fall on the ski slope. Three vertebrae had received hairline fractures, also healed now, but the spine was the central core of the neuromuscular system, and while Dr. Donnelly felt that very little damage had been done to the nerves, Sy kept suffering muscle spasms along his spine.

"I need you to turn over now," she said quietly. "Sit up first. I'll help you. Take my arm."

He smirked. "I suppose you're going to lift me."

"No. *You're* going to do the lifting, but you're going to use my arm for leverage."

"Do you know how much I weigh?"

"One-eighty," she said promptly. "This movement has nothing to do with weight."

Sy ignored that comment. "And you weigh what, a hundred pounds?"

"One-ten."

"Really big girl, huh? Okay, now *you* listen to me. I know how to turn over on my own. Just back off and let me do it."

Pam hesitated, then stepped back. "Very well." She watched him maneuver himself to his side and then onto his stomach, and bit her lip hard because his pain was so obvious. Either the medication was wearing off or his pain was intense enough to override it. She would not suggest that he take another pill, she decided. In fact, she would never again even mention his pain medication. He was not abusing it, unlike some patients who demanded chemical relief at the slightest twinge of discomfort. In truth, she admired his iron will.

Going into the bathroom, she dampened a washcloth and returned with it to wipe the sweat from his back. "I'm sorry," she murmured.

Sy didn't answer. The cool washcloth felt good on his skin, about the only thing that did feel good. He felt her adjust the towel to cover his undershorts, but he was hurting so badly he really didn't give a damn if she saw his underwear or not.

Then something else did feel good, her fingers on his spine. She started at his neck, probed gently and spoke softly. "There are three sections to the spinal column, the cervical, which I am now examining, the thoracic, or middle back, and the lumbar, your lower back. Your compression fractures were in the thoracic and lumbar regions." Her fingers drifted downward and encountered knots of muscle surrounding the thoracic vertebrae—muscle spasms, as tight as any she'd ever felt. The lumbar region was almost as bad.

She began a slow, circular movement with her fingertips on one of the knots. "Tell me if anything I do hurts you," she said quietly.

To Sy's amazement he felt his body relaxing. Or maybe it was his mind doing the relaxing, he thought. Her touch was incredible, her technique as gentle as butterfly wings. Even he knew that one massage treatment was not going to permanently loosen those knots, but nothing had felt so good in months.

"Don't move," she told him, and went over to the table where she had placed her tubes and bottles of oils and lotions. Selecting one, she returned to the therapy table, where she poured some oil into her left hand. Her next step was to warm the oil with her own hands, which took a few seconds.

"What're you doing?" Sy mumbled, unable to see her from his facedown position.

"Just making sure the oil I'm going to use on your back is the right temperature." She smiled. "I don't want to shock you into jumping straight up from this table."

"Fat chance of that happening."

Pam detected the resentment in his voice, the frustration, and she was especially gentle as she began to massage his back. She had learned something very early in her career: people relaxed more easily if she talked softly to them while she worked. The subject didn't seem to matter, it was the sound of her voice they found soothing.

"Every part of the human body is controlled by nerves," she said, while making long sweeps of her oiled hands up and down the knotted muscles along his spine, "and every one of those nerves connects directly or indirectly with the spine. I'm sure you don't think so now, but you were really very fortunate not to have received permanent nerve damage in that accident.

"The nervous system is technically and biologically understandable, yet, in some ways, still a mystery. I'm sure you've heard people say, 'My nerves are shot,' or, 'I have really bad nerves today.' And certainly you've heard of nervous breakdowns. Some doctors disdain that term. According to them, there's no such thing as a *nervous* breakdown. It's a mental breakdown. Anyhow, comments concerning one's nerves usually have something to do with emotions. Of course, actual nerve damage can cause all sorts of..." she rambled on.

Sy was only half listening. There was such an enormous difference in Pam's hands-on ministrations and Jerry's that he could hardly believe it. He was more relaxed right now than he'd been at any time during Jerry's regime, and it was puzzling. Was Pam that much better than Jerry at their craft? Was *that* the reason Dr. Donnelly had sent her to the ranch? But why not say so? What was wrong with Dr. Donnelly coming right out and telling him that Pamela Brooks was a more efficient therapist than Jerry O'Conner? Was the doctor's reticence due to professional ethics?

Sy's thoughts turned to Pam herself, and after a dozen questions about her flashed through his mind, he asked one. "What were you doing outside before lunch?"

"Walking."

"Exploring the ranch?"

"No, not at all, although I would like to become better acquainted with it. This is a beautiful ranch, Sy. You must be very proud of your home."

"I am. So you were just out walking? How come?"

She laughed. "For exercise, of course."

Her laughter charmed him, and an awareness of her nearness and clean scent began seeping through his system. She brushed aside his hair to massage his neck, and his breath caught in his throat. At least with Jerry he hadn't had to deal with feelings of a sexual nature, he thought with a frown. He inhaled deeply, slowly, and exhaled in the same slow fashion, not wanting her to catch on that he was becoming aroused.

"You'll be doing some exercising, too," she told him. "We're going to start with very simple movements, then, as you regain strength, you'll advance to more strenuous actions."

"That's your program, then? Massage and exercise?"

"Diet, exercise, massage and hot water therapy," Pam said.

"Hot water therapy? Meaning what?"

"Hot baths."

"Pam, I take showers. Getting in and out of a bathtub is too damned tough."

"I'll help you."

Sy raised his head about an inch from the table, just enough so that he could squint threateningly at her. "I don't think so, sweetheart. In my book, bathing is a private affair."

"Look at that menacing face," she exclaimed with a teasing laugh. "What do you think I'm planning to do, attack you in the bathtub?" Sy's face became flushed, and Pam laughed again. "I'll say it again, Sy, your virtue is in no danger whatsoever from me."

His embarrassment brought on a bout of stubbornness. "I'm not taking baths with you in the room."

"I'm not talking about baths, my friend, I'm discussing hot water therapy. There's a world of difference." Her eyes twinkled merrily. She couldn't help teasing him about his macho attitude. "Believe me, I do not plan to hand you the soap and watch you bathe. I don't even intend to wash your back."

"You think you're pretty funny, don't you?" Sy growled, and lowered his head to the table again.

"I enjoy laughing, if that's what you mean." Pam wiped the oil from her hands with a clean towel. "You should try it. Laughter is good medicine."

"When I see or hear something funny, I'll give it a try," Sy mumbled resentfully.

Pam let that comment pass and said brightly, "Well, I'm ready, are you?"

"Ready for what?"

"A nice long soak in the tub. Oh, which tub would you prefer using, the one in this bathroom or your own? Assuming there's a tub in your bathroom, of course."

Sy gritted his teeth. She was going to badger him into

doing what she wanted, however much he objected. Well, it wasn't going to be *all* her way!

"I'll use my own tub, and I'll soak for the rest of the day, if that's what you want, but you are not stepping one foot in my bathroom, understand?"

"Oh, but I am," she retorted. "You see, soaking isn't all you're going to be doing in that hot water."

Sy let loose with a string of curses, and Pam grinned and patted his shoulder. "There, there," she said in mock sympathy. "You really shouldn't take defeat so hard."

"I am not defeated, dammit!" he shouted.

Pam's smile disappeared, and she spoke in a very serious vein. "That's the first truly sensible thing I've heard you say. You *aren't* defeated, Sy, and you won't be as long as you hang on to that thought. Letting it slip away could very well be your downfall."

"Now you're a psychologist," he said sarcastically.

"I don't have to be a psychologist to know that a positive attitude can be the difference between good health and bad. Now, can you make it to your bathroom under your own steam, or would you like some help? I could get Cal if you're worried about me catching sight of your undies."

"You're just a barrel of laughs," Sy muttered.

"And you're the worst grouch I've ever run into," Pam said calmly. "Cute, but grouchy." She thoroughly enjoyed the color that spread from his neck to his face. "Oh," she said innocently, "hasn't anyone ever told you you're cute before? Darn, and there I've gone and let the cat out of the bag. Now you'll probably go strutting around trying to be even cuter."

"Did Donnelly send you out here to drive me crazy?"

"I don't think so. Why? Do you feel a little bit crazy?" She could tell that his blood was boiling. That was good, a whole lot better than him sitting slumped over in that wheelchair in the sunroom. At least now he knew he was alive.

Sy closed his eyes as frustration overcame any desire he'd had to best her in a battle of wits. It was obvious that she was going to have the last word, no matter what he said. And regardless of her ability to make him angry, she'd also made him feel physically better than he had in a long time.

Truth was, he didn't want to move off the table and go back to feeling the way he had before her massage.

It was as though she could read his mind, because she said quietly, "It won't last, Sy. You're feeling good now, but it's a temporary relief. It's going to take many, many treatments to get you on the path to recovery. We've only just started." She paused. "Would you like me to get Cal to help you into the bathtub?"

He gave up. "Yeah, get Cal."

"Thank you, Sy." She left the room.

Frowning, Sy raised his head a little, just so he could see the doorway. Now, why would she thank him? he wondered.

Four

Running about six inches of comfortably warm water into Sy's bathtub, Pam listened to Cal and Sy in the adjoining bedroom. She couldn't hear them clearly, as the water pouring from the spigot overrode any other sound. But it was still evident that two men were talking and moving around in the next room, and it was also evident, by tone of voice, that one of them—Sy, of course—was grousing and complaining.

Pam shook her head wryly. Even though Sy was already feeling a modicum of relief from her attentions, he was far from ready to admit that she knew what she was doing. Nor was he the least bit happy about the idea of bathtub therapy. He was undoubtedly griping to Cal about it, more or less acting like a spoiled brat, Pam thought. Had no one ever told Sy Cope what to do? In less than one full day with Sy, her impression of the man was that he had always done exactly as he pleased.

Well, she had never permitted patients to run over her with a steamroller, and she wasn't about to let Sy Cope be the first. However much he fought her tactics to get him well, she *was* going to succeed.

In truth, her oath was no more passionate in Sy's case than in any other patient's. Her dedication to her chosen profession was genuine and profoundly felt. When the doctors had done all they could for some patients, they handed them over to therapists. And when she saw improvement in a person's mobility, or when someone who had been confined to a wheelchair walked on his own, she celebrated.

There were a lot of things different in Sy Cope's case, however. She was going to be living under his roof for an indefinite period, giving him all her time and attention. Unlike Jerry, she would not be taking weekends off, for she honestly believed that two days without therapy could destroy any gains made in the previous five. Also, there were no other patients on her agenda, no one else to take her mind off Sy for even a few hours a day. Although she hadn't anticipated any such result before coming to the Cope ranch, she knew now that so much togetherness was going to intertwine their lives—they would either become friends or true adversaries. Given Sy's self-centered personality, she wondered if friendship was possible. On the other hand, the idea of him reaching the point of actually disliking her was surprisingly disturbing.

She bit her lower lip as she turned off the water. Sitting on the edge of the tub, she thought through their relationship thus far. Questions developed about it and about herself. Was she impressed with Sy's past reputation? Impressed by his good looks? Her head had never been easily turned by masculine good looks, but if she was to be completely honest with herself, wasn't she just a little bit attracted to Sy Cope?

"No, no," she whispered, shaken by the thought and denying any such attraction. He was a patient, and professionals did not fall for their patients. Why was she even thinking such a thing?

Sy, using crutches, came in, with Cal right behind him. Pam's mood lightened considerably when she saw the long terry robe Sy was wearing. In fact, she had to swallow the laugh that welled in her throat. His disability was far from funny, but there was something about his modesty that continued to strike her as comical. Why, she didn't know. Most patients guarded their modesty—why should Sy be any different?

And yet he brought out her sense of humor. Not in a normal way, though. She kept wanting to tease him, which was peculiar when she had never been a practical joker. She realized, however, that she would stand on her head in that six inches of bathwater if she thought Sy would laugh about it.

"He's all set," Cal said, a bit nervously, Pam noticed.

"Don't worry, Cal, this is not going to harm him in any way. Now, let's get rid of that robe and get him into the bathtub."

Sy scowled. "I happen to be standing right in between the two of you. You can address your remarks to me, not to each other as though I weren't here."

Pam rolled her eyes. "Still grouchy, I see." She smiled sweetly at Cal. "Is he ever nice?"

"Dammit, that's enough!" Sy exclaimed angrily. "Cal, take the crutches. I can get into the damn tub on my own."

"No, you cannot," Pam said firmly. "You are not even going to try. Cal, set the crutches down and then take his robe. You and I are going to see that he doesn't fall flat on his face in that water and drown. I haven't drowned a patient yet, and I don't intend that Sy be my first fatality."

Sy looked as though he would like to drown her. Pam merely smiled in return, and under her direction, she and Cal got Sy safely into the tub and sitting down. Privately she was amused that he'd chosen baggy bathing trunks to wear for this exercise. His first words were no surprise, though.

"I thought you said this was going to be hot water therapy. This water is barely warm," he complained.

"All in good time, my friend," she retorted. "Cal, hang

around if you wish, but we won't really need you for about an hour. Then I'd like your assistance in helping Sy get out of the tub.''

Cal seemed only too glad to vacate the premises. Pam couldn't help laughing at his haste, which earned her a dirty look from Sy, who felt like a damn fool sitting in that piddly puddle of water in bathing trunks.

Paying no mind to Sy's dark, scowling expression, Pam pulled huge bath towels from the linen closet and stuffed them around his back. She rolled a final towel into a tube and placed it behind his neck.

"Now, I want you to lean back and relax. You are very well supported and should be as comfortable as possible, given your medical condition," she said sternly, and got on her knees at the faucet end of the tub.

Sy watched her suspiciously, even though she'd been right to suppose that he was reasonably comfortable. He saw her turn on the hot water tap so that a moderate flow came from the faucet. Then she began swishing the water in the tub with her hand.

"What I'm doing," she said matter-of-factly, "is gradually bringing up the temperature of the water so your body will get used to it as it gets hotter.''

"At least you didn't sit me in a tub of boiling water," Sy said grudgingly.

She smiled. "I don't even throw live lobsters into boiling water, Sy. Can't bring myself to inflict pain on any living creature, even though I love to eat lobster.''

"So you let someone else do the dirty work.''

"I'm ashamed to say so, but yes, I guess I do. But then don't we all, in one way or another? I'm sure you don't butcher your own beef." She made a face. "This conversation is turning gruesome. If we're going to talk, let's make it about something else. The water's getting hotter.

It feels all right on my hand, but tell me if it feels too warm to you.

"Sy," she said, "you're sitting too stiffly. Let your head fall back on that rolled towel. I have a mental exercise for you. Close your eyes. Sy, *please* close your eyes! There, thank you. Now, first let your mind go blank and then picture yourself floating and weightless." The depth of the water was increasing; it was almost reaching the sexy patch of dark hair on his chest.

Pam looked at it for a moment, then at Sy's face. In repose his face was beautiful.

But she couldn't sit there and admire his natural beauty; she had work to do. She turned off the faucet.

"We're going to do a few simple exercises," she said quietly. "No, don't open your eyes. Stay as relaxed as you can." She lifted his right arm from the water and rotated his wrist. "Can you do that on your own?"

"Yes." He had no trouble in rotating either wrist or in keeping his arms above the waterline without her help.

"That's very good," she said. "Now we're going to do the same thing with your ankles." His poor legs, she thought with heartfelt sympathy. Flaccid muscles and surgical scars. No question about it, he'd gone through hell since his skiing accident. Dipping her hands into the water, she carefully brought up his right foot several inches from the bottom of the tub and then gently rotated his ankle in a clockwise motion. "Does this hurt?" she asked.

"A little. It's not bad, though."

Pam next did his left ankle, counting ten rotations as she had for his right. Lowering his foot, she began kneading his leg muscles underwater. Sy didn't react in any way until she got close to the hem of his bathing trunks.

Then his eyes opened and she found herself looking directly into bottomless blue masculinity. "Careful," he murmured softly.

She tried to make light of his veiled warning. "I'm *always* careful," she said with a smile she'd had to force. Sy Cope was pure dynamite. Her body was suddenly doing ridiculous things—her heart pounding too hard, her breath coming too short. She cleared her throat as though it would also clear her head. His thighs needed as much massage as the rest of his legs, but she moved away from those bathing trunks and concentrated on his calves.

There was a steaminess in the air that wasn't all caused by the tub of hot water, she realized uneasily. Maybe this first session had lasted long enough.

She pulled the plug and the water began gurgling down the drain. "Stay put," she said briskly, getting to her feet. "I'll go find Cal."

"It hasn't been an hour yet," Sy called out to her as she hurried from the bathroom and through his bedroom. Then she was positive he chuckled. *He chuckled!* It was a blow to her professional pride. He knew he'd gotten to her! This would not do. This would not do at all, her mind repeated as she went downstairs to locate Cal. She was not here for Sy's amusement, or to be the target of any libidious urges he might be having.

But it wasn't *his* urges she should be worrying about— it was her own, she thought in a burst of self-directed anger.

Coming upon Cal, she said curtly, "He's ready to get out of the tub."

Cal glanced at his watch and looked surprised. "Already? It's only been twenty minutes. You said an hour."

"Yes, well, I don't want to tax his strength. I don't want to tax yours, either, but do you think you can get him out of the tub by yourself? There's something I have to do." It was a bald-faced lie. There was not one single thing pressing her. Sy was the sum total of her focus on this ranch, and avoiding him right now was a cowardly thing to do.

Yet she needed some time away from him. She needed to get her bearings again.

"Sure, no problem," Cal said. "I'll take care of Sy, don't you worry none."

"Thanks, and, Cal, I'd like him to get into bed. His body temperature is up because of the hot water, and I don't want him getting a chill. Tell him I'll be in to see him in an hour or so."

"Supper's coming up in about an hour. Do you want him eating in bed?"

She thought a moment, then nodded. "Good idea. Tell him I'll see him after supper. Thanks again, Cal." She hurried off, as though something crucial awaited her attention.

What she hadn't factored into her instructions to Cal were Sy's own ideas of where and how he should spend the remainder of the day.

"I am not going to bed at four in the afternoon," he told Cal as the older man helped him out of his wet trunks. "Why would that woman even think of something so ridiculous?"

"Uh, I think she thinks you need to stay warm."

"Good God, Cal, it's at least eighty degrees in here. How warm does she want me to be?" Sy said disgustedly. "In fact, open the windows and let in some fresh air. I'm getting dressed and going downstairs."

"You seem to be moving a little easier than before," Cal commented.

"Yeah, well, I'm feeling a little better than before."

"Then Pam's doing you some good?"

"More than Jerry did, obviously." Sy cocked an eyebrow. "But don't you dare tell her I said so."

Cal grinned. "Wouldn't dream of it, Sy. What goes on between you and your therapist ain't nobody's business but your own."

Sy grinned, too, surprising Cal; it had been a long time since he'd seen a real grin on Sy's face.

"Now, that's a fact, ain't it?" Sy drawled, using Cal's vernacular.

Pam stepped through the front door of the house and breathed deeply of the cooling, late afternoon air. There was a stretch of neatly trimmed grass before her, then a set of wide stone steps, which she supposed led to the river level. Crossing the lawn, she went down the stairs and saw another stretch of grass and a second set of steps. On the final level, standing right next to the swiftly moving river, she glanced back at the house. It sat on its rise as a regal, dignified structure, architecturally perfect, beautiful to the eye.

This is a place of utter peace, she thought as she sank to the grass and watched the moving water. In the next instant a mosquito landed on her bare arm and she laughed wryly while swatting it away. Even Eden had its drawbacks apparently.

But still, even with mosquitoes looking for their supper, only natural at this still, quiet time of day, the Cope ranch and this particular spot had to be the loveliest she'd ever seen. Small wonder that Sy enjoyed the views from the sunroom. Wouldn't anyone? She, for instance, could while away hours right here, if she had the extra hours *to* while away.

She didn't, of course. Her long-range therapy program for Sy would leave her very little time for herself. Today he'd only gotten a glimpse of how strictly regimented his days were going to be, which, of course, also regimented her time. That was fine. She had no objections whatsoever to giving her all to a patient. But things weren't quite the same with Sy as they'd been with her past patients.

She wasn't the same, she quickly and uneasily amended. That was what she must be honest about, if only with herself. As disturbing and unprofessional as it was, she was attracted to Sy Cope.

He must never know, she thought next. Yes, he'd gotten a chuckle over her reaction to his comment about her not getting too close to his bathing trunks, but she must never react so foolishly to sexual innuendo again. Besides, Sy had only been teasing her. She should never have gotten so giddy and female over a little teasing, especially when she had teased him several times during the day.

Sighing, Pam brought her knees up and wrapped her arms around them. Her gaze remained on the incredible view as she tried to figure herself out. As the sun lowered in the western sky, the air got cooler and the grass began to feel damp. She finally got up and returned to the house.

In one of the small family dining rooms Sy was polishing off a meal of chicken-fried steak, mashed potatoes with country gravy and buttered corn on the cob. Every bite had been delicious—chicken-fried steak was one of Joe's specialties, and his gravy was to die for. Sy had done everything but smack his lips while cleaning his plate. He had made a decision about that irritating diet Pam thought he should stick to: he would follow it for breakfasts, snacks and lunches, but he was going to eat a normal supper, no matter what she might say about it. And, he expected, she would have a lot to say about it. But she was going to have to learn that he was not an automaton that blindly obeyed inane, unnecessary orders. Besides, he wanted to gain back some of the ten pounds he'd lost since the accident, and he sure as hell wasn't going to do that by eating steamed vegetables three times a day.

"Cal," he called out, ready for some of that peach cobbler Joe had made for dessert.

Instead of Cal appearing in the doorway, Pam looked in. Her eyes got big when she saw Sy. "I thought you were in bed!"

"Guess you thought wrong. Did you eat yet?"

"I just finished."

A devilish twinkle sparkled in Sy's eyes. "How'd you like the chicken-fried steak?"

Pam was suddenly so angry she wanted to march over to Sy Cope and box his ears. It took every ounce of willpower she possessed to smile instead and say, "It looked wonderful, but *I* stuck to my diet."

"Give the woman a gold star," Sy said with a lopsided grin that Pam saw as pure and simple defiance.

Well, from this moment on he could eat what he wanted, she decided, just as she had decided not to harp on his taking pain medication on a regular basis, as Dr. Donnelly had prescribed. She was not here to harangue Sy into getting well. If he was determined not to cooperate, only he would suffer the consequences. Surely he knew that.

"I'll take that gold star gladly," she said with the brightest smile she could muster. "What time do you usually retire?"

Sy had expected a stern lecture on the benefits of a proper diet the second Pam had walked in, and it startled him that she didn't seem to care what he'd eaten.

"Uh, around nine," he said, feeling somewhat deflated. "Why?"

"Because my agenda calls for a massage before bedtime," she responded cheerfully. "If you agree, of course."

"Uh, sure, okay," Sy stammered. "Do you want me in the therapy room at any particular time?"

"Around eight should do it." Pam walked to the door. "See you then."

Sy stared after her. Without saying one negative thing about the rich food he'd chosen over her prescribed diet for the evening meal, she had made him feel like a guilty child. He pushed his empty plate back with a disgusted snort.

And he didn't call for Cal to bring him any of Joe's peach cobbler.

There were many moods connected to massage. Pam had always attempted to lighten her patients' moods with impersonal chatter, and usually she was quite successful. This evening, much to her chagrin, she couldn't think of anything to say that *wasn't* personal. Sy's skin glistened from the oil she was using, and the contours of his back muscles seemed utterly beautiful. She thought the human body to be a work of art, in any case, but there was a sensuality to the curves and dips of Sy's torso that she hadn't noticed with other patients. It was extremely disconcerting to acknowledge that sensuality, but it was too firmly embedded in Pam's mind to dislodge.

Sy, too, was silent. Pam's hands stroking his back, stopping here and there to knead a kink or knot, were causing all sorts of internal reactions. It felt good—only God and Sy knew how really good it felt. But didn't Pam, professionalism aside, realize what she, a woman, was doing to him as a man?

Jerry had used massage on him many times, but Jerry's hands had not caressed. A man working on a man was a whole different ball game from this, Sy realized. And Jerry had had a certain roughness to his movements, which had caused more pain than relief. Sy had never relaxed during massage treatments from Jerry, and while Sy's back muscles seemed to be loosening up under Pam's hands, other parts of his body were reacting in a totally predictable way.

He had to think of something else, he realized, and wondered in the next breath why Pam wasn't talking to him as she'd done during today's first massage. Surely she wasn't upset with him because he'd teased her about getting too close to his bathing trunks.

He lay there thinking about it, trying very hard to separate her ministrations from his own feelings, to look at what she was doing to him as purely therapeutic, until he could bear the whole silent scene no longer.

"Are you mad at me?" he asked, wishing he could see her face, which was impossible if he maintained the position she had requested. She had wanted his head turned a certain way, and he wondered now if it was because she didn't want him looking at her, watching her.

Pam's answer was an immediate, "Of course not. Why would you think such a thing?"

"You're not talking, and you talked all during that other massage."

Since she couldn't explain her silence, playing ignorant seemed best. "Did I really?"

"I think you know you did." She slowly ran her hand down his spine from his neck to his tailbone, and a sexual shiver rippled through him. He gritted his teeth.

Pam felt the shiver. "Are you cold?"

"God, no," he muttered through clenched lips.

"Pardon?"

"I said no, I'm not cold." *What I am, sweetheart, is hot, and I'm getting hotter by the minute. Can't you tell the difference?*

"It wouldn't be at all good if you got chilled, which can

happen sometimes when a person is perspiring. Along with therapeutic exercise and other treatments, we must practice preventive medicine.''

"Oh, we must, must we?''

"Now *you* sound angry.''

"Guess our minds just don't meet in the same place,'' Sy mumbled. His was hovering in a particular area below his navel, and he was damned positive hers wasn't.

Pam draped a towel over his back and dried her hands on another. "That's it for this evening.'' She had planned to spend time on his legs, but there was just too much tension between them tonight. Tomorrow would be different, she told herself, a chance to begin again. She understood her patient better now. This morning she'd arrived with her usual idealistic ideas about how best to treat a person with Sy's disabilities. She had not been told anything about his disagreeable, defiant personality, nor had she expected anything from herself beyond normal sympathy. Finding herself attracted to a patient, *any* patient, was a shock she needed some time to dispel.

"Do you want some help getting off the table?'' she asked.

"No,'' he said curtly. "You can leave now.''

"I'll leave when I'm ready to leave,'' she retorted stiffly. "Actually, I plan to see you safely in bed. So, if you don't want help in getting off the table, I suggest you get to it.''

Sy pushed himself up to a sitting position, thankful for the towels he was able to bunch on his lap. Not that he was nearly as aroused as he'd been. Without her hands on him, and with that frosty tone she was addressing him in, he was returning to normal rather quickly.

He sort of resented her power over his libido and couldn't stop himself from drawling sarcastically, "You're going to tuck me in for the night?''

She spoke coolly. "Teddy bear and all. Incidentally, in case you haven't figured it out yet, I'm using the bedroom next to yours. If you need anything in the night, call my name. I'll hear you."

He raised an eyebrow. "Anything?"

Against her will, Pam flushed. "You know perfectly well what I meant," she snapped.

Sy grinned. "Guess you know what *I* meant, too."

Pam had had enough. Folding her arms across her chest, she shot him a venomous look. "I'm here to help you get well. I am not here for your amusement! Are you able to grasp that concept? You're not a nice person, Symon Cope. I've worked with many people who were much worse off than you are, and they didn't wallow in self-pity or blame the rest of the world for something they caused themselves."

Sy was stunned by her outburst. By the time she'd reached the part of her speech about his wallowing in self-pity, however, he was steaming.

"You think I shouldn't feel self-pity? And that I caused the accident so I shouldn't be upset by what happened to me? Lady, you've got a lot to learn about human nature." He slid off the table so that his feet were on the floor and sent her a look of warning. "Don't you dare come into my room tonight. Even if the damned house is burning down, you stay away from me, understand?"

Pam was appalled about what she'd said to him. There was no acceptable excuse for her outburst, her second in one day. No excuse at all. How could she have done such a thing? Miserably she watched him struggle to the wheelchair and sit down. She couldn't let him leave with this between them—she couldn't!

Racing for the door, she closed it and stood with her back against it.

"Get the hell out of the way," Sy snarled.

She lifted her chin. A sign of weakness now would forever cement the damage she'd done with her reckless anger.

But a straightforward apology was not a sign of weakness. "I'm sorry," she said evenly, belying the inner tremors she was undergoing. "Maybe I do need a lesson in human nature. One thing I do know is that anger solves nothing. I had no right to speak to you the way I did, and I apologize for every word." She added quietly, "Sy, I know I can help you. I know it."

He didn't erase the hardness from his face, but he knew she was right. In only one day under her care he was feeling better than he had in months. Oh, it wasn't an instant cure, far from it. But there was less tension in his back and legs, and was it her fault he'd been thinking of her in erotic ways during the massage? His comment about "anything" had come out of that, he knew, which he could never explain.

"Okay," he said a bit gruffly. "I accept your apology. Now, please let me go to bed."

"Thank you." Pam stepped aside and opened the door for him.

He wheeled the chair into the hall and headed for his room. "But I still don't want you tucking me in," he tossed over his shoulder in a voice that brooked no argument.

Sighing heavily, Pam began picking up the towels she'd used in tonight's treatment. She had discovered a laundry hamper in a cupboard, and she stuffed the towels into it. Her body felt weighted down and she moved slowly. It seemed to her that she was in over her head with Sy Cope, and her self-confidence was taking an awful beating.

All she could do, she realized, was to hope that tomorrow would be better. After all, she had really only just begun to put Sy on the road to recovery.

Five

Sleep didn't come easily for Pam that night. It was partly because she was listening for any telltale sounds from Sy's room, but most of her restlessness was due to inner turmoil. Always she had taken pride in her professionalism, her confident, authoritative take-charge-and-get-things-done attitude. Most people wanted so much to recover from whatever physical debility they were suffering that they eagerly welcomed any help she could give them. Arguments or debates with a patient about her methods of treatment had been few and far between during her career, thus she honestly didn't know what to make of Sy's contrariness.

At times he seemed fully cooperative, she mused while staring at the dark ceiling of her bedroom. Then, without warning or explanation, he completely rejected her advice and did what he wanted. She recalled the moment when he had suggested a new beginning, that they start over. Obviously it was the same moment that he had decided to accept her gender.

Dr. Donnelly had suspected Sy would object to his therapist being a woman, Pam thought, even though the doctor had merely suggested that Sy would object to a *change* of therapists. Also, Donnelly had not even given her a hint regarding Sy's black moods, self-pitying nature or self-righteous determination to have the world—the ranch, at least—revolve around him. Had Donnelly's omissions been deliberate, or had he never personally felt the brunt of Sy's unpleasant nature?

Regardless, and this was most disturbing of all to contemplate, she, Pamela Brooks, found Sy Cope, with all of his many faults, physically appealing.

Had she recently lost the good sense she'd been born with? she wondered with a frown.

She thought of the minor romances in her life, and then of the one big affair she'd had three years back when she had come very close to getting married. Elliot Young was also a therapist, but he hadn't been content working in Montana and had sent out dozens of résumés to hospitals, doctors and clinics, most of them in the East. Their relationship had been at its peak when he received a job offer from a renowned clinic in Baltimore. He had been very excited by the offer, Pam recalled, and he had proposed marriage and asked her to go with him to Baltimore.

She had wanted to say yes, but at that particular time she'd had a serious problem with which to contend. Her father had died several years before and her mother, Colleen, was gravely ill. Pam had moved her mother in with her so Colleen wouldn't be living alone. Elliot knew the situation as well as Pam did, and still he thought she should leave her mother and go to Baltimore. Pam had not been able to do it. Elliot had gone without her, and she hadn't resented him for it, either. She'd felt that they were each doing what they must.

They had stayed in close contact for a few months, and then things began changing. Sometimes weeks passed between Elliot's telephone calls or letters. It all came to a head one evening when Elliot called. They'd had a long, sad conversation, which had ended with a few simple sentences.

Pam, are you ever going to leave Montana?

Not as long as Mother needs me, Elliot. I'm sorry.

So am I, Pam, but this is no good. I...I've been seeing someone else.

She had never heard from Elliot again, nor had she tried to contact him. The irony of it all was that Colleen had passed away less than a month later. By then, however, Pam had recognized Elliot's selfishness and knew she would never be able to forget it. He had not been the man she'd once thought him to be, and she had never been sorry that she hadn't turned her back on her mother.

It was shortly after midnight that Pam grew so weary of lying there, going over the past, the present and the nebulous future that she got up, grabbed a robe, stuck her feet into bedroom slippers and went outside. The second-floor porch was wider than she'd expected, a very good place to stroll in the middle of a dark night, she decided.

The night air was chilly and she pulled up the collar of her robe around her throat. She walked to the far end of the porch, turned around and walked to the opposite end. She was beginning to understand the layout of the large house. Sy's room was a corner room, the last—or the first, depending on one's point of view—on this side of the second floor. That door, the one she was in fact closest to, opened into his room.

For a moment she listened at the door, then, hearing nothing, she continued pacing the porch.

Sy was awake—he'd been awake for at least an hour—and he heard footsteps on the porch. It had to be Pam out there, because no one else slept in the house. He wondered why she wasn't sleeping. Pain was keeping him awake, but what was her demon?

He began thinking about her. Even with all of her spunk and spirit, she seemed to him to be the epitome of the all-American, small-town girl. She was not the type of woman that had drawn his attention before the accident, and yet there was something about her....

But then, why wouldn't he notice her as a woman when she was the only one in sight? She was pretty, too, and very adept at her job. Maybe a little too adept for his comfort. After all, he hadn't been with a woman for a long time. Wasn't it only natural that her hands all over him, stroking, kneading, caressing, would turn his thoughts to sex?

Attempting to find a more comfortable position, Sy groaned and then muttered a vile oath. Pam's massages and the simple exercises she'd led him through had given him some relief, but his muscles hadn't stayed loose and relaxed, and the pain had returned with a vengeance. He had decided against taking a pain pill before retiring, and he didn't want to take one at this late hour because he would wake groggy in the morning. Given his acute discomfort now, it had probably been a stupid decision.

But he wanted so badly to disassociate himself completely from painkillers. He wanted to sleep without medication, to move without pain, to walk without crutches, to get around the house without a wheelchair. He wanted to be *well!*

Sy drew a deep, ponderous breath. Was Pam the person to make him well? She believed she was, and he couldn't deny that she had relieved much of his distress in the one day she'd been there. The effects of the treatments hadn't lasted through the night, but it was possible for Sy to envision a time when they would, a time when he would sleep like a baby and get up feeling refreshed.

He probably should give her a chance, and defying her good intentions was immature. But why hadn't Jerry been as good as Pam seemed to be? Dammit, why should he, Sy, have to deal with erotic sensations during treatment?

Didn't he have enough problems without that one? Maybe it should be the least of his worries, but when a man had nothing else to concentrate on but a woman's hands all over him, his thoughts were bound to turn to the erotic.

He suddenly felt resentful of Pam and her good intentions. His lips took a bitter twist. She was here to help him? Fine, he would let her. She'd told him to call her in the night should he need anything, and right now he needed, very badly, some surcease from the racking pain in his back.

Without thinking it through, deliberately ignoring his previous thoughts regarding sexual discomfort during massage, he gruffly called out, "Pam?"

Outside on the porch, Pam came to a standstill. Had Sy called for her? She listened.

"Pam?" Sy called again.

This time she heard her name quite plainly. Hurrying back to his door, she rapped. "Sy?"

"The door's not locked."

She turned the knob. Sy's room was dark. "What's wrong?" she asked.

"I need some help."

"Can you turn on a light?"

"I can barely move."

His voice sounded hoarse and strained. Obviously he was in great pain. Without further hesitation Pam felt her way to the bed, and then to the nightstand. Still feeling her way, she located the lamp and switched it on.

Her first good look at him was shocking. He was sweating, and the pallor of pain had whitened even his lips.

But she knew he would not be in this condition if he'd taken his pain medication. Her own lips thinned as sympathy fled her. There was no sensible reason for him to suffer like this. He was the most stubborn, irritating patient she'd ever cared for.

But he *was* her patient and she would do what she could for him.

The first thing she did was go into his bathroom and wet a washcloth with warm water. Returning to the bedroom, she sat on the very edge of his bed and wiped the perspiration from his face, neck and shoulders.

"You look mad as hell," Sy mumbled.

"Maybe because you could try the patience of a saint. You didn't take anything for pain tonight, did you?"

"No, and I'm not going to take any now. I'm in no mood for a lecture, either, so save your breath."

Their eyes met in an angry stare-down. Pam was the first to speak. "You're not helping yourself, you know."

"That's what you're here for."

"I can do only so much."

"I know what you can do. Stop glaring at me and just do it!"

She almost didn't. It crossed her mind to leave him in misery, pack her things and get the hell away from him. But it was a fleeting thought. It wasn't in her nature to turn her back on someone in pain.

Still, she didn't feel very friendly toward Sy at this moment, and she spoke rather stiffly. "Let's get you on your side so I can reach your back." Without thinking, she took hold of his sheet and blanket and drew them down to the foot of the bed. Her heart nearly stopped—he was stark naked!

"Sorry," she mumbled, drew the covers over him again and then hurried to the bathroom for a large towel.

Sy disgustedly closed his eyes and only opened them again when he felt the towel descend to his nether regions. She'd probably gotten a damned good look, he thought, and realized that he was actually furious that she would be so casual and careless with his body. This was the perfect argument against a man having a female therapist, which he would tell her in blunt terms if he had the strength. Right now, however, he felt as though the pain in his back had taken up residence in his brain. It was truly the only thing on which he could focus completely.

Pam decided that ignoring the incident was her best course. In the first place, nudity was nothing to be embarrassed about. Knowing Sy's penchant for modesty, she had been careless, yes, and she would be particularly mindful of that in the future. But in defense of what she'd done, it was the middle of the night and Sy was suffering. She had been concentrating on relieving his distress, certainly not on sneaking a look at his personal assets.

She sat on the edge of the bed again. "I'm going to turn you to your left side," she said calmly. "Try not to help. It will only cause you more distress." First she slid the pillow from under his head and then she reached across him, took his left arm and gently crooked it above his head. Sy groaned. "It's going to hurt, Sy, but it has to be done." *Besides, you pigheaded jerk, if you'd taken your medication as you should have, you wouldn't be in this condition!*

Using the bed pillows, she gradually got him on his side. He was breathing hard, sweating again, conveying his anguish. Her innate sympathy kicked in again, and she bit down on her lip before relaying further instructions.

"All right now, lie very still and try to relax. I'm going to run to the therapy room and get some oil. I won't be gone a minute."

Sy lay there gritting his teeth. He thought of the almost constant pain he'd lived with since the accident and wondered if he wasn't getting worse instead of better.

Pam was back almost at once. She took off her robe and

laid it on a chair; it was too bulky to work in. She sat on the bed and removed the pillows stuffed along Sy's spine. After oiling her hands, she laid them on his back. His skin felt both feverish and clammy. She began working, using long, sweeping strokes to limber his muscles. He said nothing, and she didn't break the silence. Gradually she focused her massage on specific areas along his spine, kneading the knots that were so easily detectable.

Her thoughts became questioning. Why did he keep having these awful muscle spasms? What factor of his medical problems caused such miserably painful tension? The visible damage to his body—the bone breaks—from the accident had healed. Weakness in his legs and back was understandable after such trauma, but the ongoing spasms were not.

Sometimes muscle spasms were emotionally caused. She had worked with patients who had suffered terrible muscle spasms with no previous injury at all. Was Sy doing this to himself? Not consciously, of course, but was something bothering him so much that his muscles locked up as a result?

It could be the ranch. After all, he wasn't able to get around enough to see to the ranch himself. That could be driving him up the wall, preying on his mind, keeping him tense and on edge.

If only he was friendlier, she thought with a quiet, but frustrated, sigh. Friendly enough to discuss what really went on in his mind. It could be that he needed a psychologist as much as he did a physical therapist.

But it wasn't her place to suggest any treatment outside of her own specialty. Knowing Donnelly as well as she did, she also knew that he wouldn't hesitate to tell her so.

After an hour of concentrated effort on Sy's back, Pam's own back began aching, and her wrists, as well. Sy hadn't moved or made a peep for a long time. She leaned over him to see his face. He was in such a deep sleep that he was barely breathing.

She heaved a relieved sigh, carefully got off the bed and placed the pillows along his spine again, then, ignoring the towel across his hip area, very cautiously pulled the covers from the foot of the bed and laid them over him.

It was then that she realized how exhausted she had become. Bleary-eyed, she turned off the lamp and exited Sy's room via the porch door. Returning to her own room, she crawled into bed, remembered after she'd settled down that she had left her robe behind, but deemed it unimportant. She would get it in the morning.

Yawning, she closed her eyes. There was no doubt in her mind that she would fall asleep now, none at all.

She was right.

Pam was up at five. Dressed in a sweat suit, running shoes and baseball cap, she left the house for her morning run. The ranch was coming alive. She had heard Joe in the kitchen, and, outside, men were beginning to come out of the bunkhouse. After her stretching exercises, she headed for an open field, realizing after a few minutes that roads crisscrossed the field. She knew enough about ranches to know about the many roads most of them had, necessary for pickups and equipment to get to distant pastures and other outlying regions.

There were cattle in the huge field. They paid her no mind, and she barely noticed them. As was her practice, she maintained a clear head and concentrated solely on running and breathing properly. Or rather she *tried* not to think of anything else.

It worked for a while, but then last night invaded her concentration. She felt a satisfaction that she had given Sy respite from pain, at least enough that he had been able to sleep. If she could gain his full cooperation, she would have him on his feet in weeks. How could she make him grasp and accept that concept?

The word *trust* flashed into her mind. It was the answer. Somehow she must earn Sy's whole and complete trust.

Sy awoke at seven-fifteen. The time surprised him. He hadn't slept this late in months. It was, he felt, a very good sign.

Gingerly stretching a leg, he recoiled from the jolting pain in his back. In the middle of his grimace, someone rapped on the door. Pam's voice called out, "Sy? Are you awake?"

Recalling what had happened in the night, Sy decided Pam deserved some courtesy this morning.

"Yes," he called back. "Come in."

Pam didn't know what to expect from Sy this morning. But he sounded almost friendly, and if he had awakened in a good mood, she would like to witness it with her own eyes.

Turning the knob and opening the door a few inches, she peered in. "Oh," she said in surprise, "you're still in bed."

"Just woke up." Sy was suddenly so pleased he had made it through the night without pain medication, even though he'd had to call upon Pam for help, that he felt like shouting it to the world. But then he recalled her disapproval over that very thing, so he said nothing about it.

"Sy, I think we've discussed this before, but tell me again. Have you really been showering and dressing on your own? I guess what I'm getting at is, aren't you the most uncomfortable in the morning?"

He *had* been taking care of himself in the morning, but there had been residual effects of the painkiller he'd ingested the night before to help him through the first routine of the day. He wondered now if he would be able to do it by himself this morning, although his reply to Pam was, "Mornings are no worse than any other time of day."

"Really," she said thoughtfully, wondering in the back of her mind if she had a complete grasp of Sy's physical problems. It was her experience that people suffering his type of disabilities awoke sore and stiff after a long night in bed. Even with a middle-of-the-night massage to help them along.

"Well," she said, "I'll leave you alone so you can get up." Backing from the room, she pulled the door with her.

"Pam!"

She opened the door again. "Yes?"

"Would you ask Cal to bring me a large glass of orange juice? For some reason I'm parched this morning."

"I can get it, Sy."

"No, I don't want to bother you with that kind of thing. Just ask Cal to bring it, if you wouldn't mind."

"Well, yes, of course," she murmured, and left.

Sy's lips tipped in a wry sort of grin. He'd handled that rather cleverly, hadn't he? Cal would bring the orange juice and Pam would never know that he had also helped Sy out of bed and into the shower.

There *were* disadvantages to having a female therapist, Sy thought again, recalling that moment last night when she'd thrown back his covers. His grin faded. He sure hadn't had to worry about nudity with Jerry. On the other hand, Jerry hadn't done him as much good in the many weeks he'd been Sy's therapist as Pam had accomplished in one day.

Sy heaved a sigh. He really didn't have a choice, did he? Pam was going to be his therapist and he might as well get used to the idea.

* * *

Throughout the day Pam was amazed at the change in Sy. When she asked him to do something, he did it without snapping or snarling at her. Her planned routine, which would vary little until Sy was stronger, consisted of massage, simple exercises and hot baths. The exercises would become more demanding as time went on, but he would be ready for them—she would make sure of that. If he kept on cooperating, that is. She actually prayed that his much better mood today wasn't just a temporary aberration from his normal bad humor.

During Sy's afternoon massage, she brought up an idea that had been idling in the back of her mind all day.

"Sy, I ordinarily would not suggest such an expenditure to a patient, but I believe you can afford it. If I'm getting out of line here, please just say so. Have you ever considered buying a hot tub?"

"One of those outside tubs?"

Pam was gently rubbing his back with an aromatic oil. "You could have it installed inside or out, whichever you prefer. The thing is, they're so much larger than an ordinary bathtub, and you would have a much wider range of movement in one. If you got one big enough, I could get into it with you and assist you with exercises that aren't possible in a bathtub. Actually, hot tubs are so popular I'm surprised you don't already have one."

She would get into a hot tub with him? Sy's left eyebrow shot up. *That* could be interesting.

He cleared his throat. "I don't have one because I was hardly ever here," he said. "If you think it'll help, I'll have Cal order one right away."

Pam, though concentrating on easing one of the knots in his back, nodded. "Wonderful. Will you have it installed in the house or outside?"

"Outside, I think." Sy paused a moment, then added,

"Yes, definitely outside." He had a picture in mind, which he would pass on to Cal. This was not going to be your ordinary, everyday hot tub. As for whether or not he could afford it, that idea was laughable. He could afford anything he wanted. It was just that he hadn't wanted to buy anything for a very long time. This was kind of exciting, he realized, something to look forward to. "I'll talk to Cal the minute we're through," he murmured.

"Hello, my sweet, sweet boy."

Startled by the pleasant, but strange, voice, Pam raised her eyes to see a tiny, elderly woman enter the therapy room.

Sy lifted his head a bit and smiled. "Hello, Miss Bertie."

Miss Bertie walked to the table, bent down and kissed her grandson's cheek, noticing with immense satisfaction that it was cleanly shaven. She smoothed the hair back from Sy's forehead. "How are you feeling, dearest?"

"Not too bad. Have you met Pam?"

Miss Bertie smiled at Pam. "I haven't had that pleasure." She held her hand out above Sy's back. "Hello, Pam. I'm so glad to meet you."

Pam quickly wiped the oil from her palms and fingers with a towel before shaking Miss Bertie's small hand. "Very nice meeting you, ma'am."

"You don't know who I am, do you?" Miss Bertie said with a merry little laugh. "I'm Sy's grandmother. But everyone, including him, calls me Miss Bertie. So must you. Now, you mustn't let me interrupt. Please go on with what you were doing. I'll just sit over here and stay out of the way." She moved to a chair.

Smiling at the petite woman, so appropriately dressed for the ranch in blue denim slacks and a red plaid shirt, Pam oiled her hands again. "This is massage therapy," she told Miss Bertie.

The older woman nodded. "I have great faith in massage."

"Because of personal experience?" Pam asked, again intent on working oil into Sy's taut back muscles.

"Yes," Miss Bertie replied without explanation. It was immediately obvious to Pam that she wasn't going to hear about Miss Bertie's aches and pains. "You'll see me quite often," Miss Bertie said. "I haven't lived at the ranch for a good many years, but it will always represent home to me. Sy, the color in your face is much better than it was when I was here last week. You were really quite pale that day, dear. I do believe you're finally on the road to recovery."

"He is," Pam said adamantly. "It will be weeks yet before he will be able to discard both the crutches and the wheelchair, but I would almost guarantee it is going to happen."

"You're a very positive young woman."

"Yes, Miss Bertie, I am." Pam sent the older woman a smile and received a very warm tribute in return.

"Pam suggested I buy a hot tub, Miss Bertie," Sy said. "She strongly believes in hot water therapy."

"Massage and hot water therapy. Sounds sensible to me. What else, Pam?"

"Proper diet and exercise," Pam replied. "Right now Sy's exercises are stress-free, but as his body becomes stronger his exercises will become more demanding."

"You never said anything about demanding exercise," Sy said.

Miss Bertie laughed. "Maybe she was keeping it for a surprise. Sy, you were always fit as a fiddle. You might be able to fool Pam into thinking you weren't into exercise, but I know differently. Pam, you look quite fit yourself."

"She takes long walks," Sy said. "At least she did yesterday."

Pam let that comment pass and addressed Miss Bertie. "I run three to five miles every morning, Miss Bertie, and I *also* take long walks when time permits. I don't ignore calisthenics, either."

Sy turned his head on the table to peer at Pam. "You *run* three to five miles a day? Did you do it today?"

"Yes, sir, I did," Pam replied, gently turning his head back to where it had been.

"When?" Sy asked, sounding dubious.

"Around five this morning." Pam noticed the pleased expression on Miss Bertie's face and attributed it to approval of her personal regimen. If only she could have read the older woman's mind.

That idea of mine is working out even better than I had hoped! Pam is a lovely young woman, and so bright and intelligent. Sy shaved because of her, and he is already looking healthier. I am a brilliant scamp, that's what I am.

Laughing under her breath, Miss Bertie got up from the chair. "I'll see both of you later. I want to say hello to Joe and Cal, then take a little stroll around the compound."

"It was wonderful meeting you," Pam said.

"Believe me, my dear, the pleasure was all mine." Miss Bertie left.

"Your grandmother is…" Pam started to say.

Sy broke in and finished the sentence, his tone dry. "Up to something."

"Like what? She's an absolute dear. Why would you think she's up to something?"

"Because I know her. Whenever she gets that devilish twinkle in her eyes…."

Pam did the interrupting this time. "You're imagining things. She's a perfectly delightful woman, a true lady."

"Yes, she's definitely a lady. But I'd still bet the ranch that there's something going on I don't know about."

"What do you think she's going to do, run away with the circus?" Pam laughed at the ludicrousness of Miss Bertie doing anything silly.

Closing his eyes, Sy grinned a little. Miss Bertie might not run away with a circus, but there was little else he would put past her, should she take the notion.

The funny part of his suspicion was a feeling that whatever she was up to had something to do with him.

Now, just what could that be? he wondered.

Six

Miss Bertie passed on a dinner invitation from Sy, telling Pam in his presence that she rarely drove after dark anymore. "My eyesight isn't as good as it used to be, dear. I tootle here and there during daylight hours without a bit of trouble, but it's just not safe for me to be driving at night."

"You could stay the night and go home in the morning," Sy suggested.

"You're such a dear boy, Sy, but I really must go home now." After a kiss on Sy's cheek and a hug for Pam, Miss Bertie departed the house.

Pam and Sy were then alone in the sunroom. "She's wonderful, Sy, sweet and wonderful," Pam said rather emotionally. In her opinion, Miss Bertie was the kind of woman anyone would love having for a grandmother.

Sy had been watching Miss Bertie's car travel down the driveway toward the highway. He turned his gaze on Pam. "She's also a great little actress."

"Actress! Surely you're not saying she isn't genuine." Pam was truly shocked.

"She's genuinely sweet and wonderful, as you said, and she's also genuinely a great actress, as I said."

"I have no idea what you're talking about," Pam said with a disapproving sniff.

"No, but you might if you get to know her better."

Pam showed how dubious she was about that statement by rolling her eyes. "I can't believe you would say something unkind about such a wonderfully kind woman, your very own grandmother.''

Sy rolled his own eyes. "Look, I love Miss Bertie with all my heart, but I know her and you don't. I can tell when she's up to something. The last time she was here she wasn't, today she is.''

"That's the silliest thing I've ever heard. But if she is 'up to something,' as you put it, how would it concern you?''

"I haven't figured that out yet, but it *does* concern me. Believe me, I know.''

Before Pam could reply to what she felt was a ludicrous comment, Cal walked in. "Do you want your supper served in here?'' he asked, looking from Pam to Sy. "Joe's about ready to start steaming your vegetables.''

Pam got up. "I'm going to talk to Joe about something special for dinner tonight. Sy, you decide where you want to eat while I'm gone.'' She skipped from the room.

Cal sent Sy a grin. "She's a little dynamo, ain't she?''

"I guess that's one word you could use to describe her,'' Sy replied wryly. For some reason Cal's admiration of Pam annoyed him. Of course, he was the first to admit that in one way or another almost everything annoyed him these days. It wasn't something of which he was especially proud, but facts were facts.

Cal's grin faded. "Don't you like her, S.J.? She seems to be doing you some good. That counts for something, don't it?''

Sy hesitated but finally mumbled, "Yeah, it does.''

In the kitchen, Pam was talking to Joe. "You don't even own a wok? Are you sure?''

Joe looked disgruntled. "'Course I'm sure. I wouldn't know what to do with a wok if I had ten of 'em, but I guarantee there's not one in this house.''

Pam frowned. "I see." She brightened. "I can get by without one. What I want is to prepare some stir-fry for dinner."

Joe's lips thinned. "*You're* planning on doing some cooking?"

Pam almost laughed. She'd never run into anyone so protective of a kitchen before. "You can do it, if you know how to make stir-fry. Do you?"

"Never even heard of it," Joe mumbled crossly.

Pam suspected that wasn't quite true but didn't say so. Instead she smiled warmly at the persnickety older man. "Well, it's delicious, nutritious and easy to prepare. You may watch me, if you wish. Now, I'll need a large skillet and..." She reeled off a list of ingredients.

Joe told her where to find everything and then, mumbling under his breath, turned his back on her and began working on the meal he was preparing for the men's supper. Accepting Joe as he was, including his resentment of her intrusion in his kitchen, Pam set to work.

Pam and Sy ate in one of the small dining rooms. It was a lovely room, with rose-toned fabric on the walls. The drapes at the window and the chairs' seat covers were made of the same fine material. There was a special quality to this room, and Pam suspected it had been used by Sy's parents and perhaps even his grandparents for intimate meals.

Sy had walked from the sunroom with the use of his crutches. Pam thought he was doing remarkably well today, especially when she considered what he'd gone through in the night. It was pleasant sitting across the small table from him, and she found herself admiring his striking good looks. She had noticed that he'd tied his hair back with what appeared to be a leather shoelace, and he was clean-shaven, as well, unlike yesterday when she'd arrived. Was he more concerned about his appearance now because of her presence? she wondered. Because a woman was in the house, when previously there'd been only men?

"Stir-fry," Sy said as she filled his plate from the serving bowl.

"Do you like stir-fry?" she asked, hoping he did. She passed his plate to him and for some reason thought of that *Prominence Magazine* naming him as one of the world's most eligible bachelors. She would love asking him about it. Had someone interviewed him for the article, for instance? How, exactly, had it happened?

"Yes." He actually smiled, surprising her. "Beats the hell out of steamed vegetables."

Serving herself, Pam put *Prominence Magazine* out of her mind. Maybe she and Sy would reach a stage of friendship where she could ask him questions about that article, but they were far from being on that footing yet.

"I love steamed vegetables," she exclaimed. "Do you find them hard to eat?"

"They're okay." Sy picked up his fork and took a bite. "Delicious," he murmured. "You cooked this?"

"Yes, I did."

Sy cocked an eyebrow. "Joe actually let you use the kitchen?"

Pam laughed a little. "He suffered over it, but yes, he let me use the kitchen."

"Well, I'm impressed."

She responded pertly. "Well, I'm impressed that you're impressed."

Sy took up the challenge. "And I'm impressed that you're impressed that I'm impressed."

For the first time since they'd met, they laughed together. It made Pam feel good.

* * *

After the meal was over, Sy said he wanted to sit in the sunroom until it was time for his evening massage. Pam went to the library-den to look for something to read and was perusing the shelves of books when the phones in the house rang. There was one on the desk, very close to where she was standing, but she ignored it and continued studying the quite impressive array of good books. It wasn't her place to answer the phone on the Cope ranch, and if it happened to be a call for her, someone would let her know.

The call was for Sy. Cal brought a portable phone to the sunroom and told Sy, "It's Jerry."

Sy had left a message on Jerry's home answering machine. *This is Sy Cope, Jerry. Please call me when it's convenient.*

"Hello, Jerry," he said into the phone.

"Hello, Sy. What's up?"

"That's what I'd like to know. How come you didn't come back? Do you know why you were replaced with another therapist?"

"All I know is that Donnelly put me on another case, Sy."

"Did you request the transfer?"

"Nope, sure didn't. I was wondering if maybe *you* had requested a different therapist."

"Well, I didn't. If you didn't, and I didn't, who did? Look, is this the norm? I mean, are you usually shuffled from one unfinished case to another?"

"No way. It happens occasionally, of course, but usually a therapist stays with the same patient until he is no longer needed. That's been my experience, anyway. Who did Donnelly replace me with, Sy? I could get that information myself, you understand, but I've been pretty tied up."

Sy let a few seconds go by, then spoke in a clipped, curt manner. "A woman. Pamela Brooks."

"Pam's good, Sy. I wouldn't worry about her abilities if I were you."

"That's not the point. She might be the best therapist in Montana, but I'd still like to know why Donnelly pulled you off my case and sent Pam in your place."

"Wish I could help you out with that question, but all I do is follow orders. I'm sure that's what Pam is doing, too. Incidentally, Donnelly doesn't explain his decisions. Some doctors do, some don't. Donnelly's in the latter category. Good man, though.

"Sy, you're not unhappy with Pam's work, are you? What I mean is, you *can* request a different therapist, you know. In fact, if you want me instead of Pam, just call Donnelly and tell him so. It might take a few days to re-arrange schedules, but it's your right to have the therapist you want."

"Uh, no, that's not it, Jerry," Sy stammered. In that moment Sy realized that he *didn't* want Pam leaving and Jerry returning. Their methods differed, and Pam's were helping him a whole lot more than Jerry's had. But he didn't want to explain that to Jerry. There was, after all, no reason to hurt the man's feelings.

"I was just curious about the exchange, that's all," Sy said.

"Well, like I said, it happens on occasion."

"Jerry, thanks for returning my call. Maybe we'll meet up again someday."

"Sure, Sy. Goodbye."

After breaking the connection, Sy sat there thinking. He could have said that his main objection to his new therapist was her being a woman. He could have mentioned sexual awareness and discomfort during massages. He could have said Pam was too pretty for a man not to notice, and he could have mentioned Donnelly's gall—or was it indifference?—in assigning a young, pretty therapist to a young, horny man.

Sy could feel his good mood of the day slipping away. Talking to Jerry hadn't accomplished one single thing, other than causing his dark side to resurface. If he was strong enough, he would show Pam a thing or two about men and women, he thought with a cynical twist of his lips. Her quick-witted put-downs when he got cranky just dared him to go too far. What would she do if he did? Leave the ranch in a huff?

He didn't think so. Her self-confidence appeared unshakable. She would probably never give up on a patient without an extremely powerful reason, and *he* wasn't strong enough to give her a powerful reason.

As frustration gnawed at his vitals, Sy's thoughts got darker still. Pam might be a damned good therapist, but she was also bossy, overbearing and a little too sure of herself. Truth was, and he might as well face it, he was several rungs below her on the power ladder, and this was a sensation he'd never before felt in his life. Before the accident, he'd been the big dog, the leader of any group, large or small, that he'd been with. What was he now?

He was sinking deeper into a black hole of depression, knew it was happening but couldn't seem to bring himself out of it. The sun was starting to go down, casting long shadows in the fields across the river. He watched it happen with a brooding, resentful sensation in his gut. He didn't want to have to deal with a massage and all of its sexual ramifications tonight but knew he had to. It was either that or a pain pill, and he was not taking one more of those pills, no matter how badly he hurt. Both Pam and Dr. Donnelly could like it or lump it. He still had *some* say in how he lived, dammit!

Pam walked in, smiling cheerfully. "Ready for the ther-

apy room?'' Her smile died a sudden death when she took
a good look at Sy. Just since dinner, when he'd shown a
nice side of himself, something had happened. He again
looked morose, downbeat and, yes, even angry.

"What's wrong?" she asked quietly.

"What in hell do you think is wrong?" he snapped back.

She let a few perplexed moments go by, then asked,
"Are you in pain?"

"Lady, I'm *always* in pain!"

"Sy, you seemed to be quite comfortable during dinner." She spoke gently, softly, because she didn't want to
fuel his anger. "Throughout the day, in fact." Her heart
was sinking. All day she'd been thinking of how well he
was doing, thinking, too, that it was because of her ministrations, taking pride in her work. Had he merely been
putting on an act, concealing his pain for some unfathom-
able reason? He'd said that Miss Bertie was a great little
actress. Was pretense normal for the Cope family?

Feeling deflated, Pam went to a chair and sat down. "I'd
really like to know what you're thinking, Sy," she said in
that same gentle tone. "All I'm able to see is what you
show me, and today you seemed stronger, both physically
and emotionally. You're depressed again, and there must
be a reason. Can you tell me about it? Talk about it?"

If he said that he'd only pretended all day, Pam knew
she would be disappointed enough to cry. She waited for
him to give her some kind of answer, praying he would be
honest and afraid of it, too.

"I talked to Jerry," Sy said dully.

"Since dinner?"

"Yes."

"And that depressed you?" At least he hadn't said the
whole day had been a falsehood, which gave Pam some
hope.

"That and other things," Sy mumbled. He couldn't tell her where his thoughts had gone after talking with Jerry. She didn't need to know that he became aroused during massages, nor that he'd wondered what her reaction would be to a bold and lustful pass.

But he *could* say, and he did, "Jerry doesn't know why he was reassigned, either."

"Well, I don't find that information particularly depressing," Pam said slowly. "Why did it affect you that way?"

"Because no one tells me a damned thing!" Sy shouted. "I'm the patient. Why wasn't I consulted about a change of therapists? I wasn't even given a hint about it. All of a sudden, here you are, and Jerry's out. No explanation, no nothing. I'm just supposed to sit here and accept whatever is thrown at me."

Pam stared at him as though he had just slipped a cog. "Is this the second verse of the same song you sang yesterday when I got here?" Her voice was no longer gentle. Some self-pity was natural and to be expected from patients with serious problems, but Sy could be well in a short span of time if he'd stop brooding over trivial, mostly imaginary problems and concentrate on getting well. She'd been right to suspect he was causing his own distress. He *had* been feeling better today, and now he was miserable again, undoubtedly so tense his back was killing him, simply because his chat with Jerry had reminded him that no one had told him about the exchange of therapists before it had taken place.

She got to her feet. "This is an absurd conversation. I'll be in the therapy room. Come up when you're ready." She turned at the doorway before leaving. "If you wait too long, I'll be in my room."

Alone, Sy let his head fall forward. No one understood him, no one. Oh, hell, he thought, the pain...the pain. He would do anything short of taking a pain pill to be rid of it.

His "anything" was extremely limited, he thought with barely repressed fury—Pam's massage was it.

Cursing out loud and not giving a damn who might hear him, he transferred his pain-racked body from the chair he'd been using to the wheelchair and headed for the elevator and the therapy room.

Pam worked silently for the first half hour. Sy's back muscles had been tight as a drum when she'd started, but she finally was feeling a loosening of tension in them. His eyes were closed, but she could see a less agonized expression on his face.

Never had she worked with a more stubborn, more self-destructive patient than Sy, and she would love to tell him so in plain English. She couldn't do that, of course, not tonight and probably not for several weeks yet. But when Sy was well and before she departed the Cope ranch, she was going to let him know what a difficult patient he had been. She didn't plan on being kind about it, either.

His worst knots tonight were along the thoracic vertebrae, just about on a level with his shoulder blades. She stayed with a Swedish technique—used mostly as a stress reliever—instead of the many other types of massage she had mastered, including the corrective type, which was used to correct an imbalance in the body. But it wasn't nearly as pleasurable for the patient as Swedish massage, she knew, and besides, she believed now that she had definitive evidence of Sy's spasms being stress-related.

She decided to chance a conversation about stress and the damage it could cause. She cleared her throat. "You know, we're sometimes our own worst enemies," she murmured.

Sy's eyes opened. "Meaning I'm causing my own pain?"

He wasn't dense, Pam realized. He'd caught on to her inference awfully fast. "It's not impossible, Sy," she said quietly as she continued kneading his back.

He snorted derisively. "It might not be impossible, but it's a damned preposterous theory in my case."

"Oh, is it? Haven't you ever noticed that mental or emotional tension increases the tension in your back? You got very upset over your conversation with Jerry, and what happened afterward? The stress in your mind transferred itself to your back. Think about it. Weren't you feeling much better before talking to Jerry than you did a short time later?"

Sy didn't want to believe Pam's theory. In fact, he resented her playing psychologist. He wasn't mentally deranged, for God's sake, and stress of one kind or another was all around a person. If he couldn't handle simple problems without getting knocked to his knees, what in hell kind of life was he going to have?

"If you're going to talk, change the subject," he said irritably.

She worked silently for a few minutes, then told him what she was thinking. "You really don't want to face facts, do you? Didn't Dr. Donnelly ever talk about the damages of stress?"

"Good God, I know all about stress! But so does every stockbroker, advertising executive, physician and rancher in the country. You sound as though you just invented the word. And the condition," Sy snarled.

"I'm going to tell you something, and I want you to listen," Pam said sharply. "This very minute I can feel your muscles tightening up over that outburst. And I'll tell you something else, too, Sy. You're an angry man, and until you get rid of the anger, you're not going to get well!''

She reached for the bottle of oil. ''Turn over, I'm going to massage your chest.''

''Why? *It* doesn't hurt.''

''Because your entire body is tense.''

''I suppose you never get tense.'' He'd spoken sarcastically.

''Of course I do. Everyone does. But not twenty-four hours a day, seven days a week. Turn over, please.'' It was an effort for Pam to stay calm. Sy was in a nasty, argumentative mood, and it was all she could do to control herself, to *not* give him a harsh piece of her mind. But she knew he wouldn't get any rest tonight if he went to bed so keyed up. As much as she'd love to give him a darned good tongue-lashing, she would say as little as possible and do her job.

On his own, refusing any help from Pam, Sy managed to turn over. By the time he'd accomplished the feat, however, he was pale and breathing hard.

Pam felt his very real physical discomfort in her own soul. As mule-headed and irritating as he was, he didn't deserve a life of pain. No one did. Of course, if he would take his pain medication as Dr. Donnelly had prescribed it, he wouldn't be pale and breathless over a simple bodily maneuver!

Annoyed again, Pam stuffed a pillow beneath Sy's knees.

''What's that for?'' he asked in such a demanding, patronizing way that Pam wanted to smack him one.

She remained cool and collected. ''A pillow under your knees takes a great deal of strain off your back when you're on your back.'' She looked him right in the eyes. ''Which I think you already knew. You're doing your level best to pick a fight with me, and it's not going to happen. There is nothing you can do to make me lose my temper, Sy, so why not give it up for tonight?''

Sy closed his eyes and shut her out. The ceiling light was too bright for comfort, for one thing, and he was tired of bickering for another. He was also worried. The towel over his underwear would conceal nothing should his body act up again, and he didn't want Pam knowing how sexually susceptible he was to her during massage. She didn't need to know *everything* about him, for hell's sake!

While Pam rubbed, kneaded and stroked his torso with oiled hands, Sy deliberately thought of icy showers. He even went so far as to picture himself in a blizzard, cold and shivering, just so his body wouldn't heat up.

It worked for a while, but then the pleasure of her hands on his skin began overriding his determination to stay cool. He could feel a rising tide of feverish emotions warming that icy shower and melting the snow in that blizzard. It made him mad as hell, and he opened his eyes and saw her face just above his. Her expression was intent, her gaze focused on his upper chest and her own hands.

He realized that he no longer gave a damn *what* she thought, and he raised his right arm, crooked it around her neck and pulled her head down. He got only one look at the surprised, startled expression on her face before he kissed her, and he instantly forgot it in the pleasurable feelings of a woman's mouth against his. The amazing thing was that she didn't immediately break his hold on her and back away, which gave him all sorts of erotic ideas.

Pam's initial shock was as genuine as it could get, but Sy's lips on hers was so sexually exciting that she felt the sensation ripple through her body in waves of heat. It was when she felt his tongue slide into her mouth that she regained her senses.

She forced her head up, breaking the kiss, took his arm

from around her neck and laid it on his own chest. Her heart was beating hard and fast, and her mind raced for the best way to handle what could only be an impulsive pass from a patient, however much she had enjoyed it.

She decided to laugh it off. What else could she do, act angry and say something she didn't mean?

"Cool off, sport," she said with a laugh, which, though forced, sounded genuine enough.

Sy's eyes had grown dark and steamy, she saw, and she was suddenly nervous, although she would die before letting him know how strongly his kiss had affected her.

"Kissing is *not* part of a massage," she said lightly, with another laugh. "I think we had better finish up and get you to bed." That was when she noticed the bump in the towel that could only be one thing. Her heart sank. She must have done something wrong. A man should not become aroused during simple, impersonal massage.

"Uh, maybe that's enough for tonight," she mumbled, reaching for a towel to dry her hands. She forced an impassive expression on her face. "Do you think you'll be able to sleep now?"

Sy smirked. "What do *you* think? You're a pretty good actress, too, aren't you?"

She concentrated on wiping the oil from between her fingers. "I'm sure I don't know what you're talking about."

"What I'm talking about is that you kissed back, sweetheart."

"I most certainly did not," she said, speaking calmly in spite of the fluttering she could still feel in the pit of her stomach. She dared not lose control of the situation, and she also had to let him know that she would not accept this sort of behavior from him.

She forced herself to look him in the eyes, which wasn't

easy when his were still smoldering and that damned towel was still tented.

"I hope this isn't something I have to be watching out for during future treatments," she said in her most professional voice. "I have to tell you that it's not at all acceptable."

"Even though it was the most fun you've had since you got here?"

Sy's silky tone of voice arrowed straight to the core of her, and it dawned on her that she was indeed going to have to stay very alert if she wanted to prevent future passes.

She was suddenly quite angry with Sy. He had no right to put her in this position. She'd only been doing her job, and kissing her when she wasn't looking had been proof of his self-centered arrogance.

"You think you can do anything that springs to your egotistical mind, don't you?" she said, letting her anger show. "With everyone else on this ranch you might get away with that attitude, but it's not, let me repeat, *not* going to work with me! All you are to me is another patient, and not a very nice one, to boot."

"For crying out loud, it was only a kiss," Sy said disgustedly. "The way you're carrying on, you'd think I had stormed the bastions of your chastity. Give it a break, for hell's sake."

"No, you give *me* a break!" It occurred to Pam that the longer this test of their wills went on, the more apt it was that Sy would have another bad night. And, God help her, she didn't want to have to deal with another middle-of-the-night massage, not after this.

She drew a calming breath. "Look, let's just forget it. It meant nothing to me, and I'm sure it meant nothing to you. As you said, it was only a kiss." She changed the subject before Sy could answer. "Would you like me to get Cal to help you get ready for bed tonight?"

Sy looked away with a closed expression. "I can get there myself."

"Fine, whatever you say." With her head held high, Pam walked out.

Seven

Pam had all manner of mixed feelings about Sy's kiss. The fact that she had kissed him back, as he'd so impolitely pointed out, was the most disturbing aspect of the episode. She tried desperately to understand herself and could only accept her attraction to Sy with cheerless resignation. It was her problem and something she would have to live with, even while staying alert and making sure it didn't happen again.

It was obvious that Sy didn't respect her, which she found terribly disheartening. He had barely been civil to her since the moment she arrived at the ranch, and then, without so much as a pleasant word between them, or any other kind of warning or sign, had grabbed her and kissed her as though she were public property.

The morning after it happened, Pam stood at a window of her room and watched the sunrise. She hadn't slept well, she felt tired and logy, and she was waffling on taking her usual morning run, something she rarely did. Apparently Sy had slept just fine, because she hadn't heard a sound from his room all night. Either that or he'd suffered through any bad spells he might have had by himself. Which, perhaps, bespoke of a conscience.

Pam couldn't quite make herself believe that idea, however. Picturing Sy Cope as rueful over anything he'd done in his entire life was impossible for her. A stolen kiss wouldn't bother him. He was too rich, too good-looking and too pampered. Pam suspected—from what she remembered of that article in *Prominence Magazine* and from what she'd seen on this ranch with her own eyes—that Sy had always, *always*, done as he'd pleased. From the day of his birth, undoubtedly. No wonder he viewed his present disability with such hostility. He was one of those people who'd grown up with the attitude that bad things only happened to others, never to him. It was unfortunate that he'd had to learn the hard way that fate was totally impartial.

Sighing heavily, Pam turned from the window. She might not feel like running this morning, but that was the very best argument *for* running. Exercise got one's blood pumping, and she knew she would feel much better after a hard run.

Before she could change her mind again, she quickly swapped her nightshirt for running clothes and left her room. Joe was up. She could hear him in the kitchen as she came down the stairs. She went out the front door and breathed deeply of the cool morning air while doing her stretching exercises.

When she finally began her run, her thoughts went in a peculiar direction. If *Prominence Magazine* was correct in its assessment of Sy's assets, he was incredibly wealthy. Why then didn't he have a dozen personal servants instead of just three—Joe, Cal and Sandy? Also, the Cope house was beautiful, but it wasn't a mansion. Actually, for someone reputed to possess great wealth, Sy lived quite simply.

Of course, she must keep in mind that Sy had apparently spent very little time at the ranch before the accident. Pam strove to recall the *Prominence Magazine* article better— she was sure it had been published before his accident and had boasted admiringly of Sy Cope's devil-may-care lifestyle—but she found most of it only a blurred memory and decided to look for the magazine, which she was almost certain she had kept, the next time she was home.

Reaching the top of a hill, Pam paused to catch her breath and to look back at the ranch buildings and the scenery beyond. The beauty of the place was no longer startling, but, she suspected, it would forever inspire awe. Why hadn't it been enough for Sy?

Pondering that question, she began running again. Truth was, she had to admit that Sy Cope was an unusual, unique type of man. Certainly she had never met anyone like him before. What a monumental mistake it would be to fall for him! Even taking a pass—such as the one he'd made last night—seriously would be a mistake. She'd been handy, he had kissed her, that was all there was to it. She must never think it meant more.

And if he ever tried anything again, she must look at it the same way. She would be on her guard against any such shenanigan, of course, but if he should infiltrate that guard in some clever way and succeed with another kiss, she must make darned sure that she didn't kiss him back, not even for a few seconds as she'd done last night. It really didn't matter that she found him outrageously attractive—she simply was not in Sy Cope's league.

Nor would she be his plaything while staying on his ranch. If he had no respect for her personally, he at least should respect her profession. She would make that very clear if he tried something again, she decided adamantly.

At the same time she made that decision, however, Pam felt the strangest urge to cry. Tears actually gathered and stung her eyes until she shook off the feeling. Why on earth would she cry over a man she could never have and probably wouldn't want if she *could* have him?

Her hormones were acting up this morning, she thought with a sudden burst of resentment, and it was all Sy's doing. How dared he kiss her in such a possessive, sexual fashion? And just how far would he have gone if she had let him?

Picking up speed, she forced Sy from her mind. Not only was she not going to cry over him, she wasn't even going to *think* about him! Taking a quick glance at her watch, she realized it was time to start back. She reversed directions without slowing down.

Twenty minutes later Pam was almost back to the ranch compound. She was sweaty and slightly out of breath, but, as she'd known would be the case, she was no longer in a blue funk. She would be able to face the day *and* Sy now.

She stopped suddenly and stared at the caravan of trucks of various sizes on the driveway, obviously heading for the compound. "What on earth...?" she mumbled, and took off running again.

Instead of going immediately to the house, she stopped for a breath, then walked up to a group of ranch hands, who were also watching the incoming trucks, some of which were already maneuvering into parking spots.

"What's going on?" she asked.

The men turned and looked at her, and a couple of them grinned. "You're S.J.'s new therapist, right?" one of them said.

Pam smiled. There was no good reason not to be friendly with these men. "Yes, I'm Pam Brooks. What are all these trucks doing here?"

"Delivering men and equipment to put in a hot tub," the group's spokesman said.

Pam almost laughed. There were at least a dozen men climbing out of the trucks, and she could see now that each of the trucks carried something—tools, lumber, pipe and items she couldn't identify. All for a simple hot tub? she thought, while stifling another urge to laugh. What kind of hot tub was Sy planning to have installed? This many men and this much equipment could construct an entire Roman bathhouse.

Well, it was none of her business. She was about to head for the house when a huge bear of a man walked up and offered his hand. "Hoke Brenner, ranch foreman."

Pam laid her hand in his and received a hearty hand-shake. "Pam Brooks."

"Nice meeting you, Pam. Did you meet the rest of this gawking crew?" he asked with an amused twinkle in his friendly brown eyes.

"Not by name." Pam smiled at the group. They were of various ages and description with one common factor—their clothing. Every man wore jeans, cowboy boots and a big hat.

Hoke did the honors, naming each man. Pam nodded at each, then said, "Nice meeting you all. Sorry I can't hang around and chat, but duty calls."

She headed for the house and grinned at the variety of remarks from the men as she left, from a simple goodbye to a flirty "You sure do brighten up the place, Pam!" One bold soul called out, "I've got a crick in my back! Help, I need a physical therapist!"

Pam was positive that last remark had been made by a young fellow named Tom. She couldn't remember his last name, as Hoke had reeled off the men's names so fast no one would be able to remember them all. But Tom had devilish blue eyes and she remembered them quite clearly. Easily Tom's eyes were as blue as Sy's, she thought as she entered the house via the back door, and since she apparently was such a sucker for blue eyes on a man...

No, she was not going to dwell on devilish blue eyes, not Tom's and certainly not Sy's. Staying within the maze of hallways on the first floor, she avoided the kitchen and every other room and went directly to the front foyer and the winding staircase. With all haste, she hurried up the stairs to her room, where she tore off her clothes and dashed into the bathroom for a shower.

The noise of the arriving trucks had awakened Sy. For a moment he was beset by confusion because something was startlingly different, and then a big smile broke out on his face: he had slept through the night! For the first time since the accident, he'd slept without medication or massage.

"Thank you, Lord," he whispered, so thrilled with his progress he didn't know whether to laugh or cry. But he realized after a moment that he was afraid to test his mobility. If the relatively simple act of getting out of bed inundated his body with pain again, he would be crushingly disappointed.

He sat up cautiously, using the correct method of pushing himself up with his hands and arms rather than putting stress on his back. Twinges along his spine concerned him, but so far he wasn't suffering, which renewed his hope. His robe was on the foot of the bed, and he actually held his breath while putting it on. Surprised that there were no sudden, spasmodic wrenches in his back, he reached for the crutches leaning against the nightstand, positioned them in front of himself and then gradually worked himself to his feet.

He still felt all right. He was afraid to believe it, afraid this was some kind of fluke that wouldn't last. Making no sudden moves and with the crutches supporting most of his weight, he took a few tentative steps. Nothing changed. His back was far from a hundred percent, but the agony he'd become so accustomed to feeling along his spine was no more than a dull ache.

The wonder of it hit him then—a miracle was happening.

He was getting well! Tears filled his eyes and he let them dribble down his cheeks unchecked. His improvement was Pam's doing. He was immediately embarrassed about his childish rebellion over everything she'd done or had tried to do for him. Obviously her methods and techniques were precisely the solution for his particular problems.

He had to tell her, he thought, finally drying his face on the sleeve of his robe and welcoming the eagerness that had been missing from his system for so long. And he had to thank her.

And then a thought that he never would have dreamed might be disturbing hit him, and it *was* disturbing, almost unbelievably so. How well was well to Pam? If he stayed as well as he was this morning for several days, for instance, would Pam contact Dr. Donnelly and tell him she could do no more for Sy Cope?

Sy hobbled over to the window, looked out and frowned. Why should the thought of Pam leaving the ranch bother him? It did, he realized. The idea burrowed itself into his system and caused all sorts of negative feelings. Didn't he want her to go? he asked himself. It had to happen someday—she wasn't a permanent fixture, after all.

He mulled it over for a while. Why tell Pam anything? In the first place, this morning's sense of well-being *could* be a fluke. One painless night didn't guarantee future painless nights. Or days, for that matter. And he was only getting started on Pam's exercise program. Every day that he worked with her could produce increased strength. He believed that now.

No, there wasn't one really sound reason why he should tell Pam anything. Let her discover his improvement for herself. She would see it, of course, but if he handled it smoothly enough, she would see only a gradual improvement.

And she wouldn't be leaving anytime soon.

There was something so satisfying about that conclusion that Sy's frown deepened in perplexity. Had he become so reliant on Pam's capabilities that he was leery of functioning—or attempting to function—without her?

Or was there more to it, a personal element for which he had no name nor any understanding?

"Hmm," he murmured uneasily under his breath. *That* concept was definitely food for thought.

Pam tested the strength in Sy's legs often the same way that she had done during her initial examination, by having him push the soles of his feet, one at a time, against the palm of her hand. This morning she felt such a marked improvement in pressure on her palm that her eyes widened slightly. It was the only sign she gave of the satisfaction she felt, and Sy didn't see it.

She knew that with her past patients she would have immediately said something about the positive results of this morning's test, as it was her habit to praise even the smallest improvement in whatever disability a person was trying to better. But in Sy's case, he was so prone to black depressions that she feared the slightest thing gone awry could set him off. In other words, if she praised improvement today and found a setback tomorrow, it wouldn't be good.

So she kept silent on the subject and mentioned the activity going on outside instead, while she massaged the muscles of his legs. Her routine was to limber him up, then lead him through a series of exercises.

"That must be a very special hot tub you're having installed." By this time Pam had identified electricians, plumbers and carpenters, and they were working just to the right of the front of the house. Obviously Sy did not plan to obstruct the view from the sunroom, a plan of which she highly approved.

"It'll be nice," Sy murmured. In truth, he wasn't completely comfortable with Pam this morning, something he hadn't expected before seeing her and beginning the day's routine. It was because of that impulsive kiss, he knew, even though both of them were acting as though it hadn't happened.

"I imagined a simple hot tub when I suggested it. Maybe one of those redwood models that you see so often." Pam went to the cupboard for a sheet, which she brought to the table and began tucking around Sy's hips.

"This is different," Sy said, referring to the sheet. "What're you doing?"

"Protecting your modesty. I think you're ready for more advanced leg exercise, but I have to make sure. You'll see what I mean when we get started." With the sheet firmly in place, she took his left ankle in her hands. "I'm going to do most of the work, but I want you to help, also. We're going to raise your leg from the table, knee straight, and rotate your leg at the hip." She wanted to check the mobility in his hip joints. He seemed to have made a giant leap forward in strength, which was sometimes the way it happened, but she could not advance a patient's exercise program without keeping a strict eye on joint mobility.

She completed the test with both legs and nodded. "I see no problem with your hip joints."

"Wasn't that in my medical charts? I went through every test known to mankind. It should be there."

"Perhaps I'm overly cautious, but I like to..."

Sy cut in. "Learn things about a patient for yourself."

Pam smiled. "Exactly. Did raising your legs cause discomfort in your back?"

"I felt it, but it was tolerable."

"Good, that's what I'd hoped to hear. Now, here's what I'd like you to do." Pam left the table and began sliding the exercise mat on the floor over to a blank wall. "I want you to lie on the mat with your knees slightly bent and your toes touching the wall."

"I don't get it."

"You're going to walk up the wall. This is a marvelous technique to strengthen your legs without putting stress on your back. I want you to forget you even have a back and concentrate solely on hip and leg movement."

"Aren't you going to massage my back this morning?" Sy tried not to sound as disappointed as he felt and realized at once what a change in attitude that question really was. Did he want to feel sexy and aroused this morning? Had he been waiting for one of Pam's deliciously tormenting massages?

"Later," she said briskly. "Come on now, off the table and onto the mat." She stood by and watched him follow her instructions, and she drew in a long, slow breath when she saw how much easier he moved today. There was no evidence that he'd taken a pain pill—no glazed eyes, no slurred speech—and yet he was moving almost normally.

He had to realize it, she thought. The kind of pain he'd been living with did not suddenly evolve into something "tolerable," his word, without a patient knowing it. It was odd that he hadn't talked about it. What should she make of that?

Sy walked up the wall for ten minutes, then Pam had him lie flat on the mat and slowly draw up his knees for another ten. She said often, "Do not use your back. Hips and legs only."

After that there was another exercise, and another, until Sy began showing signs of fatigue. "Okay, that's enough for now. You did great," Pam said. She was so encouraged by Sy's progress that she felt elated. She helped him up from the mat and walked him back to the table. "Now for a massage and a hot bath. How are you feeling?"

Sy got settled on the treatment table. "Tired."

"But not in pain?"

"Some." He could hardly believe that he felt only mild discomfort in his back after all that exercise. He *was* getting well! He closed his eyes as Pam began kneading his back. Her touch was pure magic, and after a while even the mild discomfort went away. Sy was a bit perplexed by it all. He'd been in very bad shape, or so he'd believed. Was it possible to recover so quickly?

Pam was amazed, there was no other word for it. Working along his spine, she could not find even one of those terrible, knotted spasms. Oh, she encountered spots of some tautness, but nothing like she'd been feeling before today.

Still, she was reluctant to pronounce him vastly improved. One week, she thought. If after a week he was still as relaxed as he was today, she would talk to him about it.

"You didn't tell me what kind of hot tub you're having installed," she murmured quietly as she worked.

Sy spoke lazily, indicating total relaxation to Pam. "There's going to be a gazebo. The tub will be installed in the gazebo. I told the contractor I wanted it ready for use by next Monday."

"Well, there's enough men and equipment out there to build a house in five days, so the timing shouldn't be a problem."

"It won't be."

Pam realized that he was falling asleep and said no more. Her thoughts continued to flow, however. If Sy continued to improve as he'd done in the past twenty-four hours, she wouldn't be here beyond a few weeks. She couldn't imagine a reason why they would ever see each other again, other than a major relapse, which shouldn't occur if she had done her job right.

Not that Sy might not have a distressed day now and then, maybe for the rest of his life. She still believed the muscle spasms in his back were emotionally caused, and if he got upset over something in the future, he could very well suffer back problems again. Since he had refused to consider her theory on that matter, it was something he was going to have to figure out for himself, and he would, she felt certain. Eventually he would.

When he reached the point of walking without crutches, he was bound to be more receptive to considering commonsense causes for any attacks of discomfort. He would, Pam repeated in her mind, connect emotional distress with the physical.

In the meantime, her course was clear. His legs were getting stronger. Along with doing whatever she could to keep his back supple, she must provide the proper treatment and exercise to reinforce and increase the strength of his leg muscles.

Sy was sleeping so peacefully on the table that she didn't want to wake him. Moving quietly around the room, she tidied it. Then, for a while, she watched the men at work on the gazebo. Time passed, and when she grew tired of standing at the window, she sat on a chair.

It was a few minutes past twelve when Cal stuck his head in the door. Pam put her fingers to her lips to caution him against speaking loudly, then got up and stepped into the hall. She spoke in a whisper.

"Sy's been sleeping for a couple of hours. I didn't want to leave him alone, in case he should get too close to the edge of the table. Would you keep an eye on him while I run down to the kitchen and get some lunch? I'll bring it back here to eat, so I should only be gone a few minutes."

"He's sleeping?" Cal looked surprised.

"He appears to be feeling much better. If his improvement continues, I expect him to do quite a lot of sleeping for a while. He's been through hell, Cal, and I believe he has a lot of sleep to catch up on."

"That's really good news, Pam," Cal whispered. "But wouldn't it be better if he did his sleeping in his bed? That table's mighty narrow, and it can't be comfortable."

"I doubt if he's aware of anything right now, least of all what he's lying on. Let me warn you about something. You may catch him napping anywhere in the house. Unless there's some sort of danger involved, let him sleep. It's an extremely good sign."

"Well, sure, whatever you say, Pam. You go ahead and get some lunch. I'll stay here with Sy."

"Thanks, Cal. Oh, if he should happen to wake up while I'm gone, it's all right if he gets dressed. He'll probably be hungry, and I can continue treatment after he has lunch."

"Okay."

Pam walked away. She should feel elated, and part of her did. Every sign pointed to Sy's finally being on the road to recovery, and that was cause for elation.

But there was a very private, very personal part of herself that felt sad and empty. When Sy Cope *was* well, he would no longer need her services.

That, of course, would be the end of their relationship.

Eight

Sy continued to improve, and by the time the gazebo and hot tub were completed, Pam was taking him for walks outside. She carried his crutches, just in case, and he didn't walk fast, but there was a confidence in his steps that was brand-new to Pam's eyes.

"The gazebo is beautiful," she said while they were out for a stroll after the last truck and carpenter had driven away. The enormous tub in the structure was already filled with water. It would be hot enough to use tomorrow morning.

"It's what I ordered."

"Apparently you knew what you wanted, and so did the contractor."

"A meeting of minds," Sy agreed, sending Pam a sidelong glance and thinking that it was his fault that *they* had never had a meeting of minds. She had arrived at the ranch brimming with good cheer and anticipation, which he strongly suspected was her normal personality, and had run headlong into his surly attitude and black moods. She still smiled on occasion, but dealing with such a contentious patient had subdued much of her natural enthusiasm.

A searing guilt assailed him as he remembered the time when he'd been known as a nice guy. A decent sort. A fun person to be around. Those had been good days. Good years. *Prominence Magazine* had even dubbed him "Montana's Playboy Rancher."

He hadn't liked the label—all he'd been doing was enjoying life—but he'd laughed it off. He didn't feel like laughing about it now. Deep down he hoped that Pam didn't read *Prominence Magazine* and hadn't seen the article. There was no way to find out, though, other than asking her point-blank, which Sy couldn't bring himself to do.

Pam had made a decision. "Sy, I think it's time we talked about how much you've improved," she said quietly. She had been assigning him more vigorous exercises with each passing day, and he'd kept up remarkably well. The simple fact he was walking outside, without aid, was proof of how well he was doing.

Sy was silent a moment. He didn't want to hear her say that she wouldn't be here much longer, and he wished she hadn't introduced the subject. How best to answer her? he wondered. *Keep it light. Don't make a big deal out of it.*

He followed his own advice by giving a short laugh. "I'm far from a hundred percent, Pam."

"Oh, I know. But you're getting there." She touched his arm. "This is far enough. Let's turn around now."

Reversing directions they began walking back toward the house. A couple of men near the bunkhouse waved and called out, "Looking good, S.J.!" Sy raised his arm to wave back and was nearly knocked to his knees by an agonizing wrenching in his back. He grabbed Pam by the arm, and she realized instantly that he was in pain again. Why? she thought almost frantically. Because he'd seen some of his ranch hands?

"Do you want the crutches?" she asked.

"No, dammit, no!"

Pride, she thought. He didn't want his men seeing him on crutches again, when he'd been doing so well. But his struggling to walk alone, as he'd been doing before the spasm hit him, was silly, and maybe even dangerous.

"Will you at least lean on me?" He was wearing his stubborn face, she saw, and it infuriated her. "Don't you dare get mule-headed on me, Sy Cope," she said through gritted teeth.

"I thought I was getting well," he said bitterly.

"You are." Something had caused this, either seeing his men or something she'd said. Pam felt puzzled as she recalled their conversation just before it had happened. They'd only been talking about his noticeable improvement, for pity's sake. Why should that bring on an attack like this?

She wasted no more time, for he was suffering, and she wound her arm around his waist. "*Lean* on me," she commanded sharply. "And don't worry about falling. I'm much stronger than I look."

Sy had experienced her strength many times and found it amazing in such a small woman. He thought it amazing, too, that she wasn't muscle-bound. Her flesh was firm, of course, but she couldn't look more feminine. And she always smelled so good. Not because of cosmetics or perfume, but from soap, toothpaste and shampoo. He wasn't missing the fact that the more he was with her, the prettier she became.

Sy didn't argue. Wrapping his arm around her shoulders, he let her lead him to the house. But he knew something now that he hadn't let himself admit before: Pam's theory about emotional upsets causing his muscle contractions was right on the money. She had started talking about his physical improvement, and he had started thinking that she was going to tell him she wouldn't be around much longer. The spasm had hit him within seconds. It could only have been caused by disruptive thoughts.

My Lord, was she really so important to him that he couldn't deal with even the idea of her leaving?

Sy's stomach churned all during the walk back to the house. Was he falling for his therapist? After years of dating glamorous, exciting women, was he discovering the real thing with an ordinary woman...? No, *ordinary* seemed an insulting word, but in all honesty, he could not label Pam glamorous. As pretty as she was, she would never dress in slinky clothing, wear scads of artfully applied makeup or flirt with every man she met.

On the other hand, dare he forget that she was the only woman he'd been near for a long spell? He'd hardly given sex any thought since the accident. Wasn't it only normal for him to respond to an attractive woman, especially when there was so much physical contact between them?

But if he really got logical about the situation and thought in terms of full recovery—or the best recovery he could make, given his serious injuries—the time was getting closer when he would be mobile enough to drive again, to leave the ranch and seek all the female companionship he wanted.

So why was he so hung up on Pam staying?

Pam had had her mail forwarded to the Cope ranch so she could keep up with her utility bills and such. While she was massaging the knots in Sy's back after their walk, Cal came into the therapy room.

"Here's your mail, Pam."

"Thank, Cal. Just set it anywhere." She wasn't expecting anything important, so she was in no hurry to see what she had received.

About an hour later, when Sy was relaxed again and resting in his room, Pam remembered her mail. Still in the therapy room, she picked up the small stack, moved a chair close to the window and sat down to go through what turned out to be mostly junk mail. But then one envelope leaped out at her—it was from Elliot!

"What the...?" she mumbled, taken completely aback. After three years of absolutely no contact, Elliot had written to her? Whatever for? She frowned at the envelope for a few moments, not positive that she wanted even to open it. She rarely thought of Elliot anymore, and she couldn't imagine a reason for him writing to her.

If it *was* a letter, of course. Maybe he'd sent her something else, information about a new therapy technique, for instance. Not that he'd ever done that before, but why on earth would he write her a letter?

She finally tore off the end of the envelope and shook out its contents. It was most definitely a letter, and she began reading it.

Dear Pam,
Bet you're surprised to hear from me. Well, I have another surprise up my sleeve, so brace yourself. I'm coming back to Montana. Never thought it would happen, but I'm actually lonesome for home. I phoned the Billings Therapy Center about work, and they said to come ahead, that they'd be glad to have me back.
    So I'm getting everything settled here—packing and saying goodbye—and plan to be on my way in about a week. I talked to Henrietta McPherson at the center when I called, and she said you were still leading the single life. Me, too, sweetheart. I think Montana isn't the only thing I'm lonesome for as I'm really looking forward to seeing you.

                                                    Love, Elliot

Pam slowly lowered the letter to her lap and then stared out the window. But it wasn't Elliot in her thoughts, it was

Sy. Elliot could write a dozen letters, a hundred, and they wouldn't affect her nearly as much as one sincere smile from Sy.

The worst was happening, she realized with a sinking sensation: she was falling in love with Sy, with a patient! She sucked in a quick, unsteady breath as the revelation took root and became more clearly defined. She wasn't falling in love, she was *already* in love. A groan built in her throat. How could she do this to herself? Sy would never love her back. She was asking for a hapless, unhappy existence.

And yet how did one alter or destroy feelings? Feelings happened all on their own. She could tell herself that professionals did not fall for their patients until hell froze over, and she would still love Sy.

Not that she had to let him know her silly thoughts, God forbid. It wasn't his burden, it was hers.

Her gaze dropped to Elliot's letter. She had no desire to see him, but there was probably very little chance of avoiding him if he was going to be working at the center again. And even if her final memories of their relationship were not good, they had once been very close. Maybe...maybe she should encourage Elliot's interest, she thought with a nervous flutter in her stomach. She didn't want to live alone for the rest of her life, and there was no chance at all of raising Sy's interest.

But could she date Elliot, or any other man, when she loved another?

Oh, she must, she thought frantically. She had to at least try to replace Sy Cope in her heart with someone else. Living out her life with unrequited love as her only companion was a chilling thought.

Pam looked at the envelope and saw that it had been

mailed three days ago. Elliot had said he would be leaving for Montana in about a week. Four days plus two or three for the trip—he would be in Billings sometime next week.

And she would see him if he contacted her, she decided with a heavy heart. If she was lucky, Elliot would make her forget Sy.

Realizing that she was grasping at straws, she heaved a forlorn sigh and rose from her chair. She dropped the junk mail in the trash can and set Elliot's letter on the small table containing her massage oils and lotions. First she would straighten the room, as she always did after using it, then she would do something to take her mind off her personal problems. Some exercise, she thought. Some calisthenics. Yes, that was what she would do. Exercise always made her feel better.

Sy had a lot to think about. He was lying on his bed, ostensibly resting, but his brain wouldn't shut down enough for a nap. A troubling, persistent question had arisen in his mind: should he tell Pam straight-out that he liked her? That he maybe *more* than liked her? The troubling part of that idea was how she might react to such an admission. She'd never given him any reason to think she might feel anything personal for him, and what if she laughed it off, the way she'd done with that impulsive kiss?

Another problem to contemplate was that maybe his feelings wouldn't last. They could stem from her being the only woman he'd been around since the accident, after all.

Annoyed with his own ambivalence, Sy carefully got off the bed and slowly wandered around the room. His back felt fine again. Pam knew exactly how to treat any discomfort he might feel. No one would ever be able to say that she wasn't an incredible therapist, that was certain.

Going to a window, Sy leaned against the frame and

scowled at the view. He was recovering rapidly and Pam would soon go on to another patient. His loins ached for her as his arms ached to hold her. Was his intense desire merely lust for her perfect body? But if that was all it was, why did he care how she might interpret another pass? Either she would reciprocate or she wouldn't. Lust was a simple emotion, and Sy knew in his soul that the feelings Pam evoked in him were not even close to being simple. The whole damned situation was too complex to unravel and comprehend, in fact.

He drew in a long, uneasy breath. If he kept thinking in this vein he was apt to feel it in his back.

Movement on the front lawn caught his eye, and he brought his gaze from the distant pastures to just below his window. Pam, wearing lavender spandex shorts and top, was doing side bends and appeared oblivious to everything else. Bending from the waist, her legs straight, she placed her hands palms-down, on the grass and walked them backward.

Sy watched as she moved from one exercise to another with all the suppleness of a young sapling. The sun shone in her hair, bringing it to its palest shade of blond. Her physical perfection reached from her sun-brightened hair to the athletic shoes on her feet. Her movements were as graceful as a ballerina's, and Sy couldn't stop staring.

At that moment his doubts vanished and he loved her more than life.

But his certainty faded when he wondered again if the feeling would last, if it was genuine. Cursing, he forced himself from the window. Watching Pam exercise on the lawn was an agony he didn't need. She shouldn't tempt him like that. If he went outside, she would stop exercising and take up the usual routine of his daily treatments.

Remembering that his crutches were still in the therapy

room, he cautiously made his way down the hall. He was gaining confidence in his returning strength, but he would not chance a fall by walking very far without someone with him or without the support of his crutches.

At the door of the therapy room, he saw the crutches leaning against the table on which Pam kept her bottles and tubes of massage oils and lotions. It was a short walk to the table, and he was about to pick up the crutches when he noticed an envelope on the table.

Curious, he picked it up instead of the crutches and saw that it was addressed to Pam and the return address cited a man's name, Elliot Young.

Shock bolted through him. It had never occurred to him that she might have a boyfriend, which was unbelievably absurd. Of course she had a boyfriend. A woman like her? She probably had hordes of men asking her out.

But maybe this guy, Elliot Young, was special. Maybe Sy Cope never had stood a chance with Pam Brooks!

"Damn," he muttered, staring daggers at the envelope in his hand. He'd never read another person's mail before, but something very important seemed to be at stake here. Still, he stood there and pondered the crime for several minutes. He was not a man with secrets himself, and he'd never been one to sneak around and snoop into other people's business. Yet he couldn't destroy the potent curiosity all but eating him alive. He *had* to find out who Elliot Young was. Looking out the window to make sure Pam was still on the lawn, Sy slipped the letter from the envelope and quickly read it.

It didn't help his mood. With grimly set lips, he returned the letter to the envelope and placed it where he'd found it. *Love, Elliot* repeated itself over and over in his mind. Apparently *Love, Elliot* had been in Baltimore for some time and now was coming back to Billings. The jerk was looking forward to seeing Pam again. Was she looking forward to seeing the jerk again?

Well, maybe he just might change her mind about that, Sy thought with a sardonic twist of his lips.

Leaving the crutches where they were—he preferred Pam not knowing that he'd been in the room—he hobbled back to his bedroom.

In her room a few nights later, almost asleep, Pam heard Sy calling her name. "Oh, no," she whispered, extremely disturbed that he would be in pain again. It appeared that he was in a stage of recovery that regressed periodically, something she hadn't expected to happen.

But every case she worked with was different, she reminded herself as she got out of bed, pulled on a robe and stuck her feet in bedroom slippers. She hurried to Sy's door and rapped. "Sy?"

She heard a muffled "Come in" through the door and turned the knob. The lamp on the nightstand was burning. Pam was certain she was going to see the effects of intense pain on Sy's face and was surprised when she didn't. Gingerly approaching the bed, she frowned. "Is something wrong?"

"I can't sleep. Would you sit and talk for a while?"

She blinked in confusion. He'd called her to his room to talk? *That* was certainly a departure from his normal attitude toward her.

But then, if he truly needed company, who else would he turn to? She was, after all, the only other person in the house at night.

"Sure," she said quietly. "I'll sit with you for a while." She moved a chair closer to the bed and settled herself on it. "Other than suffering insomnia, are you feeling all right?"

"Better than I have in months." Sy's eyes sought hers. "I owe you, Pam."

She blushed—from the blatantly intimate light in his eyes and from a compliment she would have sworn would never come out of Sy Cope's mouth.

She was so internally flustered that she stammered, "I— I'm being well paid for this job, Sy," and then winced because she had reduced his gratitude to a paycheck. It was not what he had meant and she knew it.

Sy reinforced that knowledge by saying, "I'm not talking about money. What I owe you could never be repaid in dollars and cents."

She was still flustered, but she managed a reasonably sensible answer. "You don't owe me anything, Sy. I've only been doing my job, which I was sent out here to do."

"But you do your job so well. I've been lying here thinking about it, going clear back to the day you arrived. One of the things I owe you is an apology. My behavior that day was inexcusable. I'd like to ask you something. Why did you stay?"

"I...I stayed because you needed help."

"Yeah, but I was such an intolerable jerk. Throwing that phone like a kid with a temper tantrum. God, what you must have thought of me."

Pam couldn't help smiling. "Well, that was pretty hard to take, all right."

Sy's eyes bored into her. "What *did* you think of me?"

"Um, I...I can't remember for sure."

"Try. It's important to me."

Did he really want to hear her first impression of him? Pam pondered a moment, then decided that he did. "I thought you were spoiled rotten and so used to doing whatever you wanted that you didn't know any other way to behave."

"Ouch." Sy's lips twitched with a hint of a grin. "You don't feel that way now, do you?"

He looked so handsome in the lamplight that Pam could hardly think of anything else. Oh, yes, she had it bad for Sy Cope. She felt him deep inside of herself, suspected she always would, but she didn't dare let him know the extent of her feelings for him. It was not a pleasant sensation. He didn't know it and he never would, but he inhabited a very large part of her heart. How it had happened, she would never comprehend, especially when she had guarded her emotions so carefully since the day he'd initiated that kiss.

"Not all the time," she said lightly, teasingly, so he wouldn't think this topic was making her uncomfortable. He merely looked at her for a long time, so long, in fact, that Pam finally said, a bit belligerently, "What?"

"I was wondering about something. When I'm able to leave the ranch on my own, would you go out with me?"

Pam's heart skipped a beat. Did *he* have the same kind of feelings for her that she had for him? Dared she even hope that he did?

"I...I suppose it wouldn't, um, hurt anything. Once you're no longer my patient," she added, unable to conceal completely the nervousness she suddenly felt.

Apparently Sy didn't notice. "You're saying you don't date patients?" He was frowning.

"It's really not a good idea, Sy. You see..."

"Haven't you *ever* dated a patient?"

"No, I have not."

Sy hadn't been able to get *Love, Elliot* out of his mind. "So who do you date, then, other therapists?"

He said "other therapists" as though the two words were poisonous, all but spitting them out. His disdainful tone of voice startled Pam, and she sat up straighter.

"I think we should change the subject," she said stiffly.

"I like this one."

"Well, I don't! Sy, who I date is really none of your business." Truth was, she had done very little dating since Elliot left the area, but she would bite off her tongue before telling Sy that. He was actually sounding possessive, as though she were his property! What nerve!

And then he surprised her so much she almost gasped. "I need a massage," he announced out of the blue.

"You most certainly do not," she retorted. "I know when you're in pain, and you're not in pain now!"

"I *am* in pain. Why else wasn't I able to fall asleep?"

"You said you wanted to talk."

"Only because I had hoped some conversation would relax my back. It didn't."

"When I first came in and asked how you were feeling, you said better than you'd felt in months."

"I'm sorry but it was a lie," Sy said with a forlorn face. "I'd hoped..." He stopped, unable to continue his deceit. He'd read her mail the other day and tonight he was lying to her. It was too much. He sucked in a long breath and let it out slowly. "I'm sorry, Pam. You're right, I'm not in any pain. I asked for a massage so you would...you would touch me. I wanted you to touch me," he repeated, almost sadly. He couldn't look her in the eye.

She sat there silently, digesting his confession, wondering what was really going on in his mind. If he had feelings for her—special feelings—would he use unscrupulous methods rather than romantic words to convey those feelings? She still didn't know him, did she? How sad that she loved a man she didn't really know.

Sighing, she leaned forward and brushed a lock of his wayward hair from his forehead. Their eyes met, and she saw a hot light in his. Perhaps that same light burned in hers, she didn't know. But if it did, her light was caused

If offer card is missing write to: Silhouette Reader Service, 3010 Walden Ave., P.O. Box 1867, Buffalo NY 14240-1867

NO POSTAGE
NECESSARY
IF MAILED
IN THE
UNITED STATES

BUSINESS REPLY MAIL
FIRST-CLASS MAIL   PERMIT NO. 717   BUFFALO, NY

POSTAGE WILL BE PAID BY ADDRESSEE

SILHOUETTE READER SERVICE
3010 WALDEN AVE
PO BOX 1867
BUFFALO NY 14240-9952

The Silhouette Reader Service® — Here's how it works:
Accepting your 2 free books and mystery gift places you under no obligation to buy anything. You may keep the books and gift and return the shipping statement marked "cancel." If you do not cancel, about a month later we'll send you 6 additional novels and bill you just $2.90 each in the U.S., or $3.25 in Canada, plus 25¢ delivery per book and applicable taxes if any.* That's the complete price and — compared to the cover price of $3.50 in the U.S. and $3.99 in Canada — it's quite a bargain! You may cancel at any time, but if you choose to continue, every month we'll send you 6 more books, which you may either purchase at the discount price or return it to us and cancel your subscription.

*Terms and prices subject to change without notice. Sales tax applicable in N.Y. Canadian residents will be charged applicable provincial taxes and GST.

Play The Lucky Hearts Game

and get... FREE BOOKS, a FREE GIFT... and MUCH more!

yes! I have scratched off the silver card.
Please send me my **2 FREE BOOKS** and **FREE MYSTERY GIFT**. I understand that I am under no obligation to purchase any books as explained on the back of this card.

315 SDL CNGQ

215 SDL CNGP

Scratch Here!
then look below to see what your cards get you...

Name
(PLEASE PRINT)

Address   Apt.#

City   State/Prov.   Zip/Code
                                                      Postal

A ♥	**10 ♥**	**9 ♥**	**8 ♥**
Twenty-one gets you **2 FREE BOOKS** and a **FREE MYSTERY GIFT!**	Twenty gets you **2 FREE BOOKS!**	Nineteen gets you **1 FREE BOOK!**	**TRY AGAIN!**

Offer limited to one per household and not valid to current Silhouette Romance™ subscribers. All orders subject to approval.

PRINTED IN U.S.A.

© 1998 HARLEQUIN ENTERPRISES LTD. ® and TM are trademarks owned by Harlequin Books S.A., used under license.

DETACH AND MAIL CARD TODAY!

by love. His was nothing more than desire for a woman. Probably any woman.

She drew back her hand and got up from the chair. "I'm going to say good-night now. I'm sorry you're having trouble sleeping, but I can't help you, Sy."

He knew what she meant, and he felt like a dog for trying to coerce her into making love. "You're driving me a little bit crazy, you know," he said huskily.

"You're doing that to yourself. Good night." Though her legs felt unsteady and her mind unstrung, Pam crossed to the door and walked out.

For her own sanity she had to get Sy well as fast as possible and herself off his ranch. He'd been transparent as glass tonight, but if he had been more subtle, more tactful, she might be in his bed right now.

Now *neither* of them would get much sleep, she thought rather bitterly as she threw off her robe, stepped out of her slippers and crawled into her own bed.

Nine

Pam could not remember ever feeling the same kind of cloying melancholy she did in the next few weeks. Even the breakup with Elliot had not derailed her enjoyment of simple pleasures, which was what she was now suffering because of loving a man who so obviously thought of her in only one way. Oh, yes, she knew exactly what was in Sy's mind. She felt his eyes on her often, and all she ever saw in them was lust.

It infuriated her that he would look at her so boldly, but then she would stumble over her own feelings and her anger would crash. The whole business was terribly frustrating and unnerving, and at moments she was anxious and eager to be gone, only to reverse herself and worry that the day when she would no longer be needed on the Cope ranch was approaching much too quickly.

Regardless of the ambivalence of her personal feelings, she could only be honest with Dr. Donnelly when he called to discuss Sy's progress. "He never needs the wheelchair anymore, and he walks without crutches, as well. I mentioned a cane one day, and Cal Lowe—you know who Cal is, I'm sure—produced one. He said it had belonged to Sy's grandfather. Apparently Mr. Cope had been about the same height as Sy, because the cane fits him perfectly. Surprisingly, Sy doesn't object to using it, maybe because it *was* his grandfather's. And then, of course, the addition of the hot tub to Sy's daily treatments has done wonders."

"Is he still taking pain medication?" Dr. Donnelly asked.

"Oh, no, none at all." *He stopped taking pain medication long before he should have!* Pam thought there was little point in mentioning it at this late date.

"Pam, I'd like to see Sy's progress for myself. I'm going to turn you over to reception so you can make an appointment."

Pam thought a moment. "Doctor, may I speak to Sy about it first? I'll do it at the first opportunity and then call your receptionist." She couldn't believe that Sy would refuse to see Dr. Donnelly, but neither did she feel that it was her place to make appointments for him without his okay.

"That would be fine, Pam."

After hanging up, Pam hurried up the stairs, hoping that Sy hadn't yet fallen asleep. He'd put in a rigorous morning of exercise, both in and out of the hot tub, eaten a light lunch and then retired to his room for a nap. An early afternoon nap had become a regular part of his daily routine. As she'd mentioned to Cal, Sy had a lot of sleep to catch up on, and the fact that he *could* sleep without pain was extremely gratifying.

She knocked and called quietly, "Sy?" If he didn't answer, if he was already sleeping, she would speak to him when he awoke.

But he did answer. "Come in."

Pam opened the door and, leaving it ajar, stepped into the room. Sy's clothes were on a chair, even his undershorts, and he was lying on the bed with just a sheet over him. Pam honestly hadn't known that he undressed completely for his afternoon naps, but the day was warm and only a light breeze was coming through the open windows of his bedroom, so she reasoned that maybe he'd undressed today because of the temperature.

But then she realized that she was trying to justify the quickening in her own body because Sy was in bed with just a sheet over him. Her reaction was so utterly inane when she'd grown to know almost all of his body as well as she did her own. Treating his physical problems as a professional therapist and walking into his bedroom like this were two vastly different things, however, which was also probably very silly. She'd seen him in bed nearly every day that she'd been there. It was just that it was getting harder and harder to act detached and distanced from her patient, to pretend indifference to him as a man.

"Dr. Donnelly called," she said, getting right to her reason for being there so that she could make a hasty exit. "He wants to see you and suggested I make an appointment, which I didn't feel I should do without speaking to you."

"Why does he want to see me?" Sy reached for a second pillow and stuffed it on top of the one under his head, as though settling in for a nice long chat.

Compared to his condition when she'd come to the ranch, his mobility was nothing short of amazing to Pam. And yet she knew he wasn't completely recovered. Not that he would ever be as limber and physically fit as he'd been before the accident. But even without those terrible muscle spasms she'd warred with so often all but knocking him flat, there was a resistant tension in Sy she didn't understand. She felt it most during massages, although even now, without even touching him, she sensed its presence.

"He said he'd like to see your progress for himself," she told him. "Is it all right if I make an appointment?"

Sy was silent a moment, then said, "I'd like to hear your opinion of my progress first."

"Sy, Dr. Donnelly's opinion is much more important than mine." Surely he wasn't going to balk at seeing his doctor. Why on earth would he do that?

Sy raised his hand and pointed a finger at her. "Right now, to me, *your* opinion is the only one that counts."

"That's absurd! Dr. Donnelly is a…a doctor! A specialist! You can't compare my knowledge and opinions to his."

"Like hell I can't. It wasn't him that put me back on my feet, it was you."

Weakened by a battle she hadn't expected, Pam sank to a chair. "You have some of the strangest ideas," she said, a frown creasing her forehead. "Do you really not know what Dr. Donnelly did for you, or have you simply forgotten the complex surgeries and care that made it possible for a therapist to even work with you?"

"I know exactly what Donnelly did for me, and I'll forever appreciate it. But if that had been the end of my treatment, I'd be in a wheelchair for the rest of my life. It's you who made the difference. You have to know that."

"What I did was merely an extension of Dr. Donnelly's initial treatment of your injuries. *You* have to know that!"

"You're getting angry."

"I'm getting impatient, Sy, not angry. To tell you the truth, I don't even know what we're arguing about." Pam got up. "Are you going to see the doctor or aren't you?"

A knock on the frame of the door interrupted Sy's answer. Pam looked to see who was there and saw Miss Bertie. Pam smiled at the elderly lady, even though she truly did not feel like smiling at anyone. Sy could disrupt her state of mind as no one she'd ever known could.

But she wouldn't take her bad mood out on his sweetheart of a grandmother who had been dropping in every few days. "Hello, Miss Bertie."

"Hello, Pam. Sy, are you giving this lovely child a bad time?"

Sy grinned. "This lovely child is giving *me* a bad time, Gran."

"Oh-oh," murmured Miss Bertie with an impish grin for Pam. "Whenever he calls me 'Gran,' I know he's up to something."

Pam gave Sy a pointed look. "Actually, Miss Bertie, Sy has been thinking that *you're* up to something."

Miss Bertie laughed merrily. "Oh, he does, does he?" She moved to the bed, leaned over and kissed her grandson's cheek. "Now, just what do you think an old lady could be up to, Sy?"

"Don't pull that 'old lady' stuff on me, Miss Bertie. You're the youngest person I know."

"And you're just overflowing with blarney," Miss Bertie retorted. Her expression became very loving. "You are looking so well, my dear. You look better and better, every time I see you. I couldn't be more pleased."

Pam began sidling toward the door. "I'll leave you two alone. Sy, we'll talk again later."

"Oh, did I interrupt something important?" Miss Bertie asked.

"No, you did not," Sy said emphatically.

"*I* interrupted his nap," Pam said.

"It's naptime? Then I'll also leave. Pam, do you ride? I thought I'd take a little ride on my favorite mare while I'm here," Miss Bertie said. "Perhaps you would join me?"

"Why, yes," Pam said. "I love to ride."

"I didn't know you rode horses," Sy said.

"There's quite a lot about me you don't know," Pam said with a rather haughty tilt of her chin. "See you later."

Sy frowned as she and his grandmother left the room and

closed the door. Pam was right. If you got down to brass tacks, there was very little he *did* know about her.

Funny, but he hadn't realized that before. But it didn't have to be a permanent hurdle to a more advanced relationship, did it? After all, how hard would it be to get her to talk about herself?

She was becoming a constant ache in his body. Each time she touched him, and she touched him uncountable times every day, he wondered how much more he could take without doing something unforgivable. Of course it wouldn't be unforgivable if she reciprocated. That was the fantasy that kept hounding him, the one he took to bed with him at night and woke up with in the morning. Pam, soft and loving in his arms, kissing him, wanting more than kisses.

He heaved a rough sigh.

Pam was on a mild-mannered horse and thinking, with heartfelt gratitude, that this ride had been a marvelous idea. Apparently she *could* still enjoy simple pleasures. It was a glorious day, the scenery was spectacular and Miss Bertie was a wonderful companion.

They were walking their horses, commenting on wild flowers and other impersonal topics, when Miss Bertie said, "I really must thank you, Pam. Sy has improved so much since you came to the ranch, I can hardly believe it. You must possess a very special talent for physical therapy."

"My talent isn't special, Miss Bertie. I believe that the techniques I favor just happen to fit Sy's particular needs."

"That theory is much too modest, my dear." Miss Bertie smiled at Pam. "But modesty over one's talents is a virtue and quite charming. Rather rare these days, as well. Pam, when I approached the door of Sy's room, I heard the two of you arguing. Something about Sy seeing a doctor?"

Pam sighed. "Dr. Donnelly wants Sy to go in for an examination. I reported his progress, and Dr. Donnelly wants to see it for himself. For some reason I can't begin to fathom, Sy...well, he didn't come right out and refuse, but he decided to argue against it rather than give me permission to make an appointment for him."

"He can be difficult," Miss Bertie murmured, startling Pam. "I know my grandson very well," Miss Bertie added when she saw the surprise on Pam's face. "I would bet anything that he fought your treatments every step of the way. Am I wrong?"

"No, you're not wrong," Pam said quietly.

"But you persevered, and he's getting better in spite of himself."

"He's much more cooperative than when I first arrived, but he's so...so..."

"Stubborn?"

"Well...yes."

"Pam, I'm going to speak frankly. You've done so much for Sy, and I think you're entitled to know that he's *always* been stubborn. You didn't cause it, neither did the accident. It's just part of his personality."

Pam wasn't quite sure how to reply. Miss Bertie didn't seem to notice her lapse, however, and continued talking.

"Sy was an adorable child, but he always had a very strong mind of his own. My son and daughter-in-law, Sy's parents, were much too easygoing. Lovely people, both of them, but much too lenient with a boy of Sy's nature. Then, too, Sy was an only child, so who else would they shower with love and anything money could buy? I really can't fault Sy for growing up with the idea that the world revolved around him, because his world *did* revolve around him.

"He was on a horse before he was three years old, he

drove the ranch pickups in the pastures, hell-bent for leather, when he was ten, and when he was thirteen and had decided he wanted to fly airplanes, Thomas and Corinne rushed to find the best flight instructor in the area. Sy soloed before he was fourteen. The next thing I knew, he wasn't just flying planes, he was jumping out of them. He'd taken up parachuting. After that it was mountain climbing, hang gliding, auto racing, speedboating, all sorts of activities that could have killed him. I didn't approve of the direction his life was taking and said so, but my opinion fell on deaf ears.''

Miss Bertie fell silent for a few moments. Pam was enthralled with Miss Bertie's comments and hoped the older woman would say more about Sy's background, so she, too, rode without speaking.

Miss Bertie did say more, but first she sighed rather heavily. "You know, Pam, the old saying 'Be careful what you wish for because you just might get it' is heartbreakingly true. Sy's grandfather and father had been completely contented with ranching, and I wished many times that Sy would stop traveling the globe and return to the ranch. Now he's here…I got my wish. And he's so profoundly unhappy that I would give almost anything to have the old Sy back.

"He'll never climb mountains again, you know," she finished sadly. "Or jump out of planes. I honestly believe that he will never be happy again."

Pam could hardly breathe. Now she knew what was causing Sy's underlying tension, the tension she couldn't dispel no matter how hard she tried.

But her heart wasn't aching just for Sy's misfortune. Miss Bertie was such a kind, caring woman that Pam couldn't bear seeing her unhappy, and perhaps even blaming herself for wishing that her grandson would someday be content with the ranch, as his father and grandfather had been.

"Sy is improving more every day," she said softly. "He'll be all right, Miss Bertie."

"He'll never be all right by his standards, Pam." Miss Bertie heaved another sigh, then sent Pam a smile. "You know the best thing that could happen to him now? If he met a wonderful young woman and fell in love."

Pam could feel a flush creeping up her neck and ardently hoped that it wouldn't reach her cheeks. "That...that might, uh, make him happy, yes," she stammered.

Miss Bertie's smile became broader, and a bright twinkle entered her eyes. "Do you find Sy attractive?"

Pam gulped so hard that she nearly swallowed her tongue. "He's, uh, very good-looking. I'm sure many women have noticed. He'll meet a special woman someday, Miss Bertie."

Miss Bertie hummed under her breath for a few moments, then said cheerfully, "I'm sure he will, Pam. I'm sure he will."

Around ten that night, after the ranch had settled down and all was quiet, Pam, wearing a cool cotton nightgown, took a chair from her room out onto the second-floor veranda. She had turned off the lights in her room and the front of the house was completely dark. Seating herself so that she could prop her feet on the railing, she looked up at the star-laden sky, an awe-inspiring sight. Summer was at its peak, and the night air was warm and so still that even the leaves on the trees weren't rustling.

The question that had been nibbling at Pam's mind since her horseback ride with Sy's grandmother surfaced. Had Miss Bertie indicated approval of a personal relationship between Pam and Sy? In fact, had Miss Bertie indicated hope that something personal *would* develop between them?

Pam tried to remember the conversation verbatim, and no matter how many times she examined it, she found herself returning to the same conclusion: Miss Bertie *was* hoping for a liaison between her grandson and his therapist. It was almost as if she had said, "Pam, you have my blessing. Go for it!"

Of course, Miss Bertie's hopes were strictly focused on Sy's state of mind. She wanted more than Sy's physical recovery. She wanted, with all her heart, to see him happy again.

It's nice that she thinks so much of me that she also thinks Sy would be interested, but as well as she knows her grandson, there are some things she will never know about him. I could never tell her that Sy isn't looking for a long-term commitment, for one thing. I know he has feelings for me, they just aren't the right kind. Pam sighed quietly and again raised her eyes to the starry sky. She sat like that for some minutes, then remembered something. "Oh, darn," she mumbled. Miss Bertie had gone home immediately after their ride, so she hadn't seen Sy again.

But she had given Pam something to pass on to Sy, and Pam had put it in her room and then forgotten about it. Sy had awakened from his nap grouchy and they'd argued about him seeing Dr. Donnelly again. Pam had adhered to her usual working routine with Sy for the rest of the day, but she'd been so put out with him that it had been a major effort to speak civilly. Was it any wonder she'd forgotten about that little box on her dresser?

Why, oh, why, had she fallen in love with Sy Cope? she asked herself next, sighing heavily. How could any woman fall in love with a man of his nature? He was self-centered, prone to dark moods and rarely pleasant. If she had deliberately set out to guarantee an unhappy future for herself, she could not have succeeded more. Just how stupid could a woman be?

Well, at least she wasn't stupid enough to believe that the love of a good woman would change him. Miss Bertie was going to be sorely disappointed, Pam feared. When and if Sy ever did find that special woman, he might be happy for a while, but Pam strongly suspected that he would regress rapidly. He was never going to stop resenting the fact that he couldn't do the things he'd once done so easily. The ranch had never satisfied him before, why would it satisfy him now?

And, of course, if he didn't stop resenting what had befallen him, the tension of such deeply rooted bitterness would periodically cause muscle spasms. She had once believed that Sy would figure that out for himself and attempt to alter his attitude to preclude such attacks, but she didn't believe it now. He had firmly placed his recovery and rehabilitation on her shoulders, completely ignoring any responsibility he might have in the process. He was not suddenly apt to see the light, Pam thought wryly.

She jumped when the door to Sy's bedroom opened, and quickly dropped her feet from the railing to the floor.

"Hi," he said as he stepped outside.

Pam saw at once that he'd pulled on jeans and nothing else. Nor was he using his cane. She was positive that she'd made no noise, but she was also positive that he'd known she was out here. What had he been doing, peeking through the windows?

"Hi," she said warily. "Having trouble sleeping?"

"I'm just not tired tonight." Sy moved to a post in the railing and leaned a shoulder against it. He looked at the sky. "Beautiful night."

"Yes, it is," she agreed.

"I might have to cut down on my naps during the day if I want to sleep at night."

"Which is an extremely good sign," Pam murmured. "You're getting healthier."

"Because of you."

"I'm part of it, yes, but so are you."

He snorted. "All I've done is what you've told me to do."

"If you'd care to remember, you didn't want to do anything I asked you to do when I first got here. If you hadn't started cooperating, you'd still be in that wheelchair. You really do have to start accepting some responsibility for your own recovery. And let me go one step further. It's going to be up to you to *stay* well."

"Are you lecturing me?"

"I'm saying it like it is, Sy. When I'm no longer around..."

"Don't say that!"

Pam's eyes widened. "You have the most unnerving habit of hiding your head in the sand. If you don't like something, you either throw a fit or pretend it doesn't exist. My life did not begin when I came to your ranch, and it will not end when I leave. Neither will yours. You have got to start facing what are no more than simple facts."

"They're not simple to me," Sy growled. "I need you here. I'll pay double your usual rate, triple, if you'll stay. Anything you ask."

"For the rest of our lives?" she scoffed. "Get real, Sy. You have to know that you've already reached the point of not needing a full-time therapist." A lightbulb went on in Pam's head. "You do know it, don't you? *That's* the reason you don't want to see Dr. Donnelly. You don't want to hear him say it!" Why not? she thought, her mind spinning in confusion. Why did Sy want so much to keep her on the ranch that he would offer her anything to stay? Dammit, if his reasons were personal, why couldn't he say so? If he ever did, oh Lord, if he even hinted that he cared about her as a woman and not just as his therapist, she would probably melt on the spot.

"I don't give a damn what Donnelly might say! I know what I need a hell of a lot better than he does, and I need you here!"

Instead of any sort of sweet talk, which would have sent Pam to the stars, Sy was getting angry and speaking much too loudly in the quiet night. He only wanted everything his way, Pam realized with a sinking sensation. He wasn't going to say that he had suddenly discovered that he loved her, so she might as well face facts.

She lowered her own voice, hoping he would do the same. "After I'm gone, you're perfectly capable of continuing treatment on your own. You know the exercises as well as I do. Keep up on exercise, gradually lengthen the distance of your walks, use the hot tub and try to stick to a healthy diet. If you do those things..."

"What about massage?" Sy cut in. "That's helped me more than anything else."

"No, Sy, it hasn't. Massage has been greatly relieving, I know, but..."

"Dammit, don't you think I know anything?"

"I could ask you the same question! Which one of us is the therapist, which the patient?"

Their voices had gotten loud again. Pam got up with a weary sigh. "All we ever do is argue. I'm going back to bed. Good night." She was about to enter her room when she remembered Miss Bertie's request. "Oh, I have something for you," she said. "Miss Bertie left it. I'll bring it out."

"Last time she was here I gave her my watch and asked if she would have it repaired."

"Well, she didn't say what it was. I'll get it for you."

Pam stepped into her dark bedroom and was feeling around for the light switch when she felt a pair of strong arms come around her. Her heart nearly stopped beating. Sy had followed. She felt his face in her hair, his body against her back and his arms crossed over her breasts.

"Let's not ever argue again," he whispered raggedly. "I don't like it and neither do you. I don't know why it keeps happening."

She didn't know why she let her body slump back against his—she might never know, she realized—but she found herself doing it, and also found herself thinking that nothing in her life had ever felt so good as this unexpected intimacy. The room was dark, revealed only slightly by the starlight coming through the open door and windows. They were so alone in this big house, and it struck her that they had been alone at night since she arrived, and that if they hadn't been at such odds over other things, this might have happened before tonight.

Still, she tried to cling to reason. "We...we shouldn't be doing this," she whispered.

Sy nuzzled the side of her throat and her ear, heating her skin with his breath and raising goose bumps. "I want you, Pam."

"I know you do. I've known it for a long time."

"You want me, too. Have you known that?"

She couldn't lie. Something within her, perhaps her feelings of love for this man, wouldn't let her lie. "I...I've thought about it."

Sy turned her around to face him. There was enough light for her to see his face and the dark depths of his eyes. He took her shoulders in his big hands, slowly brought her forward, and then his mouth covered hers.

Her senses went flying. His mouth on hers felt like heaven on earth, and she began kissing him back in the same hungry way he was kissing her. She'd wanted this for a long time, she thought dizzily, even if she hadn't wanted to admit it. She'd wanted it since their first surprising kiss, in fact. All the objections she'd clung to since that day dissolved like dust as Sy kisses became rougher, more demanding, and in one fleeting, heartfelt moment she forgave him for every barb and for every bad mood he'd taken out on her.

Her hands went to his bare chest to caress, to explore. Her touch was a lover's touch, the kind of touch Sy had been dreaming of, and he led her deeper into desire with more inflaming kisses. His tongue in her mouth weakened his knees and caused his heartbeat to go wild. His months of celibacy were catching up with him—he couldn't do this slowly, he had to have her now.

Breathing hard, fumbling in the dark, he got rid of her nightgown and his jeans. He took only a few moments to run his hands up and down her beautifully firm and female body and then urged her toward the bed.

Dazed by her own desire, Pam let it happen. Sy was on top of her. His kisses never stopped. His hands were everywhere.

But so were hers. She knew all of his body except for one place, and that was where her hands went, both of them. She caressed his steely, silky manhood and whimpered deep in her throat because of the feverish desire raging in her body.

Sy was so far gone that he couldn't indulge in foreplay for very long. Later, he thought. Later he would do all of the things a man should do *before* the final act, and they would make love again. But for this first time he could only think of himself, and he thrust into her with a groan and a sensation of such intense pleasure that he nearly blacked out.

It was a momentary pause, though, and then he began moving so forcefully that the bed creaked loudly in protest. Pam had never been made love to in such a rough-and-tumble way, and she loved Sy's ardor. Moaning and whimpering, she met each of his wild thrusts with one of her own. She went over the edge to that place of mindless pleasure so quickly that her emotions became unbalanced and she started crying. Sy roared her name a few seconds later and then collapsed on her.

The whole thing, Pam realized as tears continued to seep through her eyelashes, could not have lasted more than five minutes. How had she reached completion so fast?

Reality began to intrude after a few minutes of utter silence. "Your back," she whispered, wiping tears from her face. "Are you all right?"

Sy raised his head. "If I was any more all right, I'd be flying around the room." He began feathering kisses across her face and felt the dampness of her skin. "Did you cry?" There was astonishment in his voice.

"Um, a little." Some part of herself was holding back, Pam realized. She'd made passionate love with Sy, and it could be a mistake with far-reaching ramifications. It would be foolish to give him everything she was without knowing how he felt about this. How he felt about her.

"Do you always cry?"

She tried to tease, albeit in a shaky voice. "Do you always ask so many questions?"

"I might," he said slowly, as though trying to remember his past sexual experiences.

An ache began to throb in Pam's chest. Didn't he know

that he had just put her in the same category as every other woman he'd made love with? She was no more special to him than any other woman. This had been a mistake, a bad one, and thank God she hadn't done worse than she had, such as blurting out "I love you!"

She forced a huge yawn and murmured, "I am completely exhausted."

Sy frowned. He'd planned on a lot more time in her bed. Their first joining had been much too fast, even for him. Yes, he'd reached a roaring climax, and he felt pretty certain that Pam had, too, which he truly hadn't expected, given his haste. Maybe she had faked it, he thought uneasily. Some women did.

Oh hell, had she been satisfied or hadn't she? Obviously she preferred that he leave now, and he didn't want to leave, particularly with that question hounding him.

He took her face between his hands and tried, almost desperately, to see into her eyes, which wasn't quite possible in such dim light. "Did you, uh, you know?"

"Goodness, you *are* full of questions!"

"This one's important. Did I satisfy you?"

She drew a long breath. "Yes, Sy, you satisfied me." Try as she might, she couldn't stop herself from asking, if a bit cynically, "Did I satisfy you?"

"Honey, you did. You really did. Don't ever doubt it. Are you sure you're exhausted?"

Pam's spirit deflated a little more. He would make love to her as often as she let him, and without one word of romance or affection, the cad.

"I'm exhausted now and I plan to be exhausted for the remainder of my time on your ranch," she said evenly.

Sy was stunned. "But if I satisfied you...?"

"About once a year is enough for me," she said, hoping it would smash his disgustingly massive ego to smithereens.

"You're kidding."

"Yeah, I'm kidding," she drawled. "Please go now. I really am tired."

Sy left feeling so confused he didn't know what to believe.

Ten

"There was nothing loving about it," Pam whispered shakily as she ran the next morning. The night had been disastrous; she hadn't slept more than three hours, and that had been accumulated in bits and pieces. *Not* running was out of the question; it was the best way she knew to ease the sluggishness gripping her body.

Her mind, however, was not sluggish, although considering how harshly throughout the night she had condemned her behavior, it was a wonder she could think at all. But it was all there in her brain, stinging her with cruel clarity— Sy had used her, and she had let him. Worse, she had participated with embarrassing eagerness. Sure, she could blame her downfall on love, but Sy didn't know how she felt about him. To him she was a woman without morals or conscience, an easy mark. For the first time in her life, Pam didn't like herself.

As she ran, her thoughts occasionally became verbalized. "Fool, idiot," she would mutter. The small towel she'd tucked into the waistband of her shorts was used often to wipe away a self-denouncing tear.

She was almost back to the compound when she realized that she was putting all the blame for last night on *her* shoulders. Not once had she called Sy names or raged against him for taking advantage of her. Her worst thought concerning Sy was that he had used her, proof of which was how speedily he had rushed her from kisses to sex. A man who cared for a woman didn't do that.

"Oh, what do I know about it?" she mumbled in abject disgust. Most of what she knew about sex had been derived from books and magazines, and from those idiotic tests some magazines published to find out if "your man puts your pleasure before his," or to "rate your own sex appeal." It was hogwash when compared with the reality and consequences of uncommitted sex.

Not that she'd been a virgin before last night. She'd made love with Elliot, of course, and there'd been one other man before him, a long-ago, short-lived relationship that had been more experimental than anything else. It made her head pound to face the seemingly merciless fact: those few minutes with Sy last night had been the highlight of her adult life, certainly the highlight of her *love* life.

She could not escape one other fact, either; she was still in love with Sy Cope. Utterly shattered about it, she stumbled to the grassy ground and cried until she was too drained to shed another tear. Sitting up, she wiped her face with the towel. She had to get back to the ranch. Her workday awaited her. Sy awaited her. Oh, if only she didn't have to see him today!

Her thoughts expanded on that wish. Sy really didn't need a full-time therapist anymore, so why should she make herself miserable by staying? She got to her feet with a feeling of determination. She was *not* going to stay. She would phone Dr. Donnelly this morning and request another assignment. She would tell him that Sy had refused to go to Billings to see him, and that she had done all that she could for Sy. It was time for her to move on.

Yes, that was exactly what she would do. She would have to deal with Sy today, there was no way around that, but with any luck at all she would be leaving tomorrow morning, and she hoped she would never have to see him again.

Feeling slightly better, she began jogging back to the compound.

"You what?" Pam asked incredulously.

"I made an appointment to see Donnelly," Sy said. "His receptionist said that he wanted to see you, too, so I told her I'd have you drive me to Billings." It bothered him that Pam had barely spoken to him during his exercises this morning, and even worse, she hadn't once looked him in the eye. He was facedown on the therapy table now, and she'd been massaging his back and legs. He twisted his head a little so he could see her face. "Isn't that what you wanted?"

"When is the appointment?"

"Tomorrow afternoon, three o'clock."

Pam hadn't yet made her call to Dr. Donnelly. Knowing that he spent the early part of the day at the hospital seeing patients, she'd been planning to phone him at his office around eleven. Sy must have called him at the hospital.

She could still make her call, of course, but what she had to say about Sy's vastly improved condition might be better accepted by Dr. Donnelly after he examined Sy for himself.

"Is three okay?" Sy asked.

"It's fine," Pam said stiffly. "Put your head down."

Instead of doing as she'd instructed, Sy turned to his side and clasped his hand around her arm. "Pam, about last night..."

She jerked her arm free. "I don't want to talk about it. Now, turn over or this massage is finished."

"You're certainly in a mood." Sy rolled back to his stomach with a disgruntled frown. He didn't want to believe that Pam was a woman to take sex lightly, but her frosty attitude today pointed in that direction. Make love at night, forget it in the morning. He couldn't quite accept that explanation, but it was hard to come up with a different one when Pam was acting as though she couldn't stand the sight of him.

It took monumental effort for Pam to continue massaging Sy's back, and only her strong sense of responsibility and loyalty to her profession prevented her from quitting on the spot. Picturing herself doing so, saying, "I'm through, Sy, find yourself another therapist if you still think you need one," gave her a perverse sort of pleasure.

"Your bad mood is because of last night, isn't it?" Sy persisted, simply because he couldn't let it alone. Her lack of good humor *had* to be about last night. If there was something bothering her, he wanted to know what it was.

Pam would die before admitting any such thing to him. "No, it is not." She had never deliberately hurt a patient, but the heel of her palm dug too deeply into a muscle in Sy's back.

"Ouch! What in hell's wrong with you this morning? You won't look at me, you won't talk to me, and now this. I think I have a right to know what's going on."

Pam jumped back when she realized that she had just caused him pain. "You're right about one thing," she said tonelessly. "I'm in no mood for massage therapy. Go take a soak in the hot tub." Wiping her oily hands on a towel, she walked out, leaving Sy to gape at the vacant doorway and wonder what he'd done wrong. Something had set her off, but if it wasn't about last night, what was it about?

It annoyed Pam no end that the small box Miss Bertie had asked her to give to Sy was still on her dresser. She quickly scribbled a note—"This is what Miss Bertie left for you''—and took it and the box to Sy's room, where she placed it on his dresser.

Then she left the house, saddled the same horse she'd used before and rode away from the compound. Professional loyalty or not, she was going to forget Sy Cope ever existed until tomorrow afternoon when she drove him to Billings.

That, she figured, would be the end of their relationship. When they returned from Billings, she would take her things and go. Amen.

"You're not going to help me through my exercises?" Sy asked the following morning.

"No."

"And you're not going to help me in and out of the hot tub or keep up on your schedule of massages?"

"No." Pam held the door of her room in a tight grip so that it was only partially open. "You don't need my help. I left you a list of exercises and a schedule of daily activities. If there's anything you don't understand, let me know and I'll explain it to you. But you've done everything on it at least a hundred times before. So I think we can safely say that you won't be seeking my assistance." Sy's bewilderment was obvious, but she didn't give a damn.

"Well...are you going to drive me to Billings?"

"Yes."

"Pam, I don't understand. Will you talk to me about whatever it is that's bothering you?"

"No." She closed the door in his face.

They left the ranch at two in Pam's pickup. "Hook your seat belt," she told him.

"I already did." Sy spoke sharply. She hadn't even glanced his way since they'd gotten into the truck. He'd had hopes for this drive, because they would be alone and confined to one relatively small space. But apparently she still didn't intend to talk to him, which made him mad as hell. If she was all bent out of shape because they'd made love, why not say so? And if it was something else causing her cold, cutting attitude, why take it out on him?

No, he thought with an inner sigh, it had to be what had happened between them. She sure had gotten rid of him fast after it was over. Dare he forget that? She'd gotten her kicks and then had turned on him.

Trouble was, he wasn't sure she *had* gotten her kicks. Maybe she couldn't forgive his haste. Maybe she thought that was the way he always treated women in bed. Didn't she realize how long it had been for him? Didn't she know how forced abstinence for a long period could affect a man?

He sighed again. Didn't she know how incredibly desirable she was? He would have stayed with her all night if she had let him. He would have made love to her again and again, and done his best to make sure she experienced all the possible pleasures between a man and a woman.

Aw, hell, he thought disgustedly. Had he done even one thing right with Pam since the day they'd met? He'd tried getting rid of her—right in front of her, to boot—without giving her a chance, and then he'd proven himself an idiot again by fighting her methods, just because they differed from Jerry's.

Well, Pam's had worked and Jerry's hadn't. Dr. Donnelly would be mighty surprised at his progress. In fact, the good doctor might be so pleased that he would put Pam on another case, and Sy wasn't going to let that happen. He had a trick or two up his sleeve, and he wasn't ashamed of it, either. Donnelly was going to see some improvement, all right, enough for him to be happy about, but he wasn't going to see the whole picture. Maybe half the picture, Sy mused with a sudden urge to laugh.

The laugh died in his throat very quickly. He could handle Dr. Donnelly without much trouble, but what about Pam? What was her problem?

"Don't you think this has gone far enough?" he asked. "You're mad at me, and I can't even defend myself because you won't tell me what I did to make you mad."

"I'm not mad at anyone," Pam said dully, keeping her eyes on the road. She was afraid of revealing herself. Her emotional pain was too great for her to be goaded into an argument where she might say something she would forever regret, such as, "I'm in love with you, you big jerk, and you treated me like a tramp the other night."

For some reason her thoughts took another tack. People didn't choose the person they fell in love with; she hadn't made a conscious decision to fall in love with Sy. And he wasn't any different. Someday love would flatten him, same as it had her, and maybe the woman with whom he was smitten wouldn't love him. Only then would he understand what she was going through now.

No! she thought wildly. She was not hoping Sy would suffer this same awful emotional agony!

It was the honest-to-God truth. As shabbily as he had treated her, as arrogantly and rudely as he'd behaved since they met, she did not wish him anything but the best.

And maybe it was time she at least tried to be civil to him. After all, he hadn't forced her to make love with him.

She lifted her chin. "I've been…behaving badly. I'm sorry."

It wasn't enough for Sy. "Okay, but *why* were you behaving badly?"

"I do not intend to explain myself, so please stop questioning me."

"I know it has something to do with the other night," Sy persisted.

"You're only guessing, and we both know it. Please change the subject."

Sy was watching her closely, and it suddenly occurred to him that she looked rather peaked. "Maybe you're not feeling well. Is that it?"

"I'm fine," she said tonelessly.

"You don't look fine."

"Thank you. You're very kind."

"Pam, I didn't mean that the way you took it. I'm genuinely concerned. Would you tell me if you *weren't* feeling well?"

"Probably not."

"There's that attitude again. Dammit, why won't you talk to me?"

It was very difficult to be both civil and secretive, Pam was discovering. Actually, it wouldn't be this difficult if he would stop prying, she thought resentfully. She couldn't keep her anger bottled up one minute longer.

"I wouldn't think you'd have the nerve to even mention the word *attitude,*" she snapped. "You've thrown attitude all over the place since the day we met, and I'm sure it didn't just start when I got to the ranch, because it's who you are! You don't give a damn about anyone but yourself. You don't even care about your beautiful ranch. There's not an ounce of gratitude in your entire body for anything everyone trips over their own feet to do for you. No, you'd much rather wallow in self-pity and blame the rest of the world for your accident.

"Well, understand this, Sy. I don't feel one bit sorry for you. I work with people who have much worse problems than yours, and they're grateful for even the slightest im-

provement in their condition. You're back on your feet,
your pain has subsided, and are you grateful? No way."

Sy took a stunned breath. "So, that's how you feel about
me."

I love you, you self-centered jerk! "Yes, that's how I
feel about you," she said stonily.

"At least you didn't make love with me out of pity,"
Sy drawled, concealing how deeply she'd just hurt him with
a forced, almost casual cynicism. He glanced out the side
window. "Makes me wonder why you did make love with
me, though. If it wasn't pity, what was it?"

"Oh, stop!" Pam cried. "If you can't talk about something else, please say nothing!"

After several miles of uncomfortable silence, however,
Pam began wondering why Sy had so insistently pressed
her for a reason as to why she had permitted sex between
them. Why had he dug so deeply, or tried to? Well, it didn't
really matter, she told herself. This was their last full day
together; tomorrow she would be out of his life for good.

She sighed soulfully. She would get over Sy Cope eventually. She'd gotten over Elliot Young, hadn't she? She
quickly shushed the voice inside her that said this was different....

"Pam, I'm going to give Sy a pretty thorough examination, which should take about an hour," Dr. Donelly said.
"When I'm through, I'd like to talk to you."

"All right," she agreed. "Since you won't need me for
a while, I think I'll run over to the therapy center and say
hello to some friends."

Dr. Donnelly's office was several blocks from the Billings Therapy Center, so Pam took her truck. After parking,
she strolled into the building and immediately spotted a
friend in the lobby. They chatted a few minutes, then Pam

left the lobby to peer into treatment rooms. If a therapist she knew was busy, she merely smiled and waved, and if he or she wasn't with a patient, she lingered for a few words.

When she saw Elliot walking toward her in one of the corridors, she experienced a conflict of emotions. In one way she was glad to see him, but another part of her seemed to withdraw into itself. Unpleasant memories had a way of doing that to a person, she reasoned. A big smile appeared on Elliot's face when he saw her, and he hurried his step.

When they met up she let him hug her, although she cut it very short. "Pam, you look fantastic," he exclaimed. "How are you?"

My, she thought, his opinion of how she looked certainly differed from Sy's! Speaking of looks, she added to herself, there was nothing wrong with Elliot's. He wasn't as strikingly handsome as Sy, but then who was?

Telling herself that she liked shortly clipped, sandy-colored hair and hazel eyes just as much as she liked long dark hair and blue eyes, she said, "I'm very well, thank you. How are you?"

"Glad to be home. I heard you were working out at the Cope ranch? I was going to call but I knew you would be busy and decided to wait until you had some free time. Are you back now?"

"Almost."

"Wonderful! Are you in town for the day?"

"No, I really only have about another—" she looked at her watch "—twenty minutes." She had longer than that, but she wanted to be back at Dr. Donnelly's office before the hour was up, just in case he finished with Sy sooner than he'd thought.

Elliot took her hand. "Time enough for a cup of coffee. Let's go to the cafeteria."

Armed with large disposable cups of coffee, they sat at a table. Elliot couldn't seem to stop grinning, and Pam felt her earlier trepidation fading. If nothing else, they could be friends.

"I really missed you," Elliot said after a sip of hot coffee.

That comment seemed out of sync to Pam. She might have been the one to cause their initial separation by refusing to go to Baltimore with Elliot, but she had not been the one to start seeing someone else and phoning to tell her so.

"I think you've just recently convinced yourself of that, Elliot," she said calmly.

"No, that's not true. I *always* missed you, Pam."

"Even while you were seeing someone else? Elliot, let's not get off on the wrong foot, okay? I'm glad to see you and maybe you're glad to see me. Let's leave it at that."

"Well, sure, if that's what you want." Elliot's face brightened. "Hey, it's not that far to the Cope ranch. How about dinner together on Friday night? I'll drive out and pick you up."

"I don't think I'm going to be there that long, Elliot."

"You'll be back in town?"

Pam set her cup on the table. "That's what I'm hoping for, yes."

"Great. Then I'll pick you up at your apartment. Let's set a time. You say."

Pam wondered if she should date Elliot. She knew he always put himself first, so maybe it was best if they kept things purely platonic.

But didn't Sy also put himself first? And didn't she hope with every fiber of her being that she could find a man that would knock Sy Cope completely out of her system? Maybe Elliot wasn't the best place to start, but he was handy and willing, and he was doing his utmost to make her think he'd never forgotten her.

There was always the chance that he'd changed, slim though it be.

"All right," she agreed. "Seven o'clock on Friday evening." After a sip of coffee she asked, "Did they put you to work full-time?"

"Fortunately, yes. I have several challenging cases...."

Pam tried very hard to appear interested in Elliot's workload, but she wasn't completely successful, not when her thoughts were on Sy and how pleased Dr. Donnelly must be with his progress. She would undoubtedly hear all about it when she got back to Donnelly's office.

Only a moment later she realized how bored she was with Elliot's stories. Bored with Elliot himself, in fact. How sad, she thought. This is not going to work. She'd made a date with him and she would keep it, but only because she couldn't bring herself to hurt Elliot's feelings with a stumbling explanation of why she'd changed her mind so soon.

She made a big thing of checking her watch. "I've got to run," she exclaimed. "Thanks for the coffee, Elliot."

"I'll walk you out."

"No need." Pam got up and pushed her chair under the table. "Stay and finish your coffee."

Elliot got to his feet. "If you're sure..."

She forced a smile. "Bye for now."

"See you on Friday."

Pam hurried from the cafeteria, back through the center and out to her truck. Seated behind the wheel, she covered her face with her hands and groaned. What had possessed her to think that Elliot might make her forget Sy? It would never happen, and now she'd put herself in an awkward situation.

"Damn," she whispered.

* * *

Leaning heavily on his cane, Sy again limped very visibly across the room for Dr. Donnelly's benefit.

Donnelly was frowning. "And you're feeling pain in your back and legs?"

"Mostly in my back." Sy hoped his lies wouldn't send him to hell, but if Donnelly thought he was as well as he really was, he would discharge Pam. And Sy was willing to risk the consequences of a few lies for such a good cause.

The doctor sat on the stool in his examination room. "Well, you're not nearly as recovered as Pam led me to believe. I'm glad you came in, Sy. There's definite progress, but not enough to discontinue therapy."

Sy glowed within, but he put on a sadly disappointed face.

"Don't worry about it, Sy," Dr. Donnelly said sympathetically. "You've made exceptional forward strides, and I'm quite certain the trend will continue. Not without further physical therapy, however. I'll discuss it with Pam. Get dressed and then go to the waiting room. I'll check with reception to see if she's here."

He punched a number on the wall phone. "Is Pamela Brooks in reception? Good, please send her to my office." After hanging up, Donnelly walked to the door. "I'd like to see you again in two weeks."

"I'll make an appointment on my way out," Sy said solemnly.

Dr. Donnelly stopped at the door and turned. "Oh, perhaps I should ask how you and Pam are getting along? Are you satisfied with her as your therapist?"

"She's an exceptional therapist, Doctor, and she's extremely satisfying in, uh, ways I hadn't expected when she arrived."

"Good, very good." Dr. Donnelly walked out.

Alone, Sy chuckled under his breath. Pam was in for one very big surprise. How would she handle it?

Pam stopped at the open door of Dr. Donnelly's private office. He was seated behind the desk. "Come in, Pam. Please sit down."

"Thank you," she murmured, taking a seat.

"I'd like you to intensify Sy's treatments for the next two weeks," he said as he wrote something in a folder, which Pam thought was probably Sy's file.

Pam blinked in total shock and stared at the doctor. "I beg your pardon?"

Donnelly raised his eyes. "I was under the impression from our phone conversation that Sy was much more advanced than he is. He's made good progress, unquestionably, but he's still not where I want him to be. Where I *know* he can be."

"But...but, Doctor, he...he's doing almost everything for himself now, and he walks without support, and he..."

"You don't think a cane is support?"

"Well, yes, of course a cane is support, but he rarely uses it anymore."

"Really. Pam, obviously you and I are seeing Sy's condition very differently."

Pam was so confused she didn't know what to say. She finally thought of something. "You examined him? Tested the strength in his legs and back? Did you check everything—his mobility in particular?"

"Young woman, I don't think you're qualified to advise me on how to conduct an examination."

"I'm sorry," she murmured with a perplexed frown. "I just don't understand. He...he's been doing so well."

"Not as well as you think, apparently. I told Sy that I'd like to see him in two weeks, and I'm telling you now that

I want you to heighten the intensity of his treatments. He explained what exercises you've had him doing, and they should be gradually advanced to a more exacting, strenuous stage. When he's better able to get around, he should do more walking. Use your judgment on that, but please don't hold him back.''

Hold him back? This was so opposite to what Pam had expected to hear Dr. Donnelly say that she couldn't seem to grasp it. Beset by confusion, she found herself doubting the type of examination Donnelly had performed, regardless of his stern put-down when she'd asked him about it.

Dr. Donnelly rose from his chair. "I have patients in the waiting room. Call me if you need anything."

Pam left with her head down and an ache in her midsection. How could she have been so wrong about Sy's progress?

Eleven

Pam ducked into the ladies' room on her way out. Confused and terribly unsure of anything—especially herself—she bathed her temples with cool water. Her heart seemed to be pumping in overdrive, making her feel edgy and out of breath. Never before in her career had she so badly misjudged a patient's progress. Where had she gone wrong?

Donnelly was a specialist with an impeccable reputation; she could not doubt his diagnosis. But she couldn't stop herself from wondering what he'd seen in Sy's condition that she had not. Yes, Sy still used his grandfather's cane on occasion, but mostly he got around on his own. And did it very well.

She was disappointed enough to just let go and wail—she would be at the Cope ranch for another two weeks—but the destruction of her sensible plan to put distance between herself and Sy wasn't nearly as disturbing as her erroneous opinion of his physical improvements.

Shaking her head in dismay, she left the restroom, traversed a short hall and entered the waiting room. Sy looked comfortably seated, as did four other people waiting their turn to see Dr. Donnelly, and he smiled at her. She didn't smile back as she walked over to him.

"We can leave now," she said quietly. She offered her hand to help him get up, and he took it with a murmured "Thanks." Leaving the office and then the building, Pam saw how heavily he was leaning on the cane. Apparently

Donnelly had put him through the paces and Sy was feeling the result of some very taxing tests. Besides, it was possible that she'd been mistaken all along about his increasing mobility. She wondered, uneasily, if she had let her emotions, her feelings for Sy, influence her normal good judgment. Maybe she'd been wanting so badly for him to be well that she had seen much more in his progress than she should have.

When they reached her truck in the parking lot, however, Sy startled her by jumping into the passenger seat with an amazing agility. Pam stood there stunned. She'd been prepared to help him get in, and he hadn't even taken her hand!

More puzzled than ever, she rounded the front of the truck and climbed into the driver's seat. Questions bombarded her, mainly revolving around what kind of tests Dr. Donnelly had conducted.

Before she could ask, however, Sy said cheerfully, "I'm starving. Let's have dinner. Is Gunderson's still open? It was always my favorite restaurant in Billings."

"Gunderson's is still in business, yes, but it's a little early for dinner." Pam started the motor. She didn't want to have dinner with Sy in a restaurant like Gunderson's, which had a marvelously intimate atmosphere, dim lighting and the best wine cellar in town. Not that she would drink and drive, but she had a feeling that Sy would indulge, and she wanted some serious conversation with him, not an intimate meal with him giddy from wine.

"But I'm hungry," Sy protested.

"I'll stop at a fast-food outlet. Take your pick."

"I see that your mood hasn't changed any," he said dryly.

Pam drove from the parking lot and cautiously entered the traffic of a busy street. "My *mood* has changed drastically," she retorted sharply. "What kind of tests did Donnelly give you?"

Sy shrugged nonchalantly. "The usual."

"The usual what? Sy, tell me exactly what he had you do."

"There's a hamburger place up ahead. Stop there. I'd rather eat at Gunderson's, but I guess a burger will do."

Pam stiffened. He would probably order fries with his hamburger and ingest more fat than he should eat in a week. To hell with it, she thought irately, and she pulled into the drive-through lane. Apparently she was wrong about everything else she'd been doing, so she was probably also wrong about what he should be eating.

Sy ordered onion rings *and* fries with his burger and soft drink, and Pam ordered a diet cola. When the food was passed through the window and Sy had paid for it, Pam started the drive back to the ranch. Sy ate with relish, and she sipped her diet cola whenever traffic permitted.

"These are great," Sy remarked, holding out the sack of onion rings. "Have some."

"No, thank you," she said stiffly.

"Don't you ever relax?"

She sent him a venomous look, then, gritting her teeth, returned her gaze to the road. Did she ever relax, indeed! What was it he thought she'd done with him the other night? Another two weeks with this awful feeling in the pit of her stomach...could she bear it?

Traffic got lighter as the city dwindled into widely spaced homes and then open country. Sy crumpled the wrappers and tucked them into the paper sack in which his food had been served.

He settled back. "That was good. Thanks for stopping."

"You're welcome," Pam mumbled. Something was terribly amiss, and it had to do with Dr. Donnelly's examination. "Will you tell me now what Donnelly's examination consisted of?"

"What do you want to know?"

Pam's voice became sharper, conveying impatience. Sy was deliberately being obtuse. "I want to know what tests Dr. Donnelly conducted."

"Well, let's see," Sy said lazily. "The nurse took my blood pressure and temperature."

"Dammit, I don't care what the nurse did! What did Dr. Donnelly do?"

"What's bothering you, Pam?" Sy asked calmly, knowing full well that she had expected a much different diagnosis from Donnelly.

She couldn't tell him that she'd been planning—hoping—to be taken off his case as of today. She couldn't tell him that he was causing her too much internal agony and that she feared the longer she worked with him, the deeper that torment would go. Two more weeks with him might forever cement her feelings for him, and she didn't want to live out her life with a broken heart. If he was a different sort of man, one who didn't constantly put himself first, she wouldn't be so worried about her future.

But he was who he was, too rich, too good-looking, too pampered and spoiled, and she was a very ordinary woman. Instinct told her that he was never going to fall in love with her, not in two more weeks, not in two more years. But the upcoming two weeks were going to wreak untold damage on her already shaky self-control. She feared, with every fiber of her being, that if he made another pass, she would not be able to say no.

It made her angry. "You are deliberately evading a direct answer," she accused.

"Pam, there's nothing to tell. Suffice it to say that Donnelly was pleased with my progress. So am I, and so should you be. All three of us know it was because of you, so where's the problem? Why are you so upset?"

She shot him a suspicious glance, not certain why she suspected something awry but convinced that Sy was at the heart of it. "You're capable of anything, aren't you?"

Sy heaved a big sigh. "I used to be."

"I was *not* referring to your physical capabilities."

Sy put on a puzzled expression. "No? Then what were you referring to?"

She was getting nowhere. "Forget it," she muttered. "Just forget it."

"You're angry. Let's talk about something else. I like your truck. It looks brand-new, but it's about two years old, right?"

"Yes." She didn't want to talk to him at all. Her stomach was churning and her head was aching. He was the most irritating person she'd ever known. How in God's name could she have fallen in love with a man of his ilk? She didn't deserve this.

"Obviously you've taken very good care of it."

"Yes."

"Do you let other people drive it?"

"Occasionally."

"How about letting me drive it?"

Pam's mouth dropped open, and she sent him an astonished look. "You're not talking about now, are you?"

"Of course I am. It would feel incredible to drive again. Pam, we haven't seen another car for five minutes, and I know this road like my own hand. Let me drive, please. I'm a good driver, and I promise you one thing. If I put even a tiny scratch on your truck, I'll buy you a new one."

"That's the silliest thing I've ever heard," she scoffed. "I'm not objecting to your driving my truck because I'm worried about a scratch. If I am to believe Dr. Donnelly's diagnosis, you should not be driving anything.''

"And what else *should* you believe, right? He is the doctor, after all.''

Pam was beginning to smell a very large rat. Her confusion was finally dissipating, and she was able to think logically again. For example, if Donnelly had seen Sy jump into her truck in the parking lot, he would not have prescribed another two weeks of intensive therapy. Not that Sy had reached the point of requiring no therapy at all. He was going to have to exercise on a regular basis for a long time to come to maintain his mobility. But he knew the routine, and he could follow it without the aid of a full-time therapist. Perhaps Donnelly would want Sy to come into the therapy center a couple of times a week for a while, but that was only standard procedure.

But Sy had somehow convinced Dr. Donnelly that he still needed a full-time therapist! For God's sake, why?

No, wait a minute, Pam thought. That idea was just too far-out. Why on earth would he want Dr. Donnelly to think he was worse off than he was? It made no sense.

Confused again, Pam barely heard Sy speak. "Excuse me?" she said.

"I said that I wanted to drive. Come on, Pam, be a sport.''

She had no fight left in her. Never would she be able to best Sy in a contest of wits. He was too used to having everything his way and a master at the game of evasion.

Without a word she wheeled to the side of the road and slapped the shifting lever into park. Sy grinned. "Hey, this is great! Thanks.''

Pam unhooked her seat belt, got out and walked around to the other side of the truck. Sy slid across the bench seat. In a few seconds they were back on the road, with Sy projecting the elation of a child with a new toy. Completely disgusted with him, with herself and, yes, even with Dr. Donnelly, Pam stared straight ahead and said nothing. But she was thinking. Oh, yes, she was definitely thinking. Someway, somehow, Sy had conned Donnelly. She didn't know how he'd done it or why he'd done it, but she no longer harbored even a tiny doubt that he had. People in pain did not sit behind the wheel of a vehicle the way Sy was doing, the damned fraud. At that moment Pam didn't even like Sy Cope, let alone love him. Maybe she *would* be able to get through the next two weeks without permanent emotional damage, she thought with a thinning of her lips.

"I know what you did," she said coldly.

"About what?" Sy asked innocently, although he could just barely keep from laughing. He hadn't had this much fun in months. Damn, it felt good to be driving again. And he had at least another two weeks with Pam. He had no solid plans for those fourteen days, but now she wouldn't be leaving before he figured himself out. He had some very unusual feelings for Pam, and he couldn't let her leave until he knew what they meant.

"About what?" she mimicked in a derogatory voice. "You know exactly what I'm talking about, you...you... con artist!"

"Now, that hurts," he said in the most injured tone he could manage.

"Yeah, right," Pam drawled with heavy sarcasm, and turned her face to the side window. In two seconds her head jerked around so she could kill him with a murderous look. "What I'd like to know is why you did it."

"Did what, sweetheart?"

"If you don't stop treating me as though I'm a total

moron, I swear that the minute we get to the ranch, I'm going to pack my things and leave!"

"You can't leave. Donnelly prescribed two more weeks..."

"I can do anything I want to do, Sy Cope, and you damned well better believe it!"

"You mean to say that you'd go off and leave me only partially recovered? Donnelly wouldn't like that, honey."

"Do you think he'd like to hear how you pulled the wool over his eyes today?"

"He wouldn't believe it."

"There!" she cried exultantly. "You just admitted what you did."

Sy shrugged. "So hang me."

Pam's eyes narrowed menacingly. "I'm going to give you one more chance. Either tell me why you did it or I'm through as your therapist."

Sy shot her a glance and saw from the determined expression on her face that she meant what she'd said.

"Okay, I'll tell you—" he scanned the countryside "—in about three minutes."

"Why wait three minutes? Do it now!"

"Hold your horses. We're almost there."

"Almost where?" Sy made an abrupt right turn onto a dirt road, and Pam sat up straighter to look around. "Where are you taking me?" Her voice was laden with suspicion.

Sy drove into a large stand of trees and stopped the truck. Turning off the ignition, he sent Pam a wickedly teasing grin. "*This* is where I'm taking you."

"Why?"

"Take a wild guess." He flipped open his seat belt, slid across the seat and pulled Pam into his arms. His mouth covered hers in a kiss so sizzling hot that her system immediately caught fire.

Somewhere in her befuddled brain a small voice cried, "No...no!" but the rest of her, every inch, was melting into a piece of malleable clay that wanted more...more. She opened her mouth for his tongue and felt his hand slide under her dress and up her bare thighs. She'd put on the dress for the trip to Billings and she shouldn't have; it made it too easy for Sy to do what he was doing!

But she didn't want him to stop, and she adjusted her position to make it even easier for him to attain his goal. When he did, when her bikini panties were no longer a deterrent and he was stroking her most sensitive spot, she moaned in her throat and kissed him so wildly, so passionately, with her fingers threading into his hair and her breasts pushing into his chest, that both of them began gasping for air.

Sy raised his head a little, just enough so each of them could catch a breath, then kissed her again. She was going to be satisfied *this* time, he vowed ardently, and long before he was, if he could help it. No part of his past personal life had ever seemed as crucial as his giving Pam full and complete satisfaction. He wanted no perturbing questions gnawing at him after it was over. He wanted to know for sure this time, and he was *going* to know, come hell or high water!

Later he realized that he had never once doubted her cooperation, and for a good ten minutes he had it. He was deliberately going slowly, caressing her in the right places, mating their mouths again and again in breath-stealing kisses. He was so hard and ready himself that he hurt, but he gritted his teeth and told himself that he could take it.

And then, without warning, she began struggling. Tearing his mouth from hers, she grabbed his hand from between her legs. "No!"

He was dazed with desire, almost frenzied from it, and

he couldn't believe she meant it. "Pam," he whispered hoarsely. "Please don't say no. Don't do that to us." He kept trying to kiss her again, and she kept turning her head. "Pam, please," he pleaded.

"What kind of woman do you think I am?" she cried.

"You're a beautiful, sexy, intelligent woman. What else would I think?"

She pushed his errant hand away from her, the one that had done so much damage to her normal good sense.

"You think I'm easy," she said accusingly. "You think that just because *you* want sex, you can have it with the nearest available woman." With unsteady hands she tried to smooth the wrinkles from her clothes.

"Pam, that's not true." But he had to wonder if she wasn't right. He wanted her, no question about it, but she was also the closest available woman. His emotions were in shambles. His body ached with a desire that he knew now was not going to be gratified. Why had she let him go so far if she'd had no intention of following through?

Pam was asking herself a similar question: why on earth had she kissed him back? Where was her self-control hiding these days? Maybe she loved him madly, maybe she was losing her mind, but whatever her malady, she couldn't deny the power he had over her senses. It wasn't right. It wasn't fair.

She felt his eyes all but bore holes into her, but she ignored them and dug into her purse for a comb. "Have you had enough driving for today?"

"I haven't had enough of anything," he muttered darkly. "Neither have you."

She looked at him then, with eyes as hard as marbles. "You're wrong about that. I've had enough of your egotistical games to last me a lifetime. Now, either get my truck moving or get out of the driver's seat so I can do it."

"You know, when we first met I thought you were incapable of making a remark like that egotistical crack. Guess I was wrong about a lot of things." Sy slid back behind the wheel.

"And since you've always believed that you're never wrong, it must be a terrible blow to your ego to discover otherwise."

Before Sy started the engine, he looked at her with eyes almost as hard as hers. "Why are you so angry? You were a willing participant, no matter what you think *my* motives were."

"Because..." Her mouth was suddenly dry. Why *was* she so angry? Because she loved him and knew she would never have him? Because in some ways she was putty in his hands and knew in her heart that her response was only what he expected from women?

She could say none of that. Grasping at straws, she mumbled, "I'm angry over what you did in Donnelly's office."

He smirked. "First of all, you don't have a clue about what I did or didn't do in Donnelly's office. Second, if I did mislead him, who did it hurt?"

"Deceit always hurts someone."

"Oh, really? Well, suppose you tell me who I hurt today."

Pam stared daggers at him, but something within her was wilting. The only person he'd hurt was her, and since she couldn't explain how he'd hurt her, she didn't know what else to say. The question remained, of course, as to why he'd done something so utterly nonsensical. What possible benefit would he derive from having deceived Dr. Donnelly?

"You don't have an answer for that, do you?" Sy said. "I knew you wouldn't, because my little prank didn't harm one single person."

"Little prank?" Pam tried very hard to convey disgust, but he was getting the better of her again and she came off sounding desperate. She did have one last salvo to hurl at him, however. "You always do exactly as you please, don't you?"

"Doesn't everyone?"

Why, he believes it! Pam thought, astounded. He actually believed everyone lived as he did. It was too much to swallow in silence.

"No, Sy," she said with as much sarcasm as she could muster, "everyone does not ride roughshod over other people to get what they want! The question is why you wanted to deceive Donnelly in the first place. You must have had a reason for behaving like an adolescent. What was it?"

He grinned. "Are you sure you want to know?"

"Would I be asking if I didn't?" she shrieked. Her patience had come to an end. She could take no more of his evasive tactics.

"Hey, I didn't mean to make you crazy." His eyes narrowed on her for a moment, then he said quite calmly, "Nope, I'm not going to tell you. You're not ready to hear it, and maybe I'm not ready to say it." Turning away from her, he started the truck.

Pam was struck with such an all-consuming fury she actually saw spots before her eyes. "You...you..." The names she would love to call him got stuck in her throat, only because she didn't use such vile language, not even in anger.

Sy sent her a casual glance, then got the truck turned around and began the drive back to the highway. "What were you going to call me? Was it darling? Or sweetheart?"

"Guess again, you...you insufferable jerk!"

Sy chuckled. "Feeling a little bit frustrated, sweetheart?

Well, take heart in the fact that I, too, am suffering from unrequited passion.''

"I am *not* suffering from unrequited passion!"

"Now, now, there's no point in denying it. Only a few minutes ago you wanted me just as much as I wanted you."

"That's it! The second we get to the ranch, I'm taking my things and leaving! If I never see you again it will be too soon!"

"Oh, come on, Pam, why make such a big drama out of this? Can't we disagree about something on an adult level?"

She felt totally defeated. She knew she was going to stay the additional two weeks that Dr. Donnelly had requested of her, even though it was entirely to maintain her reputation as a responsible therapist. This bickering with Sy had to stop. He was only going to tell her what he wanted to tell her, and no amount of begging, pleading or harassment on her part would change his mind.

"Fine," she said dully, turning her face to the side window. "Whatever you say is fine."

Sy sent her a startled look, saw only the back of her head, then returned his eyes to the road and chewed on his bottom lip. She'd done an awfully fast turnabout, which, considering how long this argument had gone on, was the last thing he'd expected to happen.

But he cheered up very quickly. He had two more weeks with Pam, and if he didn't understand his unusual feelings for her by the end of those fourteen days, he probably never would. And he was driving again. Life was getting better by leaps and bounds.

It was all because of Pam. Whatever else did or did not take place between them, he was at least big enough to admit that she'd brought him back to life.

Twelve

There could be clues to explain Sy's peculiar behavior in Donnelly's office today, Pam decided as she lay in bed that night. For one, he'd told her he would answer her questions in three minutes, then had driven into that grove of trees and kissed her. Had that kiss been his answer? It was the only one he'd given her, after all.

But it seemed so unreasonable to think that he had devised such a deceitful scheme in order to keep her on the ranch for another two weeks that she kept shying from that conclusion. A lover might do something like that, or a man *in* love. But Sy loved no one but himself, with the exception of Miss Bertie, of course.

No, she could not accept that explanation. She never had possessed much of an ego where men were concerned, and dealing with Sy hadn't boosted it any. She could not believe that he'd deliberately tricked Dr. Donnelly into thinking he still needed a full-time therapist just to keep her from leaving. It had to be something else.

And then, out of the blue, she remembered that she had made a date with Elliot for Friday night. Groaning, she pulled a pillow over her head. She didn't want to go out with Elliot. Who knew what he would expect from a renewed relationship, and if one more man started thinking that he could direct her life, she would scream.

In the next moment she realized the ramifications of what had just run through her mind. Despite her many denials of the concept, some part of her did believe that Sy had manipulated her time and life today!

For heaven's sake, why?

It was around midnight when Sy awoke in pain. He couldn't move even a leg or an arm without feeling it in his back. Discouraged because he'd thought—believed—that he was past this kind of attack, he lay there breathing deeply and attempted to alleviate the spasms through relaxation.

Pam had told him the best way to relax when he had trouble sleeping. *Lie still. Clear your mind and then think,* Feet, relax. *Feel them going limp. Work your way up your body, ankles, knees, thighs, and so on. You can make this work, Sy. I've done it many times. The most important part of this exercise is not to let your mind wander to something else. It's also the most difficult part of the exercise, but with practice you will be able to do it.*

Sy decided to try Pam's advice. His alternatives were to endure pain-filled, sleepless hours until morning or to wake Pam now for a massage. Something inside of him rebelled at the idea of disturbing Pam's sleep. He'd done it before, quite a few times, and it hadn't bothered him an iota; tonight it did.

Damn, they had a strange relationship, he thought uneasily. Everything was so complicated with Pam. Why was that?

Well, it wasn't something he could unravel tonight. *Concentrate. Clear your mind.*

The relaxation exercise helped a great deal, and Sy was finally able to move his legs without pain jolting through the muscles along his spine. But he didn't yet have complete relief, and he thought of the hot tub outside and how great it would feel to submerge himself in hot, rushing water.

Slowly raising his arm, he switched on the bedside lamp. His crutches were in one corner of the room, the wheelchair in another, and the cane was leaning against a nearby chair. He wondered if he could make it downstairs and out to the tub using only the cane. When he'd finally managed to get out of bed and was standing on his feet, weaving rather weakly, he decided to take no chances and to use the crutches.

It was then that he remembered he was nude, and leaning heavily on the crutches, he went into the bathroom and wrapped a towel around his hips. Moving as quietly as he could manage, he left his bedroom, rode the elevator down to the first floor and went outside through the front door.

The cool night air gave him a bit of a shiver, and he hurried the best he could to the gazebo and eventually to the hot tub. Dropping the towel and crutches, he turned on the jets and maneuvered himself into the water. Laying his head back on the edge of the tub, he closed his eyes in sublime relief. He might hurt again when he got out, but nothing hurt at the moment and all he felt was an incredibly pleasurable sensation.

It was the way he'd felt most of the time before the accident, he realized. Freedom of movement should never be taken for granted, and he'd done it all the time, the same as every other person who had never experienced painful, restricted mobility.

For that matter, he'd taken everything for granted back then—his good health, the wealth of his family, his athletic prowess and his popularity with everyone he met. How things have changed, he thought with a frustrated sigh. The only item on that list that he still possessed was wealth. His health would never be the same, athletics as he'd known them were gone forever, and he himself had destroyed his previous popularity by being rude to friends when they'd come to the ranch to see him.

Why had this happened to him? Had he done something to deserve it? His lips thinned over questions he'd asked himself a thousand times since the accident.

Upstairs in her bed, Pam opened her eyes. It took a minute for her to realize that the humming noise she heard was coming from the hot tub. For a moment she frowned and tried to get her bearings. Had Sy told his men they could use the hot tub? Not that there was anything wrong with that idea, but in the middle of the night? The noise of the motor and jets had awakened her. Wouldn't it also awaken Sy?

She must get to the bottom of this, she decided, and slipped out of bed to check on Sy. His bedroom door was open, and the light from the nightstand lamp fell on his empty bed. Sy was outside!

"Well, for Pete's sake," she muttered. Why on earth was he out in that hot tub alone at this time of night? Almost at once her irritation evolved into worry. Sy should not be in that tub without someone close at hand! Not that she'd come right out and said so, but didn't he have enough common sense of his own to know that?

Forgetting that she was wearing only a nightshirt, Pam ran down the hall to the stairs and then ran down the stairs to the front door. From there she ran to the gazebo, which was dark; Sy had not turned on any lights! It wasn't like her to let fear rule her emotions, but she was suddenly scared to death. He could have fallen. He could have slipped and gone under. He could have struck his head.

"Sy?" she cried, loudly enough to be heard over the noise of the tub.

He opened his eyes and made out Pam's shadowy form across the tub from where he sat. "What is it?"

Her knees nearly buckled with relief. "Why don't you have a light on?"

"I didn't want a light."

Pam cautiously made her way around the tub in the dark. "Why are you out here at all? Don't you know what time it is?"

"Calm down, for God's sake. I'm perfectly all right, and what difference does the time make?"

"If you're all right—*feeling* all right, I mean—why did you need to use the tub?" Pam sank to the floor about a foot from where Sy's head appeared above the tub's rim. "You scared the living daylights out of me."

She was telling him the truth; he could hear it in her voice. Merely to alleviate her concern, he explained that he had awakened in pain and what he'd done about it.

Pam became very still, and when he was finished with his explanation, she said almost sadly, "Do you realize how distinctly you proved tonight that you no longer need me here?"

Sy's heart sank. All day he'd done everything but stand on his head to prove that he *did* still need her services, and now he'd demonstrated exactly the opposite. He should have called her to his room when he first woke up. He should have had her relieve his distress. He should not have even worried about disturbing her sleep!

He didn't know what to say, so he said nothing. Pam asked quietly, "Aren't you going to answer me?"

"What do you want me to say?"

"How about the truth?"

The truth. What if he told her the truth tonight and then it wasn't the truth tomorrow? Why in hell couldn't he sort out his own emotions? Why was he fighting so hard to keep her at the ranch now, when he wasn't sure that he would want her there next week or next month? He'd always been changeable, getting all charged up about something and then losing interest after a while and going on to a new and more interesting challenge.

He didn't want to hurt her, of that he was certain, but maybe she *should* know the truth about him. Maybe he owed her that much.

"Okay, I'll tell you the truth as it is this minute," he said flatly.

Pam's eyes widened. "Are you saying your truths change with the clock?"

"Are yours set in concrete? Have you never changed your mind about something?"

"Sy, we're talking about you. Let's stick to the subject."

"We're talking about both of us. You see, the truth I referred to is about you."

Pam's heart skipped a beat. "I think I can guess what it is," she said slowly. "I know you deliberately misled Dr. Donnelly to keep me here for another two weeks." She paused for a moment, then added, "What I don't know is why."

"Yes, you do. You might have trouble admitting it, but you know the reason I don't want you to leave."

"You...you're talking about the...the other night?" Her face flamed, though it was too dark for Sy to see the high color in her cheeks.

"That, yes, and something else. I think I'm in love with you."

Pam's mouth dropped open. Before she could close it and respond to that startling confession, Sy quickly said, "The key word in that sentence is *think*. I've been hoping that I would know for sure in another two weeks. So, there's my truth. Is it what you wanted to hear?"

She clenched her hands into fists. In all of her life she had never been so deeply wounded. He *thought* he might be in love with her? What unmitigated gall! Did he think she would be thrilled to hear something so degrading? How did he have the nerve to say such a thing to her? Well, this was it, the final insult. She would take no more!

She began scrambling to her feet, but a big hand snaked out and caught her by the ankle. She struggled to escape it, tripped instead and felt herself falling into the water.

She came up sputtering. "You...you adolescent jerk!"

Sy had let go of the side of the tub before she hit the water. He'd only intended to stop her from leaving in a huff, not to half drown her. "Pam, I'm sorry. Just a sec." He reached out and hit the switch to turn off the jets, then took the two steps that separated them in the large tub and pulled her into his arms.

"Don't you dare!" she screeched, and struggled to get away.

He held on. "Say anything you want, only please keep your voice down. I don't want to wake up everyone on the ranch."

"Who gives a damn what *you* want?" But she spewed her venom in a much quieter voice.

"What are you most angry about—the fact that I might be in love with you or the fact that I don't know for sure?"

"Do you think that sort of ambiguity would flatter any woman? Should I kiss your hand because you *might* be in love with me?" she spat.

"I'd much rather have you kiss my mouth." Sy yanked her forward, clasped the back of her neck and pressed his lips to hers. It was spontaneous combustion. Despising her weakness for this man did nothing to strengthen Pam's resolve. In two seconds she was kissing him back as though starved for his touch. Her hands skimmed down his broad back and it was then that she realized he was stark naked.

As for her nightshirt, it was sodden and clinging to her body. Sy rid her of it in one swift movement, drawing it up and over her head. It floated on the water around them, unnoticed as they kissed hungrily, again and again. Dazed by desire, Pam was barely aware of being slowly but accurately led to one of the seats under the water.

Sy placed her on it and nestled his hips between her legs. His mouth devoured hers as his hands moved over her wet and slippery skin. Her nipples became hard and erect in his palms, and then he dipped his head and sucked on first one and then the other.

Even though she was lost in passion, a glimmer of reason floated through Pam's brain. She should not be doing this with Sy. How could she make love with a man who only thought he loved her? He'd made it very clear that he wasn't sure of his feelings, and how could she forgive him for that most cutting of insults just because he had kissed her?

The answer was easy to come by and difficult to face: she loved *him*, obviously too much to deny him anything! How had sensible, realistic, down-to-earth Pamela Brooks come to this? Obviously she wasn't as sensible as she'd always believed. She could blame Sy for that, too.

All thought fled her mind very quickly. Sensation, hot and delicious, seemed the only thing that mattered. Sy's bold hands were everywhere, teasing, caressing, inciting her own boldness. It occurred in the murky depths of her mind that he wasn't hurrying her along as he'd done the first time, and she sank deeper and deeper into pleasure as the need for fulfillment became more controlling. She herself took his throbbing manhood and placed it at the aching cleft between her legs, at the same time whispering, "Make love to me."

In the very next heartbeat, a shattering thought made her turn her head and push against his chest.

Sy didn't step away from her, he couldn't. He was at the very threshold of the most pleasurable act between a man and a woman, and she'd been with him every step of the way. Now she had just confused him beyond belief. "Pam?"

She could hear puzzlement in the way he'd said her name. "We took one chance," she whispered hoarsely. "We can't take another. Do you have protection?"

"Not out here, no." Sy placed his forehead against hers and groaned. "Sweetheart, I want you so bad I'm in agony."

"I know, but..." She bit her lip for a moment. Stopping at this point was agonizing for both of them. Sy wasn't the only one feeling it. Breathlessly she whispered, "Consider the consequences if I got pregnant."

Sy nearly choked. He'd been terribly remiss their first time together and hadn't considered the possible consequences, not even slightly. "You could already be pregnant," he mumbled thickly.

Pam tried to swallow the sudden lump in her throat. "Yes," was all she could get out of her mouth. If she was pregnant and he decided that he didn't love her...

"Do, uh, you think you are? I mean, can a woman tell this soon?"

"I'll know in another week or so."

He hated this clinical conversation and told himself that she couldn't possibly be pregnant. The fact that he would hate any conversation that might put an end to their frenzied lovemaking didn't completely escape him, but it wasn't something he wanted to think about right this minute. He tipped her chin and kissed her, thinking, *To hell with it!*

Pam tried desperately to hang on to reason, but his hot, hard arousal was slowly inching its way into her, and his onslaught of kisses, one after another, was too much to combat.

She gave up and wound her legs around his hips, drawing him deeper inside of her. Sy's growl of approval from deep in his throat brought her need for him and what he was doing to her to an explosive stage. She could feel that wonderful, mind-boggling tension building in the pit of her stomach, and their kisses became wilder, of shorter duration, just as their thrusts and parries under the water were becoming wilder. There was no longer a possibility of stopping; they had both forgone that opportunity several minutes before.

But neither was thinking of that. Neither was worried about pregnancy. The chemistry between them was astonishing, so incredibly perfect that their thoughts, such as they were, seemed to be more connected to the stars than to anything earthly.

The water sloshed in the tub as their movements became more frenetic. And when it finally happened, when they were both soaring somewhere in outer space, they cried out, loudly and without the slightest concern that they might be overheard and that one of the men might come out of the bunkhouse to investigate voices in the middle of the night.

Sy fell to the seat next to Pam and put his head back. Hers was already resting weakly on the lip of the tub, and there they sat, completely exhausted, utterly sated.

After a while, as was bound to happen, they descended back to earth and to earthly realities.

Pam's first lucid thought was, *If he tells me now that he loves me, I will believe him.*

Sy's was, *I must love her to feel so much for her, I must.*

But he didn't say it. He knew himself too well to put much trust in what he was feeling. Instead he slid his arm around Pam's shoulders and kissed her willing lips. "Did I ever tell you how beautiful I think you are?"

Pam sighed. "Not in those words, no. Besides, I know I'm not beautiful."

Sy was truly mystified by her response, until he remembered that when she'd first come to the ranch, he had thought of her in terms of being pretty, not beautiful.

Well, he'd certainly changed on that score. Right this minute she seemed to be the most beautiful of women, wet, dripping hair and all. And it was something he believed in, so he could argue his attitude with the utmost confidence.

"Don't ever think you're not beautiful," he told her. "I've known hundreds of beautiful women, and you're right up there with the best of them."

Pam felt as though icy hands had just clutched her heart. He had the most uncanny knack of saying the wrong thing after making love.

She couldn't stop herself. She turned her head so that her face was an inch from his. "You really are an adolescent jerk, aren't you?"

"What?"

Pam stood up. "I surprised you. Well, that's just too bad, Sy. You're one surprise after another for me, so maybe a taste of your own medicine is what you need most." She looked around for her nightshirt, which was nowhere to be seen. It must have sunk to the bottom of the tub.

She didn't care. Climbing out of the tub, she picked up Sy's towel and wrapped it around herself.

Sy was almost frantic. What had he done to make her angry again? He too climbed out of the tub, only he had nothing with which to cover himself.

"Pam, for God's sake, don't leave without telling me why you're mad at me again. What'd I do this time?"

She looked at him for a long moment, then shook her head. "You would never understand. Good night."

Naked as the day he was born, Sy followed her into the house, pleading with her to tell him what he'd done to make her angry. In the foyer, though, they separated, because he was afraid of taking the stairs without help and Pam wasn't offering any. He went to the elevator while she stoically climbed the stairs.

She made it to her room before the elevator reached the second floor, and she went in, locked the door, dropped the towel and crawled into bed. She was crying into her pillow, berating herself for being the biggest fool of the century, when Sy pounded on her door.

"Pam? For hell's sake, talk to me! This isn't fair, dammit!"

"Get away from my door," she shouted furiously.

Three hours later, she quietly got up, packed her things and tiptoed from the house.

She cried all during the drive to Billings, but it was no more than she'd expected to happen.

And it's no less than you deserve, she told herself. You only got what any fool deserves, and if ever there was a fool, it's you!

Sy was positive he wouldn't sleep a wink the rest of the night, but when he woke up at seven-thirty he realized that he'd slept very well.

He also realized that he felt good, damned good. Stretching his arms and legs to their limit caused not the least ripple of pain in his back. Pam would be glad to hear that.

But then he recalled how they had parted in the night, and his mouth tightened. What was wrong with that woman? Making mad, passionate love with him one minute and being furious with him the next. Over nothing, too. At least *he* couldn't figure out why she'd gotten so ticked off. Well, it would probably pass. She'd gotten mad at him before and she'd gotten over it.

He was getting up, moving slowly to make sure his well-being remained intact, when someone rapped on the door. He grinned, thinking it was Pam. She was probably over her spell and ready to begin the day's therapy.

"Come on in," he called out cheerfully.

Cal walked in. "Morning, S.J. Um, how're you feeling?"

"Great, Cal, just great."

"That's good to hear."

There was something in Cal's eyes that gave Sy a sense of foreboding. "What's wrong?"

"Maybe nothing. If you already know about it, it's probably nothing."

Sy could feel his body tensing up. "If I already know what, Cal?"

The older man cleared his throat. "Uh, Pam's gone."

"Pam's gone where?" Sy said sharply.

Cal looked as though he were getting mighty nervous. "Guess you didn't know, did you? She's just gone, Sy. I checked her room and she took her clothes with her."

"She took everything?"

"Everything." Cal cleared his throat again. "Um, anything you want me to help you with?"

Sy shook his head and felt the simple gesture in his back. With a groan of pure misery, he returned to the bed and crawled under the covers.

"S.J.," Cal said with no small alarm, "you can't stay in bed all day."

"Leave me alone, Cal," Sy growled. "Just leave me the hell alone."

Thirteen

It was still dark when Pam parked her pickup in her garage.
She hauled her luggage up to her apartment, set it down in
the laundry room, continued on to the bedroom, threw off
her clothes and climbed into bed. Her own bed felt good,
and she pulled the covers over her head, leaving only her
face exposed, and closed her eyes.

Three hours later she awoke to daylight and the ringing
of the telephone. She never moved, but she listened as the
answering machine switched on. "I can't come to the
phone right now," her own voice said brightly. "So leave
your name and number and I'll call you back. Bye!"

She stiffened when she heard Sy's voice. "Pam, I know
you're there. Pick up, dammit!"

"Jerk," she mumbled, furious all over again that he had
the nerve to sound angry. Well, he could stay angry for the
rest of his life for all she cared.

Tears filled her eyes. She *did* care, damn him. She was
going to care for a very long time.

But she wasn't going to take his calls. In fact she wasn't
going to take anyone's calls today, and maybe not even
tomorrow. She needed to be completely alone for a while.
Turning over in bed, she went back to sleep.

When she finally got up, late in the afternoon, there were
six calls from Sy on the machine, two from Dr. Donnelly's
office and one from Elliot Young. Sy's messages changed
drastically through the day, evolving from anger to pathos

to pleading. None of them altered Pam's resolve to ignore him. Donnelly's receptionist merely requested that she call in when she got home. Elliot's message was the one she listened to most closely.

"Pam, honey, tomorrow is Friday. Just checking in with you about our dinner date. Give me a call at 555-6638. That's my condo number and I should be home around six. Incidentally, I'm really anxious to show you my condo. It's brand-new and I'm not totally settled yet, probably won't be for weeks, but it's a great place. I have a lease option on it and will probably end up buying it. Great location. I'm sure you'll like it. Call as soon as you can. I'm really looking forward to tomorrow night."

Out of habit Pam wrote Elliot's new number on a pad, but then she groaned and pushed the button that would erase all messages. Going out with Elliot tomorrow night was the last thing she wanted to do. Well, maybe not quite the last, she thought irately. Seeing Sy again would be much worse than seeing Elliot.

But, dammit, she didn't want to see either one of them! For that matter, she didn't want to see anyone. Nothing looked so appealing as just hibernating in her apartment for a good long time, at least until the misery she'd caused herself had abated some.

Of course she could get away with that for only a day or two. She would call Donnelly's office in the morning, and if she was going to cancel tomorrow night's date with Elliot, it was best if she did it before he got home from work, because she didn't want to have to explain anything to him.

Reluctantly she dialed his number, glancing at the clock to check the time—4:15 p.m. Prepared to talk to Elliot's machine, she nearly choked when he answered on the second ring. "Hello?"

"Uh…uh…hello," she stammered.

"Pam?"

"Uh, yes. Didn't you say you'd be home around six?" *Why is that cloud of misery still hanging over my head? He's not supposed to be there!*

"Got off early today. How've you been?"

"Uh, fine, just fine."

"You don't sound fine. What's wrong, honey?"

You have no right to call me honey! No man does. "Really, Elliot, I'm perfectly all right." She knew she sounded impatient, but it was impossible for her to speak any other way today. In time, things would get back to normal. *She* would get back to normal. In the meantime, people would just have to accept her the way she was or not at all. It was up to them.

"Okay, I'll take your word for it," Elliot said. "Hey, I'm really looking forward to seeing you tomorrow night."

"So you said on my answering machine," Pam remarked dryly.

Elliot chuckled in her ear. "Guess I did. Anyhow, I'll pick you up at seven. I was wondering if you were home or still at the Cope ranch, so I called the ranch and…"

Pam cut in. "I wish you hadn't done that."

"Heck, honey, whoever it was that answered was as nice as pie. He said that you'd left early this morning."

"*Very* early."

"Anyway, that was when I called your apartment and left that message. Tomorrow night is going to be so great, Pam. You know, we've got a lot of catching up to do. I can hardly wait."

Pam drew an unsteady breath. Now was the time she should tell him that she was not going out with him, not tomorrow night, not any night. But she opened her mouth to do so and nothing came out of it. Pamela Brooks, you're nothing but a sniveling coward, she thought, furious with herself once again.

"Elliot, there's someone at my front door," she lied.

"Oh, all right. I'll say goodbye in that case. See you at seven tomorrow night."

Pam waited until he'd hung up, then slammed her own phone down hard enough to break it. Why did she keep letting men walk all over her? At what precise point in her life had she lost her backbone?

Totally disgusted with herself, she marched into the bathroom for a shower.

Pam was eating a bowl of soup for dinner when the phone rang again. She sat at the table and listened. It was Sy.

"Pam, if you're there, please pick up. I'm so confused I don't know which end is up. Obviously I did or said something wrong last night, but I can't figure out what it was. I've tried to figure it out all day, and all I do is go in circles. For me, last night was perfect. Where did I disappoint you? How did I disappoint you? Please talk to me, please." After a few moments of silence, he sighed. "Guess you're not going to. Maybe you're not at home. I hope you're not. That would be easier to accept than knowing you're just ignoring my calls. Bye for now. I'll call again."

"No, don't call again," she whispered. "Please don't call again." She placed her spoon in her bowl and gave up on dinner. Her stomach felt upset and queasy. She got up from the table and walked into the living room, breathing deeply to allay the threatening nausea. The hardest thing to accept in this whole mess was that she was still in love with Sy, and every time she thought of her stupidity, she felt like crying.

The pealing of the front doorbell startled her so much she jumped a foot. The thought of seeing anyone made her stomach roll, and if the person on her front stoop should happen to be either Sy or Elliot—Sy *could* have called from the corner pay phone—she was not going to open the door! Moving quietly, she went to the foyer and peered through the door's security peephole. "Oh, no," she whispered, deeply shaken to see Miss Bertie standing there.

She couldn't be rude to Miss Bertie, however much she preferred not seeing or having to talk to one single person. She unlocked the door and pulled it open.

Miss Bertie smiled. "Hello, Pam. How are you, dear?"

"I'm all right," Pam said quietly. "Please come in."

Pam directed the elderly woman to a comfortable chair in the living room. "May I get you something, Miss Bertie? A cup of tea, perhaps?"

"Nothing, Pam, thank you. Please sit down. I know I've surprised you, and I won't stay long, but I simply had to see you for a few moments."

Pam sank to a chair. "You're welcome in my home anytime, Miss Bertie."

"That's a very nice thing to say, Pam, but then I knew you were an exceptional young woman at our first meeting."

"I liked you right away, too," Pam said. "Sy is very fortunate to have you for his grandmother."

"I'm very fortunate to have Sy, Pam," Miss Bertie said gently. "The older one gets, the more important family becomes, and Sy is my only family."

"You're here on his behalf, aren't you?"

"He's terribly worried about you. I went out to the ranch today, just one of my usual visits, and found Sy pacing the house like a caged lion."

"He was pacing? With or without crutches or cane?"

Miss Bertie's eyes lit up. "My goodness! He wasn't using either. That's a very good sign, isn't it? I should have realized."

"He's almost fully recovered, Miss Bertie. We all know he will always have to live within certain physical limitations, but his life should be pretty normal. Normal to most people, that is."

"You sound bitter, Pam, and that breaks my heart. Did Sy break yours? Oh, goodness, there I go prying, and I told myself I wasn't going to do that."

Heaving a sigh, Pam fell back in her chair. "I know he's your grandson and you love him dearly, but he's…he's not a nice person, Miss Bertie." Pam tempered that opinion by adding, "Not always."

"I know Sy's personality better than anyone else ever could, Pam. But I saw some very positive changes in Sy after you started tending him. I can only conclude that you bring out the best in him. I'll tell you plainly that I had extremely high hopes for the two of you. Now, here you are, obviously unhappy, and Sy's at the ranch, also unhappy, and don't you think we should do something about that?"

Pam sat up straighter. "Miss Bertie, you don't know the whole story, and I…I can't tell you everything."

"Of course you can't, dear. Some things are too personal and private to tell anyone, but don't forget that I was once young and in love, just as you and Sy are today."

Pam's jaw dropped. "Sy isn't in love with me, Miss Bertie!"

"Oh, yes, he is, Pam. He just hasn't faced it yet," Miss Bertie said serenely.

Pam stared at the older woman. "How…how do you know that?"

"I know my grandson. Now, if you love him, and I feel

certain you do, not speaking to him on the phone and doing your best to pretend he doesn't exist could destroy something very precious. I think you have to ask yourself how badly you want him. Pam, get in the ring and put on the boxing gloves. Fight for him! I want you for a granddaughter, and one of these days Sy is going to realize that he wants you for his wife. Child, whatever you do, don't give up!''

Pam was stunned to near speechlessness. ''I...I don't know what to say.''

''I know,'' Miss Bertie said sympathetically. ''He's as mulish as they come, and overbearing. My, yes, he really can be overbearing. But underneath all that bluster and attitude, Sy's a darling. You'll have to trust me on that, because he probably hasn't shown you that side of himself.''

''He...he was pleasant...and charming...a few times.''

Miss Bertie smiled. ''Imagine if he was pleasant and charming all of the time. He would be with the right woman, Pam. I know that as surely as I know anything.''

''And...and you think I'm the right woman.''

''Not think, dear, know.'' Miss Bertie pushed herself from the chair to her feet. ''I'm going to leave now. You have a lot to mull over. Oh, by the way, I think it would be best if Sy never heard about this little chat. May I count on your discretion?''

Pam got up. ''Yes...of course.''

Miss Bertie moved closer to Pam and kissed her cheek. ''You're a very special young woman. Don't, for heaven's sake, let Sy daunt you.'' Miss Bertie smiled impishly. ''Let's not forget that he is, after all, just a man, or that women have been the stronger sex since Eve. I know you can win him, Pam, but you can't be a shrinking violet about it. Throw everything you have at him. Goodbye, my dear. We'll talk again.''

After escorting Miss Bertie to the door, Pam returned to the living room and collapsed on the sofa, feeling as though she had just received some sort of shock therapy. Should she take Miss Bertie's advice seriously and go after Sy with both guns blazing? My Lord, could she even do something like that? Never in her life had she chased a man. Could she start now? But start where? How? What would be her first move? Her second, if the first was rebuffed?

And then Pam recalled what Sy had said to her just last night. *I might be in love with you, but I don't know for sure.* "My God," she whispered, shaken to her soul. Miss Bertie was right! Instead of getting her feelings all hurt and wounded and leaving the ranch like a thief in the night, she should have stayed on Sy's turf and fought for the man she loved!

Yes, she certainly did have a lot to mull over, much more than she could have imagined in her wildest dreams. Miss Bertie had been right about that, as well.

Sy had a plan. On Friday he took great care with his exercises, both in and out of the hot tub, for he wanted no sudden tensing of muscles and resulting pain to undermine that plan. He already knew he could drive, so getting to Billings was not going to be a problem. Neither had obtaining Pam's home address been a problem; it was listed in the phone book, along with her phone number.

The biggest problem of the entire day, in fact, had been Cal. "S.J.!" Cal had exclaimed excitedly when Sy told him he was driving to Billings that evening. "You shouldn't be going off by yourself like that, especially not at night."

Sy hadn't debated the matter. "I'm going, Cal," he'd stated firmly.

"Well, heck, if you have to go, let me take you."

"Nope, but thanks for offering."

And so it happened that Sy left the ranch shortly after dinner and drove to Billings. His thoughts were grim, as they'd been since Pam had sneaked away in the night, but he didn't let them get so grim as to cause tension in his back. He intended to confront Pam on his feet, not as a semi-invalid. Without her, the ranch didn't even feel like home, and he knew in his heart that she had become very, very important to him. She *had* to talk to him; he was going to stand on her doorstep—if that's what it took—until she did.

Once in Billings it took a while to locate her address. It was in a newer section of the city, one that he wasn't familiar with, but he finally stopped in front of a small apartment complex. Parked at the curb, he turned off the ignition and cautiously climbed out of his car. There was an uneasy churning in his stomach, but he wasn't able to control every part of his body. As good as he was becoming at controlling tension that might land him on his back, no one could dominate every portion of their body, he told himself as he walked up the sidewalk to Pam's front door.

Inside, Pam was nervously pacing. She had tried to reach Elliot all day so she could cancel their dinner date, but she'd been told that he had the day off and no one knew where he was spending it. At any rate, she expected him to ring her doorbell at any moment. She hoped when he saw her jeans, T-shirt and sandals that he would understand at once that she didn't intend going out with him. At the same time she realized that she could be in for an unpleasant scene with Elliot. Regardless, she was adamant about letting him know that she was in love with another man and that she never should have made this date with him.

She winced when the doorbell rang, stopped for a deep breath, then went to the door to face Elliot with squared shoulders and a determined tilt to her chin.

Only it wasn't Elliot on her little porch, it was Sy, so handsome in dark slacks and a white shirt that she didn't breathe for a good thirty seconds. They just stood there looking at each other, drinking in the sight of each other, each thinking the exact same thought: *I'm so much in love with this person that I'm dizzy from it!*

For Sy it was a shock of enormous proportions. For Pam it was hope renewed. She finally managed a weakly stated, "Hi."

Sy cleared his throat. "Hi. May I come in?"

"Yes...yes." She was still so breathless that speaking normally was difficult. But she had enough wits left to step back so he *could* come in, and after shutting the door, she brought him to the living room. "Sit, uh, anywhere."

"Thanks." Sy lowered himself into a chair that, though nicely upholstered had a straight back. Pam perched on the edge of a sofa cushion, too unnerved to make herself comfortable.

"How...how are you feeling?" she asked, much too aware of the thumping of her heart.

"Good...I'm feeling good."

"That's good."

"Uh, yes, it's good that I'm feeling good."

Neither of them realized how inane they sounded. Mentally Sy was still standing at Pam's front door, reliving that momentous shock when he'd realized that he was in love with her. Pam was wondering with what ammunition she should load those imaginary guns she was supposed to use to fight for him, to "win" him, as Miss Bertie had put it.

"Oh?" she exclaimed, jumping to her feet. "Can I get you something to drink?"

"Ice water." Sy's throat was dry and getting drier. Was that how it happened to other people, he wondered, one second not knowing anything for sure and the next knowing everything with irrevocable certainty? Another question, even more complex than the first, began gnawing at him. Should he just say it, without preamble, without romantic words or even a warning? *Pam, it just hit me like a thunderbolt. I am in love with you. I think I have been for a long time.*

But that seemed so cold, so callous. Women wanted romance. Hell, *he* wanted romance.

Pam returned with two glasses containing ice cubes and water, one of which she gave to Sy. "Thank you," he said quietly.

Resuming her perch on the sofa, she frowned slightly. He was…different. Was she?

They sipped water and looked at each other. "Well," Sy said. "You have a nice little apartment here."

"I like it." After a moment she said, "Your coming here is surprising."

"I suppose so. But you wouldn't take my calls and…"

"And what, Sy?"

"Well, it just didn't seem right, I guess, you and I not talking, I mean."

"If it didn't seem right to you, then it must have seemed wrong," Pam murmured. "Was that it?"

"Yeah, I guess that was it."

"So you came here to right a wrong?" For the first time since she sat down, Pam leaned back. "How do you propose to do that, Sy?"

He smiled wanly. "You don't plan to make this easy for me, do you?"

Pam's heart skipped a full beat. He was so utterly gorgeous. His long hair was brushed smoothly back from his handsome face, and never had she ever seen eyes like his. It struck her, quite painfully, that she wanted him naked, in her bed, in her arms, inside of her, and that she would always want him in that same impassioned way.

She licked her dry lips and took another swallow of water. "Make what easy for you, Sy?" Her voice came out all whispery and breathy, and she felt that if he couldn't tell from that where her mind had been, he would never know anything about her.

Sy drained his glass of water, then placed it on the table next to his chair. He got up slowly and walked to the sofa and sat very close to her, so that their thighs and arms were touching.

Pam felt as though she were melting, with the core of all that heat centered precisely between her legs. "You were saying?" she said huskily.

"I wasn't saying what I was thinking, but that's what I'd like to do now." He took her free hand in his and lovingly held it.

Almost frantically Pam looked for a place to set her glass. Finally she lowered it to the carpet and promptly forgot about it. Sy had something important to say to her, and it was all she could think of.

"Yes, say it," she whispered raggedly. "Please say it."

At that very moment the doorbell rang. Pam's eyes grew big as saucers. Elliot! My God, she'd forgotten about Elliot! *No, no, not now! Not now!*

"Someone's at your door," Sy said.

"Uh, I know." Sliding her hand from Sy's, she tried desperately to think, but nothing brilliant or even intelligent came to mind. Sy had been on the brink of talking about love, she knew it in her soul, and now this. How would she ever make him understand that she loved him, too, but had still made a date with another man? It didn't even make sense to her, so how would Sy interpret it?

The bell pealed again. "I think you'd better answer it," Sy said quietly.

Sick to her stomach, Pam got up. Her legs felt shaky as gelatin, and she marveled that she didn't fall flat on her face as she stumbled to the foyer. It occurred to her then that if Sy remained on the sofa, he wouldn't be able to see who had rung the bell. If she could keep Elliot outside, that is.

Well, she had to stop him from coming in, that was all there was to it. Opening the door a mere crack, she slipped through it before Elliot could do more than smile at her.

His smile vanished. "What're you doing?"

She began talking very fast and very quietly. "Elliot, something's come up and I have to cancel dinner."

"What came up?"

"Um…" She saw Elliot look at the car at the curb, and she looked at it herself, realizing it was an ultracostly, luxury sedan. "A friend," she said with great haste. "A friend dropped in."

"A friend who drives that? A man, Pam?"

"Elliot, please don't get angry. I tried to reach you today to cancel…"

"But you said he just dropped in. Why were you going to cancel earlier? Pam, there's something you're not telling me. You know, I think I'd like to go in and meet your friend." He brushed past Pam and pushed open the door.

"Elliot!" she cried. "Stop right where you are!"

But he was already in the doorway between the foyer and living room, and when she peered around him, she could see Sy getting to his feet. The two men stood glaring at each other, and Pam wished the earth would just open up and swallow her whole. Anything would be easier than trying to explain this to Sy.

She ducked around Elliot and faced him, putting herself

between him and Sy. "I want you to leave," she said with scalding force behind her words.

"In a minute," Elliot said to her, then glared at Sy again. "I'm Elliot Young, and Pam and I had a dinner date tonight. Who're you to ruin it for us?"

"The name's Sy Cope."

"*The* Sy Cope? World's most eligible bachelor, millions of bucks and all that other junk? Okay, guess that does it. Doubt if I could ever compete with your dough, pal." He gave Pam a mocking salute. "So long, babe. See you around. Oh, and good luck with the playboy here. Methinks you're gonna need it. Can't blame you for trying for the brass ring, though. Can't blame you a bit."

Even before the door slammed behind Elliot, Pam was trying to explain. "That was not what you're thinking, Sy. In the first place, I wouldn't care if you didn't have a dime, and in the second..."

"Probably not," Sy cut in with deadly calm. "I think I'll be running along, too, Pam. Sort of tired. I'm sure you understand."

She leaned against the frame of the doorway, because she was honestly afraid that her legs were going to fold. "Did you ever wonder before tonight if I made love with you because you had money?"

"No, it never crossed my mind."

"But you're wondering now."

"No. I'm not."

"Then why are you leaving? You were about to say something when Elliot got here. I think it was something important."

Sy shrugged. "It wasn't. Just forget it, okay? I need to leave because I'm tired." It was a lie. He wasn't one bit tired. But he was angry. And glad, very glad, that he hadn't told Pam how much he loved her.

"Did you like making love to me?" It was the most difficult question that had ever come out of her mouth. She didn't talk to men that way.

"What?"

"You heard me."

Sy's lip curled cynically. "Yeah, I liked it. I liked it a lot." He wanted to make her hurt, as he was hurting. "You've got a great body, and if you offered it right now, I'd use it again. Is that what you wanted to hear?"

"No," she whispered around the lump that formed in her throat. "That wasn't what I wanted to hear." She moved away from the doorway, continuing clear to the opposite side of the room. "Good night, Sy," she said sadly.

"Goodbye." Sy walked out of her apartment, and a few seconds later she heard his car drive away.

It was over. She knew it now, and the strange part of it was that she couldn't even cry about it. The pain she was feeling was too deep for mere tears.

She would get over it, of course.

Someday.

Fourteen

Pam went back to work at the Billings Therapy Center. It wasn't the same, nothing was. Even the career in which she had taken such pride, and which had always seemed so worthwhile to her, couldn't lift her cheerless spirit. Friends noticed the drastic change in her, and some of them asked questions. Her answer was always the same—"I'm fine. Nothing's wrong." How could she tell anyone the reason for her unhappiness?

One thing unnerved her terribly. Every time she ran into Elliot he made some snide remark such as, "How's your rich boyfriend?" He did it whether they were alone or with other people, and Pam actually cringed whenever she spotted him. She realized one day, after overhearing a giggled, whispered discussion between two female co-workers, that everyone working at the center probably knew about her relationship with Sy, or at least they had heard Elliot's version of it. It made her sick to her stomach that he would do something that spiteful, and the knowledge that her co-workers were talking about her behind her back made going to work every morning an ordeal.

She was very tempted to corner Elliot and tell him off, but common sense prevailed, and instead she concentrated on avoiding him. After all, what would she accomplish by ranting at Elliot except to provide more fodder for the gossip mill? He would probably love having new material to spread around about her.

The thing was, of course, that no one would be gossiping at all if the man referred to in Elliot's degrading comments and stories was anyone other than Sy Cope. Relationships came and went around the center, they always had. But Sy, being the man he was, wealthy, ultrahandsome and with a bad-boy reputation, titillated people's imaginations. It was Henrietta "Retta" McPherson, one of Pam's closer friends at the center, who said to her one day, "Don't let it bother you, Pam. Next week they'll be talking about someone else. What I really don't understand, though, is why Elliot would be such a worm. Weren't the two of you engaged a few years back?"

"Almost engaged, Retta," Pam said with a heavy sigh. "Before he went to Baltimore."

"Well, he's letting his jealousy of Sy Cope control his good sense, if he ever had any to begin with, that is," Retta said wryly.

That little chat stayed with Pam. It hadn't occurred to her that jealousy was at the root of Elliot's hateful behavior, but something was, and Retta's jealousy theory made sense. All she could do about it, she decided, was to act totally unconcerned until Elliot got over it. He would, eventually.

Weeks went by—they were approaching the end of summer—and the gossip had started to die down, however hard Elliot tried to keep it going. Pam was beginning to feel a little better about life in general. Not that she would ever forget Sy. Nor would she ever love anyone quite as much again, she was certain, but daily routines were keeping her busy enough that he was no longer the only thought in her mind.

Then, on a Monday morning, she awoke with almost choking nausea and barely made it to the bathroom in time. Once it was over, it was over. The nausea was completely gone, and while brushing her teeth, she wondered what on earth had brought it on. Something she'd eaten last night? A mild—*very* mild—virus?

Or...? "Oh, no," she whispered, and dashed from the bathroom to the calendar on her kitchen wall. The dates blurred before her eyes as reality struck—she had missed two periods!

Sinking weakly to a kitchen chair, she sat with her head in her hands. This couldn't be happening, it couldn't!

But how many women in the history of the world had thought that same thing and then given birth seven or eight months later? "Oh, God," she moaned.

I can't think about this now. I just can't! Jumping up, she returned to her bathroom to take her morning shower.

On her way to work Pam stopped at a drugstore and purchased a home pregnancy test kit. When she got to the center, she went to the most remote restroom in the building, locked herself in a stall and administered the test.

It came out positive.

In moments of complete honesty, Sy could do nothing else but give Pam full credit for his recovery. But thinking of Pam never failed to unnerve him, so he did his best not to think of her. He succeeded pretty well, too. During the day, at least. It wasn't possible to control his dreams, however, and he often woke up at night suffering the after-effects of a dream with Pam in the starring role. Sometimes the dreams were erotic, sometimes not, but every one of them was disruptive and disturbing, and he usually had trouble falling asleep again.

The days just kept getting better, though. He faithfully followed Pam's regimen of exercise and even advanced himself from walking to jogging. Rarely did he feel a spasm in his back anymore, and his legs were once again strong and muscular. Sy was his own therapist now, and he bought and read several books on the subject. He knew now that underlying tension could wreak havoc with his back, and he also knew that most of the tension he'd suffered before and even during Pam's tenure had been caused by frustration.

He was no longer frustrated because he had finally accepted, albeit reluctantly, the irrevocable facts of his physical capabilities. He would never be fit enough to climb mountains; a hard landing from a parachute jump could permanently cripple him; his reflexes would never again be quick enough to drive race cars or boats; downhill skiing was out, unless he wanted to ski the beginners' slopes, which he would never do; and things like hang gliding, surfing during storms to catch the biggest waves and riding a motorcycle hell-bent for election would be foolish risks for him to take.

He consoled his hunger for excitement by making a mental list of the things he *could* do. Cross-country skiing, for instance. He felt certain that he would be strong enough for that when this winter's snowfalls permitted the sport. He could swim and was, in fact, having an indoor pool in a new building constructed not far from the house. He hadn't yet gotten on a horse, but he would very soon now. He could drive ordinary vehicles and thanked God for that ability every time he got into one. He could go where he wanted, when he wanted. He could fish. He could walk!

Instead of sitting around feeling sorry for himself, as he'd done before Pam had come along, Sy now leaned toward the positive aspects of his life. It was quite an awakening. He even began taking an interest in the operation of the ranch, surprising Hoke, he knew, by asking the foreman to spend a half hour with him each day to keep him apprised of what job the men were doing, in what portion of the ranch the herds were grazing and so on.

Sy's days were full and he was no longer miserable about the blow fate had dealt him on that perilous ski slope. And yet, in his heart, he knew something crucial was missing: Pam. As many women as he had known before her, he had never really been in love before, and when he had one of those disturbing dreams and couldn't go back to sleep, he tortured himself with thoughts of what might have been. Not willingly, not deliberately, God forbid, but because in the darkest part of a long, silent night, it simply wasn't possible for him to direct his thoughts away from her.

But he also felt that she couldn't care less about anything he might think. She had Elliot Young back in her life again. Making love with Sy couldn't have been any more than casual sex to her. He thought no less of her for it, either. After all, casual, meaningless sex had been a way of life for him and many of his former friends for a very long time.

Strangely, Sy never longed for sex. Maybe the strenuous exercises on which he spent so much of his energy saved him from that particular discomfort, or maybe he deliberately eluded the issue because when he did think of sex, he immediately saw Pam in his mind's eye. Whatever the reason, sex, or the lack thereof, wasn't a problem for him.

Miss Bertie seemed to have a different point of view about it, though. During one of her visits to the ranch, she brought up the subject. "You're a young man, Sy, and, thank the good Lord, you're healthy again. According to Cal and Joe you're always here, and there aren't any women around that I know of, so what are you doing for female companionship?"

"Is that a sly way of asking if I'm living a celibate life?" Sy said with a laugh.

"Are you?" Miss Bertie asked bluntly.

"Gran, you never cease to amaze me."

Miss Bertie sipped from her cup of tea and smiled sweetly. "Pam was so dear, wasn't she? You must miss her. Or perhaps you and she stay in touch. Do you?"

"No, and that's the last question I'm going to answer about my personal life."

"You needn't get testy, Sy. I was only thinking of you."

After Miss Bertie left that day, Sy felt an overwhelming urge to phone Pam. Just to ask how she was doing, he thought, just to find out if she was all right. He battled with the idea for a while and finally talked himself out of it. He would probably get her answering machine and she wouldn't return his call, so why put himself through that again?

The days and nights became weeks.

Pam took an afternoon off from her job and drove to Bozeman to see an obstetrician. She was completely honest with him. "I'm a member of the Billings medical community and unmarried. Word could get around about my condition before I want it to. That's why I came to you."

The doctor was understanding and efficient. After an examination he pronounced Pam marvelously healthy, gave her some pamphlets to read about pregnancy and asked if she intended to see him again.

"Yes. For a while, at least. My plans are...well, right now I don't have a plan."

She didn't. All during the drive back to Billings she fought depression. She was single, totally without relatives, pregnant and in love with her baby's father but without a dram of hope for any sort of future together. Plus, her child was going to be Miss Bertie's great-grandchild, and maybe that was the saddest thing of all. Miss Bertie would never meet her great-grandchild, nor would the baby ever know his wonderful great-grandmother.

That thought brought tears to Pam's eyes, and she had to dash them away quickly so she could see the freeway clearly. However, there was nothing she could do about the ache in her chest; her heart felt heavy as lead. Her spirit was at an all-time low, and she couldn't even begin to formulate a sensible plan for her and the baby's future.

When she got home, she fell on her bed and wept.

It did nothing but clog her nose and redden her eyes.

Pam had to forcibly pull herself out of the deep sleep into which she had fallen. Someone was at her front door. The bell kept ringing...and ringing.

Hauling herself off the bed, she hurried through the apartment and opened the door. Still groggy, she stared blankly at Miss Bertie.

"Oh, my dear!" Miss Bertie exclaimed worriedly. "Are you ill?"

It struck Pam how truly awful she must look. Crying oneself to sleep always resulted in red, swollen eyes and nose, and her hair was probably a mess, and her clothes were probably wrinkled and...oh, it was all too much!

She started bawling again and found herself in Miss Bertie's gentle arms. "There, there," the elderly lady said. "Nothing can be that bad. Come on now, let's get you inside."

Pam let Miss Bertie take over completely, and she found herself lying on the sofa with an afghan over her. Miss Bertie disappeared and returned in a moment with a cool wet washcloth, which she placed on Pam's forehead. She then sat alongside of Pam, perching on the very edge of the sofa's middle cushion, and peered sharply into Pam's swollen eyes.

"I insist on knowing what's wrong," Miss Bertie said firmly. "Did someone in your family pass away?"

"I have no family," Pam said, and started crying again.

"You need some tissues. Where might I find them?"

"The kitchen and...and the bathroom."

In seconds Pam had a handful of tissues. "Blow your nose, honey," Miss Bertie instructed. Pam obeyed. "Now, my dear, let's do a little talking. What's all this blubbering about?"

Panic rose in Pam's throat. "I...I can't tell you."

Miss Bertie's gaze remained steadfast, and Pam saw how bright her eyes were, and how blue, almost as blue as her grandson's. Tears again filled her own eyes, for she was beginning to feel hopeless as well as depressed.

"You can't tell anyone, or you just can't tell me?" Miss Bertie asked.

On top of feeling hopeless and depressed, Pam also began feeling trapped. Miss Bertie was nobody's fool. Pam could tell that the elderly woman suspected her fragile state of mind had something to do with Sy.

"Please, Miss Bertie, don't ask," she whispered, wishing with all her heart and soul that Sy's grandmother hadn't visited her today. Normally she would just be getting home from work, and she would have offered dinner to her guest. Instead, her guest was taking care of her! How embarrassing.

"Evasion will not work with me, young woman. I *am* asking. I believe we are friends. Am I wrong in that assumption?"

"No, you're not wrong."

"Well, in my book, Pam, friends help each other get through trying times. I cannot help you through anything without first knowing what it is."

"I know, but..."

"But it's about something Sy said or did and you're afraid of hurting my feelings because he's my grandson."

"Yes...no...uh, it's no more his fault than mine."

Miss Bertie looked at her shrewdly for a moment, then got to her feet, whereupon she began walking around the room. Pam wiped her eyes and blew her nose again, keeping a close and very nervous eye on Miss Bertie because she was so afraid of the older woman figuring it out.

Which, of course, Miss Bertie had already done. She turned at the fireplace and looked at Pam. "You're expecting a child. I'm going to ask you this because I have to hear it at least once. Is it Sy's child?"

Pam turned her face to the back of the sofa and began sobbing. Miss Bertie rushed over to sit next to her. "Pam, you must answer me. Is Sy the father of your baby?"

After a moan of pure misery, Pam whispered, "Yes."

"Oh, joy!"

Startled beyond belief, Pam turned over and saw tears in Miss Bertie's eyes. "You...you don't hate me?"

"Hate you! My dear, you've made me the happiest woman in all of Montana. You're in love with him, of course."

"Oh, yes," Pam said in a shaky little voice. "But he doesn't love me, Miss Bertie. He really doesn't."

"Nonsense. Besides, who Sy does or doesn't love matters very little at this point. Your child is a Cope, and he or she is going to have the Cope name."

Pam frantically clutched at Miss Bertie's hand. "You can't tell him, Miss Bertie, you can't! He will never forgive me."

"Forgive you for what, getting pregnant?" Miss Bertie sniffed derogatorily. "Unless the world has gone completely topsy-turvy in the past forty years, it still takes two to make a baby. At least, that's how I remember it. Pam, this child is as much Sy's responsibility as it is yours, and I guarantee you that he will not only face that responsibility, he will do so in a decent and forthright manner. The Copes have always been honorable people. I will accept no less from Sy.''

Pam covered her face with her hands and whispered, ''Oh, God.'' She could see it all, a forced marriage and Sy's rage—perhaps withheld in the presence of his grandmother, but a very strong, abiding part of his already self-centered personality, nonetheless. It wasn't what she wanted, not for herself and certainly not for her baby.

''Miss Bertie, I...I won't marry Sy. I'll have the baby alone. You may see him whenever you wish. But I will not live with a man who doesn't love me. I don't deserve that kind of life, and I...''

''Just stop right there, young lady. I figured on Sy's stubbornness, but not on yours. You are bringing a new life to this world, a *human* life, and that's God's greatest miracle. Are you going to minimize it, trivialize it by taking away your child's father without even giving Sy a chance? I don't think so. No, I simply will not stand for it. You and Sy are going to be married. Don't worry, I'll be the one to talk to him about it. Now, if either of you possesses the brains I've been giving you both credit for having, you'll make your marriage work, for your child's sake if not for your own. Goodness, I can't believe you would consider any other solution.''

Miss Bertie got to her feet. ''It's too late today, but I'll drive out to the ranch first thing in the morning. Where will you be?''

''At work,'' Pam said timidly. In all of her life she'd never come up against anyone with Miss Bertie's determination. ''The therapy center.''

''I'll find the number in the phone book.'' Miss Bertie bent over and kissed Pam's wet cheek. ''Cheer up, Pam. Everything is going to be just fine, you'll see. No, don't get up. I can see myself to the door. I'll be calling you after I talk to Sy. Goodbye, my dear. Try to get a good night's rest.''

Miss Bertie walked to the foyer and then through the front door with her head high. Pam just stared after her with her mouth ajar. She felt as though she'd been flattened by a freight train, a sweet, gentle, soft-spoken freight train, to be true, but one that was definitely constructed from steel. And tomorrow morning, Miss Bertie was also going to flatten Sy!

Pam pulled the afghan over her head and groaned out loud. Sy was going to despise her. He would think that she had gone to his grandmother to plead with the elderly woman to force him to marry her. Dear God, how would she ever convince him that it hadn't happened that way? That Miss Bertie had dropped in on her on a day when she'd been upset and uncertain and more depressed than she'd ever been in her life? Sy would never believe her, never! Right or wrong, he was a man who believed in only what he himself was certain of. Who knew that better than she?

This was going to be the marriage from hell, she thought with a dismal sigh. And it wouldn't last, it would never last.

How could it?

Fifteen

Sy had a pleasant surprise the following morning—Miss Bertie arrived at the ranch early enough to eat breakfast with him.

"This is nice," he told her as he held the chair for her to sit at the table in the lovely rose dining room.

"Yes, it is, but I can tell that you're very curious about such an early visit." Miss Bertie poured milk into her cup of coffee while Sy took his seat.

"Well…yes," Sy admitted with a laugh. "Can never fool you, can I, Gran?"

"Only once in a while, dear, only once in a while." Cal came in with a large tray from which he took bowls of oatmeal and placed them in front of her and Sy, and then he set a bowl of cut-up fresh fruit between them. Small plates and forks for the fruit were part of the place settings. Cal also unloaded a pitcher of milk, containers of honey and sweeteners and hot whole wheat toast.

"Good morning, Cal," Miss Bertie said brightly. "This looks marvelous."

"Thank you, Miss Bertie. It's a lot different from what Sy used to call breakfast, ain't it?"

"Yes, it certainly is."

"Anything else I can get you, ma'am?"

"No, Cal, thank you." Miss Bertie sent her grandson a tender, loving smile as Cal left the room. "You've changed your habits a great deal, haven't you?"

"Had to, Miss Bertie. It was either change old habits or sit in that damned wheelchair for the rest of my life." He passed the pitcher of milk. "Are you going to tell me what brought you out here so early this morning?"

"In due time, dear. Let's enjoy our breakfast first. You know, I noticed a touch of fall in the air this morning." Miss Bertie finished preparing her oatmeal and began eating.

"Yes, I think summer is coming to an end."

"It was a wonderful summer, don't you agree?"

"Unusual, at any rate."

"You look fit as a fiddle. And I'm so pleased that you're becoming involved in ranch affairs."

"Yes, well, I needed something to occupy my mind, Gran. The ranch seems to be doing it."

"I'm very proud of you, Sy. I hope you know that. I love you and I'm very proud of you."

Sy smiled. "I love you and I'm proud of you, too, Miss Bertie."

"What do you think was the most important factor in your recovery? I have my own ideas on that, but I'd like to hear yours."

"That's an easy question to answer, Gran. Pam made all the difference. When she came to the ranch I was a mess. She's responsible for my recovery."

"Yes," Miss Bertie murmured. "That's exactly what I was thinking." She spooned some of the fruit from the bowl to her plate. "Have you done any riding yet?"

"Not yet. Soon, though."

"You seem quite happy."

"I think I am happy, Miss Bertie. It took a major adjustment in attitude, but I feel like I'm on the right track now."

"I feel you are, too, and that makes me very happy."

"More coffee, Gran?"

"No, thank you, dear. My doctor prefers that I give up coffee entirely, but I cheat a little and drink one cup with breakfast."

Sy's expression became concerned. "You're not unwell, are you?"

"For my age I'm very well, Sy. I don't want you worrying about me."

"Then why can't you drink all the coffee you want?"

"For the same reason you're eating oatmeal and fruit for breakfast, when I know you love bacon and eggs, dear. To *stay* healthy. Don't look so doubtful, Sy. Really, you must believe me. I have no serious medical problems."

"Some minor problems, then?"

"Goodness, you're a persistent boy. All right, yes, I have a few minor problems, but I will not have you worrying about me." Miss Bertie's eyes twinkled. "Believe me, dearest, I plan to be around for a good many years."

Sy fell silent, then said quietly, "I don't know what I'd do without you, Gran. You're my only family."

"And you are *my* only family. That will change, though."

"It will?"

"When you marry, Sy," Miss Bertie said serenely.

"Oh, sure, but who knows when that will happen, if it ever does?" Sy sounded gloomy, which Miss Bertie didn't miss. She smiled, and they finished eating with chitchat about the ranch.

Miss Bertie pushed her chair back from the table. "Now, I know you have things to do, but I need a few more minutes of your time. May we talk in the library?"

"Of course." Sy escorted Miss Bertie from the dining room to the library, where they each chose a favorite chair and sat down.

"I always loved this room," Miss Bertie said, her gaze sweeping the walls of bookshelves and the splendid old furniture.

"It's a great room," Sy agreed, patiently waiting for his grandmother to introduce whatever topic had brought her to the ranch so early in the day.

She did it with her very next sentence. "I saw Pam yesterday."

Sy's pulse rate increased in speed and he sat up straighter. "How is she?" he asked casually, as though it really didn't matter to him how Pam was doing and he was merely making polite conversation.

Miss Bertie stole a quiet breath. "She's pregnant."

The first thing that flashed into Sy's mind was Elliot Young. "That bastard!" he said, instantly furious. He got to his feet to go to the window and stare out.

"I beg your pardon?" Miss Bertie was stunned. She had not expected an outburst like that one from Sy.

"Sorry for the language," Sy mumbled. His mind seemed to be racing from one thing to another. Elliot Young, that jerk, and Pam, together and making love—Sy winced—and Pam telling Miss Bertie that she was pregnant, and Miss Bertie rushing out here to tell him. What in hell was going on?

He turned to look at his grandmother. "Why did you think I would be interested in that sort of news?"

"Because it's your baby, Sy."

Sy was floored. Didn't Miss Bertie know about Elliot Young? What kind of game was Pam playing? He opened his mouth to talk about Elliot Young, then closed it again. He'd get to the bottom of this himself, and he'd do it without smearing Pam to a woman who so obviously cared about her well-being.

"Pam told you it's my baby?" he said, exercising supreme effort to control the level of his voice.

"Yes, Sy, she did. Of course, I told her that you were an honorable man and would marry her. In all honesty, Sy, I'm very excited about the thought of a baby, and a wedding."

Sy inhaled a long breath. "Yes, well, we'll see about that."

Miss Bertie displayed shock. "The Copes have always been honorable people, Sy. Surely you wouldn't turn your back on your own child."

"I would never turn my back on my own child, Grandmother. I will take care of this, trust me."

Miss Bertie sat back rather suddenly. Before her very eyes her grandson had become a man of dignity. Even as a child he had called her Miss Bertie. Sometimes he called her Gran, usually when he was teasing her about something, but never, not once, had he ever called her Grandmother. Until now.

"Yes," she said quietly, "I do trust you."

"Thank you."

Miss Bertie knew she had done all she could do. Driving out here, she had thought of several possible scenarios for this most serious of conversations, but none were even close to what had actually occurred. She got up from her chair, went over to Sy and put her arms around his waist.

"My dearest grandson," she said softly. "My heart is so full."

She was so small that Sy had to bend over to hug her. "So is mine. I love you very much, Grandmother."

"I love you, Sy." After a moment, Miss Bertie stepped back. "I'm going to leave now. Please let me know what you and Pam decide."

"I will, I promise. Oh, do you know where she'll be today?"

"At the therapy center."

Sy walked Miss Bertie out to her car and saw her off, then, grim-lipped, he returned to the house and began his daily routine of exercise. It felt good to sweat and strain his muscles, and he put off thinking about what he had to do later. He would have plenty of time for that particular activity during the drive to Billings.

Sy thought of nothing else during the drive. If the baby was his he would, without hesitation, offer marriage. If there was no Elliot Young, there would also be no doubts in his mind, he realized. But he'd seen the man at Pam's apartment with his own eyes. The baby could be Elliot's child. Maybe even Pam herself didn't know for sure.

But she had still gone to Miss Bertie, Sy thought with a surge of bitterness. Sy Cope was a much better catch, financially speaking, than Elliot Young could ever be.

And yet Pam had never struck him as a gold digger, and he'd met more than a few of that type of woman before, make no mistake. Sy slammed the steering wheel with the palm of his hand. He didn't want to believe that Pam was capable of that kind of deceit, but how would he ever unearth the truth?

Recalling that Elliot hadn't been in Montana when Pam first came to the ranch gave Sy some hope, and he began calculating dates. Or trying to. The summer had gone by so fast, and it was frustrating to realize that he couldn't remember which had come first, Elliot's letter announcing his impending return or the night *he* and Pam had made wild, crazy love in her bed.

It was a critical point and he racked his brain for a clear memory. It simply wasn't there, but something else was.

Pam had not left the ranch even once after her arrival until the day she'd driven him to see Dr. Donnelly. That appointment had definitely come after the session in her bed. Then they'd made love in the hot tub and Pam had run away.

Yes, he at least had that much straight. Maybe the most important answer he could seek was: just how pregnant was Pam? In terms of time, that is. Since she could not have had relations with Elliot until after she'd gone to her own home in Billings, it all had to do with timing, didn't it?

Sy's lips thinned when he thought of the short span of time in which so much had taken place. If Pam's pregnancy was still being measured in weeks, there was no way of him coming to any sensible conclusion about the paternity of her child. He was going to have to make a decision merely from talking to her. Of course he could always demand a blood test to prove paternity, but that seemed like a very dire step to take. If the baby really was his and Pam knew it, she would probably never forgive him if he did that to her.

"God, what a mess," he muttered under his breath.

Arriving at the therapy center, he parked his car and strode into the building through the glassed-in front doors. Inside he looked around. Several people were working behind a large, circular counter, and he headed that way.

"Holy cow!" a young woman whispered to another. "Take a look at the hunk who just walked in."

"I'm in love," the other woman sighed with a mock swoon. "Who is he?"

"I have no idea, but I'm going to find out." She moved to a prominent place at the counter so Sy would have to talk to her.

Sy walked up without a smile. He was in no mood for chitchat of any kind, and he especially had no desire to flirt with this young woman, who looked as though that were her primary goal for the day. "Would you please contact Pamela Brooks and tell her that Symon Cope is in the lobby and would like to see her?"

The woman visibly gulped. "Symon Cope? Yes, Mr. Cope. I'll page her right away."

"Thank you."

Sy walked away and the woman rolled her eyes at her friend and mouthed, "Did you hear?" After receiving a silent nod, the first woman picked up the phone and punched two numbers. Sy could hear the page come through the public-address system.

"Pamela Brooks, please come to the lobby. Mr. Symon Cope is…uh, he's waiting to see you."

Pam was on her way to a specialty therapy room to confer with another therapist regarding the care of a partially paralyzed stroke victim. The page echoing throughout the building made her knees go weak. Not a single person in the entire center could have missed hearing it. Hurrying her step, she dashed into the appointed room and told her coworker, "I have a page."

"I heard it. We'll talk later."

"Thanks." Leaving as hastily as she'd arrived, Pam made the first turn in the corridor before the reality of Sy's actually being there caught up with her. She ducked into an alcove to collect herself, because she was shaking like a leaf and knew in her soul that she could not face Sy in a weak and sniveling state.

In fact, she had never needed emotional strength more than she did now. This wasn't her idea, she didn't like what was happening and if Sy dared to imply anything else, she was going to let him have it. She hoped Miss Bertie would understand, should that occur.

Finally realizing that she could hide in this alcove all

day and still not feel calm, Pam squared her shoulders, lifted her chin and reentered the corridor leading to the lobby. Her determination to maintain the upper hand in this confrontation stayed with her until she was at the immense entrance of the lobby and saw Sy, and then everything within her went to hell.

He wasn't looking her way; he was near one of the huge front windows staring outside. He was gorgeous, tall and straight and all man in dark blue jeans, a blue-and-white-striped shirt and low-heeled black boots. His long hair was tied back with a leather string, and he was wearing sunglasses with black lenses.

There seemed to be a peculiar hush in the lobby, and Pam's eyes darted around to find out why. Everyone was watching her and watching Sy. People who shouldn't be in the lobby at all were peering around doors, and she even spotted Elliot, trying to remain inconspicuous behind a tall pillar.

"Good Lord," she mumbled in abject disgust. Obviously everyone who'd heard the page and hadn't been involved in something they couldn't leave for a few minutes had come to the lobby to see the show.

Well, maybe she'd give them one, she thought angrily. Maybe she just might stand their hair on end.

That blustering resolve weakened the closer she got to Sy, however.

Hearing approaching footsteps, he turned from the window, fully prepared to treat Pam respectfully but coolly until he knew what to do next.

But seeing her, looking into her beautiful green eyes and feeling her pull again completely destroyed his sensible intentions, and before he even knew what he was doing, he had pulled her into his arms and kissed her fully on the lips.

Hearing a collective gasp from everyone in the lobby, Pam permitted the kiss to last only a few seconds. She didn't permit herself to enjoy it, although she would die on the spot before giving *that* away to her nosy co-workers.

The one thing she couldn't control was the burning heat in her cheeks. Glaring up at Sy, she whispered furiously, "You still believe you can do anything you want! Let go of me, you cretin!"

It finally sank into Sy's brain that a dozen people were watching them. He'd embarrassed Pam in front of the people with whom she worked, and he was embarrassing himself.

But even red-faced, he felt a crazy kind of joy. Any woman trying to trap a man into marrying her would not be calling him names!

"Pam," he said in an undertone. "Will you marry me?"

Her eyes widened. "This wasn't my idea, Sy."

"May we talk about that later? Answer my question. Will you marry me?"

"You only want your baby," she whispered.

He knew at that moment that the baby was indeed his. "Yes," he said. "I want my child. I also want its mother to be my wife."

"For the sake of propriety."

"Call it what you will, Pam. Are you going to marry me?"

She turned her head just a little and again saw how avidly the people she'd known for years were watching. And she saw Elliot again, as well, for he was now standing in front of the pillar, in plain sight. She suddenly wanted all of them to think she was the happiest woman in the world, and while tears slid down her cheeks, she nodded her head and whispered, "Yes."

Sy misunderstood those tears and thought they signified

happiness, so he grabbed her into a big hug and shouted for all to hear, "She said yes!"

Elliot scowled and women whispered behind their hands to one another, but finally everyone crowded around Sy and Pam and offered congratulations. Pam's heart softened. Yes, they had talked about her behind her back, and some of them had believed Elliot's insulting fabrications, but they were still her friends. She smiled at them all, noticing that Elliot was no longer present.

"We're going to lunch," she announced then, and took Sy by the hand and led him outside. "Where are you parked?"

"Over there."

Pam let him hang on to her hand and open the car door for her. When he got in and grinned at her, though, she said coldly, "You can drop the act now. I know you don't want to marry me any more than I want to marry you, and we both know we're doing this only because Miss Bertie insisted on it."

Sy's face fell, but he quickly recovered and shot back at her, "Yeah, well, we can live with it. I can, anyway. Guess you're the only one who knows what you can live with." He started the car. "Where do you want to have lunch?"

"I don't. It was the only excuse I could think of to leave for a while. Just drive around, if you don't mind."

"Fine," Sy said stiffly. He drove from the parking lot to the street. Out of the corner of his eye he saw Pam wiping away tears. "What're you crying about?"

"What do you think I'm crying about?" she snapped.

"I couldn't begin to imagine," Sy drawled.

"I'm sure it couldn't have anything to do with being forced into a marriage I don't want," Pam said with scathing sarcasm.

"Hey, if you don't want to marry me, don't do it."

"Sure, make me the heavy. Dammit, I don't have a choice!"

"You've got a lot of choices. What about Elliot Young? He'd probably marry you in a New York second."

"Oh, don't be ridiculous. We can't stand the sight of each other."

"Didn't look like it to me that night at your apartment."

Pam turned to glare suspiciously at him. "Well, suppose you tell me how it did look to you."

Sy shrugged. "Pretty chummy."

"Are you insinuating something?"

Sy hesitated, but decided against even hinting that he'd wondered if the baby was his or Elliot's.

"No, I'm not insinuating anything, other than the fact that you and Elliot seemed to know each other pretty well."

Pam faced front again. "We did…a long time ago. I don't want to talk about it. It's in the past and that's a good place for it. Leave it there."

"You know, you're not being very nice about this."

"Oh, and I suppose you're just overjoyed."

"I'm taking it on the chin, Pam. You know, that's something I've had to learn how to do this summer. Learned my lessons pretty well, too, if I do say so myself."

Pam felt her anger fading. "Are you all right? Have you been doing your exercises every day?"

"Every day," he confirmed. "Can't you tell by looking at me?"

She ran her eyes over him from the top of his handsome head to the toes of his polished boots. "You are looking well. Are you still having spasms in your back?"

"Nope."

"None at all?"

"None. You see, I learned an awful lot from a spunky little gal this summer."

"You're talking about me."

"Who else?" Sy took a breath. "Pam, we're going to have a baby, and unless you change your mind, we're going to be married. Let's make the best of it, okay?" He knew now that Pam wasn't now, nor ever had been, in love with him, but he also knew that he would love her forever. They could make a go of it if they tried.

She startled him by bursting into tears. Her heart was permanently broken. "Making the best of it" was not how she had visualized her someday marriage. And it hurt so much to know that Sy would never love her the way she loved him. He was doing the honorable thing, because the Copes had always been honorable people. Actually, he was marrying her because Miss Bertie had flattened him this morning, the same way she'd flattened Pam yesterday.

But she, too, was an honorable person, and marrying the father of her child was the least she could do for a baby who hadn't asked to be brought into this wretched world.

Wiping her eyes, she nodded. "I'll try."

"I'll try, too, Pam."

"You can take me back to the center now."

"All right." Sy made a right turn. "When do you want to get together to plan the wedding?"

"This coming weekend would work, I guess," she said listlessly.

"Pam, I was thinking that we should get married this coming weekend."

"So soon?"

"Why put it off?"

"My job..."

"Hell, go back in there and quit your job. You're not going to keep on working, are you?"

"I...I haven't given that any thought." Confusion struck her. Quit her job? Her career? But she was going to have

a new career now, wasn't she? She was going to be a
mother, and raising a child was the most important job any
woman could ever do.

"Well, please do."

"Am I going to be living at the ranch?"

Sy looked at her as though she'd lost half her marbles.
"Where else would you live? Pam, you haven't given this
any thought."

She sighed. "No, I guess I haven't."

Sy shook his head in disbelief. And to think he'd been
worried about Pam plotting to marry a Cope. He was a
grade-A sap, that's what he was. Having reached the center's parking lot, he pulled into a space and stopped.

He turned to face Pam. "Let's make our plans right now.
I'd like to have a small wedding in Grandmother's church
this coming Saturday. Then we'll go somewhere afterward,
anywhere you want, and spend some time together away
from everyone else. What do you say?"

"That sounds...fine." Her voice was hoarse because of
the tears in her throat.

"Good, then it's settled. Think about quitting your job,
okay?"

"Yes, I'll think about it."

Sy leaned forward and kissed her on the forehead. "I'll
go by Grandmother's house before I leave town and tell
her about our plans."

"When did you start calling Miss Bertie 'Grandmother'?"

Sy looked taken aback. "I'm not sure. That's odd."

Pam sighed. "Lots of things are odd, Sy." Opening her
door, she got out. "Bye."

"I'll call you this evening."

"If you want."

Sy watched her walk into the building and realized that

he felt like shedding a few tears himself. If he ever said, "Pam, I've been in love with you for a very long time," what would *she* say?

He probably would never find out.

Clearing his throat, he put the car in gear and drove away.

Miss Bertie was ecstatic. "I'm going to call Pastor John right this minute about holding the wedding in the church this coming Saturday."

Sy knew there was no way to slow his grandmother down, let alone stop her, so he merely smiled and let her make the call.

She put down the phone with a bright smile for her grandson. "It's all arranged for two in the afternoon."

"Good. Now, do we order flowers, or what?"

"Would you like me to take care of the details?"

Sy laughed. "Yes, I would."

"Then you just go on your merry way and let me do it. Oh, I'll need to talk to Pam."

"Call the therapy center," Sy said wryly.

"She's working today, that's right. I forgot."

Sy was thinking hard, and after a few moments he said, "Gran, would you do something else for me?"

"Oh-oh, he called me Gran." Miss Bertie's eyes twinkled mischievously. "What do you want me to do, you scamp?"

"Convince Pam to quit working."

"She isn't planning to?"

"I'm not sure, but I think a dose of your special brand of nudging might sway her in that direction."

"You *are* a scamp. Special brand of nudging, indeed!" Miss Bertie then laughed. "Yes, I'll be happy to discuss it with Pam."

Sy humorously rolled his eyes. "She doesn't stand a chance against you, Miss Bertie. I know already that she'll soon be among the unemployed." He kissed his grandmother's cheek. "Bye. Gotta run."

"Goodbye, you scalawag!"

Humming happily, Miss Bertie began looking through the phone book for the number of her favorite florist shop. Sometimes life was just too wonderful for words. Sy married and happy on the ranch, Pam as her granddaughter-in-law and a great-grandbaby to look forward to in the bargain? Oh my, yes, life was indeed sweet.

Sixteen

Pam tried to keep her mind on her job that afternoon, but people kept interrupting her, either to congratulate her again or to ask questions. Some of her co-workers' questions were slyly put, as though she had a dirty little secret and they were cleverly attempting to find out what it was. In some cases Pam realized that her friends and so-called friends were connecting today's events to Elliot's gossip. About midafternoon she felt sick at heart. Yes, she had received some genuine good wishes, particularly from Retta, but for the most part she was picking up little more than abnormal—and perhaps even snide—curiosity from those who accosted her.

It struck her in one fell swoop: they were laughing at her behind her back! After all, who was she to land a fish as big as Sy Cope?

Sad to say, she felt very much that way herself. Without the baby, Sy would never have contacted her. They never would have seen each other again.

Around three she was on the verge of breaking down, and she gathered her things and went to the lobby to sign out. Katie Hand, who answered the telephone and kept an eye on the employees' comings and goings, raised an eyebrow.

"Got a heavy date with lover boy?" she inquired in a saccharine tone.

Pam had suddenly had enough. She looked Katie in the

eye. "Why I'm leaving early is none of your business, Katie. I'm gone, and that's all you need to know." She walked out with her head high.

Her courage came and went during the drive to her apartment. Memories of the summer, good and bad, flashed through her mind. Sy's good mood today gnawed at her. *I'm taking it on the chin, Pam.* She had no choice *but* to take it on the chin, but he did. Honorable ancestry or not, why had he acted as though they should both be happy over a shotgun wedding?

The answer came swiftly. Her baby was a Cope, and both Sy and Miss Bertie were willing to do anything to guarantee a close relationship with her child, even to making her a part of the Cope family!

Pam's lips thinned angrily. They were manipulating her into an ill-fated marriage, and just when, exactly, had she lost her last dram of courage?

Arriving home, she parked in the garage, lowered the door and stormed from her truck into the apartment. To hell with gossip, she thought fervently. She was *not* marrying Sy, and people could talk about her till their tongues fell off and she wouldn't care. She wasn't the first woman to bear a child without a husband, and she sure as hell wouldn't be the last!

Going directly to the kitchen phone, she reached for it to call the Cope ranch, when it started ringing. She grabbed it and brought it to her ear. "Hello!"

"Pam, are you all right? I phoned the therapy center and a woman said that you'd left for the day. I took a chance on your having gone home, but I instantly became worried that you might not be feeling well."

"Miss Bertie," Pam said weakly, and sank into a chair. She couldn't imagine a circumstance that would justify rudeness to Miss Bertie, not even when she knew so adamantly that the elderly woman was collaborating with Sy to get his child by any means. "I'm not ill, Miss Bertie."

"I'm certainly glad to hear that, my dear. Pam, I have everything arranged for Saturday. The wedding is set for two in the afternoon and Pastor John Fairmont will preside. I've ordered flowers—pink and white bud roses—and the rings you and Sy will exchange are family heirlooms. What I need to know is how many guests you wish to invite. I'm planning an intimate little reception at my home after the ceremony, and it would help so much if I knew how many people will be attending."

"I...I'm not sure," Pam stammered.

"Well, you can think about that and call me back." The longer Miss Bertie talked, the weaker Pam got. "Of course," Miss Bertie said, "you and Sy will have to obtain your marriage license tomorrow. A couple can't get married without a license, you know."

"No...they can't." *Oh, God, what am I going to do? It's all arranged.*

"Do you have an adequate dress, dear? I would be very pleased to take you shopping in the morning, if you don't. I'd like to see you wearing a lovely dress."

"I have a dress."

"What color, dear?"

"Pink."

"Perfect! Well, let me see. Have I covered everything? I believe so. Oh, I've been on the phone with Sy several times, and I'm sure you'll be receiving a call from him regarding the license."

Pam simply could not come up with a reply, and after a moment Miss Bertie said, "Pam? Are you still there?"

"Yes, Miss Bertie."

"Well, you probably have a million things to do, so I'll

say goodbye now. Call me when you decide on your guest list, dear.''

"Yes, Miss Bertie.''

"Goodbye, dear.''

"Goodbye, Miss Bertie.'' Pam put down the phone and then sat staring into space. It was several minutes before her mind started functioning again, and her first lucid thought was a rather panicky, I can't let this happen!

But neither could she lay siege to Miss Bertie's cheerful determination. Sy was going to have to deal with his grandmother, she couldn't do it. If that made her a coward, she thought, so be it.

Again she reached for the phone, and this time it didn't ring. She dialed the Cope ranch, Cal answered, and she asked to speak to Sy.

"Hold on, Pam,'' Cal said. "I think he's outside.''

"Thank you, Cal.'' Two or three minutes ticked by, and Pam gripped the phone with white knuckles. Finally she heard a door slam and footsteps, then Sy's voice in her ear.

"Pam?''

She got right to it, knowing that if she procrastinated for even a moment, she might never say it. "The wedding's off, Sy. We are not getting married on Saturday or any other day. Please tell Miss Bertie. That's all I had to say. Goodbye.'' She hung up.

"Pam, wait!'' But the phone was dead. "What in hell?'' Sy muttered. He banged the phone down and stood there trying to figure out Pam's startling change of attitude. Why was the wedding off? What had happened since he'd seen her only a few hours ago?

"Dammit, anyway,'' he mumbled. Fumbling with the phone book, he looked up the therapy center's number and dialed it. "Pamela Brooks, please,'' he said curtly.

"I'm sorry, sir, but Pam isn't here."

"Do you know where she is?"

"No, sir."

"Okay, thanks." He dialed Pam's home number and was surprised when she answered. But he wasn't in the best of moods and the first words out of his mouth were, "What in hell is going on?"

"Don't call me again, Sy." Pam hung up.

Cursing under his breath, Sy all but ran through the house and out to his car. She was going to talk to him if he had to tie her to a chair, he thought angrily, and he drove away fast enough that the wheels of his car spun and squealed.

Pam felt much better than she had all afternoon. She knew now what she was going to do with her life, or rather *not* going to do with it, and the fact that her future did not include a farce of a marriage was amazingly comforting. Not that she would ever completely get over Sy, but she would learn to live with feelings that would never see the light of day.

She made another decision and felt good about it, as well. She would never attempt to stop Sy from seeing his child or Miss Bertie from seeing her great-grandchild. Regardless of the ill will between her and her baby's father, every child deserved to know his family.

With those consoling thoughts in mind, Pam went to the bathroom and took a nice long shower. She would, of course, return to work in the morning, and she would announce to anyone who was interested—and she knew that most of her co-workers would be avidly interested—that she was not marrying Sy Cope. She might even include the fact of her pregnancy in that message, as everyone would figure it out very soon, anyhow. It was probably best to get it all out at one time. They could gossip their little hearts out, and they would, but then it would become old news and the gossips would go on to something else.

Stepping out of the shower, Pam toweled off and dried her hair. Inasmuch as she wasn't planning on leaving the apartment for the rest of the day, she put on a nightgown and bathrobe.

In the kitchen a short while later, she checked her refrigerator for something to fix for her dinner. She had plenty of fresh produce on hand and decided that steamed vegetables were as good as anything. Taking them to the sink, she began cleaning them for the steamer.

Chopping celery and carrots, she started thinking of Sy and wondered if he had called Miss Bertie yet. She hoped so, because until Miss Bertie was informed, the cancellation of the wedding really wasn't official. The idea of Miss Bertie still planning on a Saturday wedding and reception when there was going to be neither was disturbing for Pam, but she couldn't bring herself to phone Miss Bertie and tell her herself. That was for Sy to do. This whole fiasco was his fault, and he should be the one to correct it.

Someone leaned on her doorbell so that it didn't stop ringing, and her heart sank because she knew it was Sy at her door. She didn't have to open it, she realized. She didn't have to do *anything* she didn't want to do, and she wasn't going to, either.

But was she afraid to tell Sy to his face what she'd told him on the phone?

"No way," she declared out loud, and she marched through the apartment to the front door, still holding the butcher knife.

She yanked it open. "Do you think I'm deaf or something? Get your hand away from that doorbell!" Sy rudely

pushed past her. "Well, do come in," she drawled sardon-
ically, and slammed the door shut.

"I want to know what in hell's going on!"

"Don't you dare take that tone with me!" Pam waved
both hands in front of Sy's face, forgetting that one of them
held a large, sharp knife.

"What're you planning to do, scalp me?"

"What?" Seeing the knife, she dropped it on an end
table. "I'm sorry. I forgot I had it. I was chopping vegetables when the doorbell rang. And rang and rang and
rang," she added caustically. "Sy, you wasted your time
coming here, and I wish you'd leave."

"I'm not leaving until you explain yourself."

"I did that on the phone!"

"Like hell you did. You dropped your bomb and hung
up!"

"All right! You want to hear it all, fine! I am not marrying a man who thinks of no one but himself. I worked
hard this summer to make you well, and most of the time
you were wallowing in self-pity or lashing out at someone
because *you* would never be able to climb a stupid mountain again! Well, isn't that just too bad? Believe me, you
do not have my sympathy over something so utterly inane.
You are self-centered, completely insensitive and spoiled
rotten. I will not live your kind of life. And I will not marry
you just to satisfy your egocentric idea of nobility. I'm
perfectly capable of raising my baby alone, and I don't give
two whits what anyone will ever think about it, including
you. Does that answer your question?"

"Quite...clearly." Sy sank to the sofa and sat with his
forearms on his knees and his head down. "Did telling me
off make you feel better?" he finally asked, turning his
head to look at her.

Pam was still on her feet, and she felt her stomach sink

clear to her toes. Letting Sy have it should have lifted her spirits to the sky, but it hadn't. All she felt was a ponderous sadness, for herself, for her baby and for the Copes.

After a few moments Sy realized that she wasn't going to answer his question, which raised further questions in his mind. But he decided against asking them and said instead, "Pam, we didn't argue or disagree all the time this summer."

She took an unsteady breath. "No, not all the time, just most of the time."

"Pam, I know I was disagreeable and tough to deal with, but if you thought so, why did you…you know…make love with me?"

"Probably because I'm a fool," she said as she weakly sank onto a chair. It was strange how anger was no longer burning a hole in her stomach, she thought. Why wasn't she still angry with Sy?

"You're not a fool," he said quietly.

"Well, there are other names for women who behaved as I did."

"Don't say things like that."

"Are you telling me that *you* didn't think I was an easy mark?"

"I never thought that either of us did anything wrong. No, I never considered you an easy mark."

She shrugged. "You have your opinion, I have mine."

Sy raised his eyes to hers. "Can't you tell I've changed?"

"You're healthier, if that's what you mean."

"You know it's not what I mean. Pam, I hated the world after that accident. When you came along I was positive that I was going to be in a wheelchair for the rest of my life. Why would I think you could help me any more than

Jerry had? Besides, you were a woman, and I still had *some* pride left.''

"Where is this conversation going, Sy? I already knew everything you just said.''

Sy looked at her for a long time, and Pam looked back only because she was not going to let him daunt her. She was glad that she was no longer enraged, but she still was not going to permit Sy to intimidate her.

"You know a lot about me,'' he said, "but not everything.''

"I missed something? What was it? Did you throw another telephone when I wasn't looking?''

"No, I fell in love with you when you weren't looking.''

Pam's whole body went numb. When she was able to speak again, she scoffed, "You would even try that to get me to marry you? Let me tell you something, Sy. You don't have to marry me to have your child. I don't mean that you can have him, but you can see him as often as you wish. I don't intend to deprive my child of his father, or of his great-grandmother. You see, I understand how important family is to a person. At least you have Miss Bertie. I have no one.'' She took a breath. "But I will.''

"I appreciate your attitude about the baby, Pam, but I didn't say what I did to coerce you into marrying me. I was going to tell you how I felt about you the night...well, the night Elliot interrupted us right here in this apartment.''

Pam suddenly found it hard to breathe. He *had* been on the verge of saying something important that night, she remembered.

But then she also remembered the rest of that evening just as clearly. "You let Elliot's arrival stop you from telling me that you loved me? Sy, how can I believe something so...so silly?''

"I knew who he was because...because I read the letter

he sent you from Baltimore. I thought you were still in love with him.''

"You read my mail?'' She was appalled and showed it.

"I'm not proud of it, but yes, I did.''

"And from one letter, which, incidentally, said very little, and because I had made a date to have dinner with a man I'd known for many years, you decided that I must be in love with him.'' Sighing heavily, Pam laid her head back. "You're as big a fool as I am.''

"Meaning?'' Sy cautiously asked.

Pam got up and began pacing the carpet. "You want the whole truth? I might as well tell you everything. What have I got to lose at this point? *I* fell in love with *you*, probably the first day we met. Do you think I really cared that you threw that telephone? You staggered me, Sy. You shattered every image I'd previously had of the man I would someday fall in love with.''

Stunned, Sy got to his feet. "Pam...''

"No, let me finish. I felt it happening, and I tried very hard to stop it from happening, but it just kept getting worse. On top of that I met Miss Bertie and fell in love with her, too. Still, I told myself that you were nothing but an immature, self-serving grouch. When you said to jump, poor Cal jumped. You were nasty to him, to me and, I would imagine, to everyone else who had the misfortune of having to deal with you.''

She gave a gritty little laugh. "I vowed that before I left the Cope ranch I was going to tell you what a horrible patient you were.''

"But you weren't going to tell me you were in love with me.''

"Oh, I thought of doing that, too, but you made it impossible. Do you realize that immediately after we made love—both times—you talked about other women?''

"I most certainly did not!"

"You most certainly did!"

"Are you in love with me now?"

Pam stopped pacing and looked at him. "Let's not get into that, okay? This is all very serious to me, Sy, and I'm not sure it is to you."

He held out his hands in a helpless gesture. "How can I prove that it is?"

"I don't know. Frankly, I think we've talked long enough. Please leave now." She saw him walking toward her. "No, Sy, you're not going to influence me with a pass."

"This isn't a pass, you little idiot. I'm in love with you." Sy took her by the shoulders and pulled her up against himself.

"No," she moaned, because as she'd done twice before in his arms, she was losing all sense of reason. She felt the warmth of his breath in her hair, and her self-control slipped another notch.

"Pam, maybe you're right. Maybe we've both been fools, but should we let past mistakes destroy the future? My God, we're going to have a baby, and we love each other. Don't deny it, I know now that you do love me. Well, I love you, too. I have for a long time. I tried denial, same as you did. I kept asking myself if the feelings I had for you would last. Nothing ever had before—why would this?"

She leaned back to see his face. "Nothing ever lasted? Sy, what were you looking for?"

"Damned if I know, but I sure tried hard to find it." He laid his hand along her cheek. "Maybe it was you."

"When you were fifteen years old and jumping out of planes? No, I don't think it was me."

He smiled a little. "You're right, of course. Something

was driving me, but I have no idea what it was. That awful restlessness is gone, you know. I lost it sometime this summer.''

"How can you be sure? If nothing ever lasted..."

"That was before, Pam, this is now. You've known two men, each of them named Symon Jacob Cope. The better man came out on top. I could go on and on about that particular subject, and if you give me the chance, someday I will. Not now, though. We've got something a lot more important than that to discuss." Sy looked deeply into Pam's eyes. "You are the love of my life."

It was a declaration she hadn't been prepared to hear, and it affected her so strongly she felt breathless. "Oh, Sy," she whispered emotionally. "Am I really?"

"I've never been in love before."

She stared, she blinked, she stared, and then she exclaimed, "That is utter hogwash! Wait here." Leaving him openmouthed, she ran to her bedroom and dug into the bottom drawer of her nightstand. Running back to the living room, she held up an old copy of *Prominence Magazine.* "What about this?"

Sy looked disgusted. "Aw, hell, do you read that thing?"

Pam was flipping pages. "I certainly read this issue. Listen. 'When asked about his love life, Sy Cope laughed charmingly and said, *Lou, I fall in and out of love three times a week.*'" Pam's expression was accusing. "Did you say that?"

"Pam, you have to understand the kind of man I was then."

"That's what I'm trying to do. Did you tell Lou, whoever he or she is, that you fell in and out of love three times a week?"

"Lou is a woman, and she interviewed me for that article. It seemed like fun at the time, and I went along with it. I told her anything she wanted to hear, and when that issue came out naming me one of the world's most eligible bachelors, I laughed it off. Pam, I did not fall in and out of love three times a week. There were women, yes, and I'll tell you about every one of them, if you want to hear about it. But why would you?''

''I don't.'' Feeling just a little bit foolish, Pam looked down at the magazine in her hand. She didn't want to talk about Elliot, so why would Sy want to talk about old flames? But something still bothered her, and she had to bring it out in the open. ''You obviously lived a very glamorous life. Why would you fall in love with a woman like me?''

''You don't want to believe it, do you? You're in love with me, I've told you that I'm in love with you, and you don't want to believe it. Why not, Pam?''

It all came together then, hitting Pam with such force that she felt as though she'd just been struck. She took a breath and released it and wondered in her soul if she had the courage to tell Sy the truth.

''Why not, Pam?'' Sy repeated, almost sternly.

''Because…I'm afraid,'' she whispered.

''Afraid! Afraid of what?''

She couldn't hold it back any longer, and it came tumbling out of her mouth. ''You could have any woman you wanted!'' she cried.

''It doesn't appear that way to me, not when the one woman I do want is doing her best to argue me out of loving her.'' Sy had had enough of this ridiculous debate. He took the magazine out of Pam's hand and tossed it away, then put his arms around her. He felt her shiver against his chest, and he stroked her hair with a gentle touch. ''I used to wonder about love,'' he said softly. ''Not often, not all the time, but once in a while I'd see a couple that were so in love they seemed to glow. Pam, that's how you make me feel, as if I were glowing. Can't you put aside your fears and just accept that?"

"I...want to. Oh, Sy, I want to." She leaned back to see his face. "I keep wondering if we really know each other. Do you feel like you know me?"

"Yes, I know you. I know you're unselfish and intelligent, and I know you're as beautiful on the inside as you are on the outside." He smiled, albeit a bit wickedly. "And I know how passionate you can be." Slowly, with his eyes holding hers, he untied the sash of her robe. "I know that I want you," he said, smile gone, voice husky. "In my bed, at my side, as my wife."

Her legs had started trembling. She had asked every question, she'd voiced every doubt, and there was nothing left inside of her except love. Love for this man who had given her the highest highs and the lowest lows of her life throughout the summer.

"Yes," she whispered tremulously. "Yes to everything you just said."

A hot light appeared in Sy's eyes. "You'll marry me?"

"I'll marry you, I'll stand at your side through thick and thin, and I'll share your bed."

Overjoyed, he laughed. "Right now, let's share yours."

She slid her arms around his neck and laughed too, and it was the same bubbly laugh that Sy had heard when she had first come to the ranch. It sobered him, because it was his fault that she had stopped laughing.

"I'll never hurt you again," he said in a thick, teary voice.

Pam saw the moisture in his eyes and realized what a truly amazing moment this was. "If you cry, so will I," she said gently.

Sy shaped a shaky smile. "They're good tears, sweetheart. I'm happier than I've ever been."

She nestled contentedly against his chest. "Oh, Sy, so am I. So am I."

One stray thought gladdened her heart even more than it already was: And so will Miss Bertie be happy.

She was right. Miss Bertie was ecstatic.

*   *   *   *   *

Here's a preview of next month's

——World's Most——
Eligible Bachelors

Sheik Jefri
the exotic ruler of Jalameer from

THE SEDUCTIVE SHEIK
by
Tracy Sinclair

A large, burly man answered the Sheik's door. His suspicious gaze was a little disconcerting. Even after Holly had given her name and stated her business, he didn't invite her inside.

"I believe Sheik Jefri wishes to see me," she said firmly. "Will you please tell him Holly Barnett is here."

Before he could give her an argument, the Sheik came out of the next room, rolling up his sleeves. He had removed his jacket and tie, and unfastened the first few buttons of his white shirt. The opening revealed part of a broad chest shadowed by dark hair. The effect was very sexy.

The man lived up to his reputation, Holly thought. No wonder women swooned over him. He was more than just handsome. That lean body was as taut as an athlete's. He was a big man, but he moved with the grace of a dancer— or perhaps a stalking jungle animal.

A tiny shiver ran up her spine. There was something almost feral in his unblinking inspection of her, as though the rules of civilized society didn't apply to him. But that was crazy, she told herself. He was one of the most urbane, sophisticated men in the world.

Holly's evaluation was correct. The Sheik was very polished, but he was also used to getting what he wanted. And he couldn't help feeling a stab of desire as he stared at Holly. She was incredibly lovely with that long mane of auburn hair drawn back from the delicate face of an angel.

He wanted to free her hair from its restraining band and run his fingers through the shining strands. And then he wanted to remove those severe clothes she wore and caress the lovely body they concealed. Her long, slender legs promised beguiling perfection.

A bad idea, of course. One did not mix romance with business. It would make things awkward if he had to fire her, which was entirely possible.

"You aren't what I expected," he said finally.

"I realize that you aren't used to seeing women in management positions," she began carefully. "But I think you'll find that I'm very competent. The Sunset Palms is one of the best run hotels in the city."

"Yet you had a crisis today."

"A hotel this size has many of them. The important thing is that I handled it."

"Tell me about it."

Holly explained what had happened and the way she resolved the problem. "I'm afraid that sooner or later the Contessa will need more care than we can give her. She's a lovely lady, but she's getting more and more erratic."

"She sounds like my Aunt Fatawa."

His unexpected grin transformed his entire face. Holly could see the devilish charm that had attracted so many women. The intimidating imperiousness disappeared as his eyes brimmed with laughter. They weren't black like his hair, as she had thought, but a very dark blue that lightened or darkened according to his moods.

"I'm glad you understand why I wasn't there to meet you this noon," she said, feeling more relaxed. Everything was going better than she expected. Underneath that autocratic manner was a man like all the rest. She could handle him, Holly thought confidently. "I hope you received a proper welcome." She smiled.

The Sheik's dark eyes were enigmatic. "Do you consider yourself a good judge of character?"

Holly's slim body tensed. It had been a mistake to dismiss him as just another playboy to be charmed into submission. The man was sharper than she thought. While she looked for a safe path through the minefield, a pleasant looking man came from one of the other rooms.

"You have a telephone call, Your Highness," he said.

"Why are you bothering me with it? Take a message."

"I thought you might want to speak to Miss Carmody," the man murmured.

The Sheik's frown was replaced by a pleased expression. "Tell her I'll be right with her." He looked at the thin gold watch on his wrist and said to Holly, "We'll have to postpone our talk. Come back in half an hour." Without waiting for a reply, he stood and strode into the other room.

Holly left the apartment fuming over being dismissed like a servant! She held a position of importance in this hotel. Their meeting should have taken precedence over a phone call from an oversexed blonde. "Miss Carmody" was undoubtedly Annissa Carmody, the famous supermodel. Well, maybe she'd keep the Sheik so busy he'd let Holly do her job without interference.

This March Silhouette is proud to present

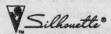

SENSATIONAL

MAGGIE SHAYNE
BARBARA BOSWELL
SUSAN MALLERY
MARIE FERRARELLA

This is a special collection of four complete novels for one low price, featuring a novel from each line: Silhouette Intimate Moments, Silhouette Desire, Silhouette Special Edition and Silhouette Romance.

Available at your favorite retail outlet.

Look us up on-line at: http://www.romance.net

PSSEN

If you enjoyed what you just read,
then we've got an offer you can't resist!

Take 2 bestselling love stories FREE!
Plus get a FREE surprise gift!

Clip this page and mail it to Silhouette Reader Service™

IN U.S.A.	IN CANADA
3010 Walden Ave.	P.O. Box 609
P.O. Box 1867	Fort Erie, Ontario
Buffalo, N.Y. 14240-1867	L2A 5X3

YES! Please send me 2 free Silhouette Romance® novels and my free surprise gift. Then send me 6 brand-new novels every month, which I will receive months before they're available in stores. In the U.S.A., bill me at the bargain price of $2.90 plus 25¢ delivery per book and applicable sales tax, if any*. In Canada, bill me at the bargain price of $3.25 plus 25¢ delivery per book and applicable taxes**. That's the complete price and a savings of over 10% off the cover prices—what a great deal! I understand that accepting the 2 free books and gift places me under no obligation ever to buy any books. I can always return a shipment and cancel at any time. Even if I never buy another book from Silhouette, the 2 free books and gift are mine to keep forever. So why not take us up on our invitation. You'll be glad you did!

215 SEN CNE7
315 SEN CNE9

Name	(PLEASE PRINT)	
Address	Apt.#	
City	State/Prov.	Zip/Postal Code

* Terms and prices subject to change without notice. Sales tax applicable in N.Y.
** Canadian residents will be charged applicable provincial taxes and GST.
  All orders subject to approval. Offer limited to one per household.
  ® are registered trademarks of Harlequin Enterprises Limited.

SROM99   ©1998 Harlequin Enterprises Limited

A marriage of convenience?

SPOUSE FOR HIRE

This January, don't miss our newest three-story collection about three resourceful women who hire husbands for a limited time. But what happens when these three handsome, charming and impossibly sexy husbands turn out to be too good to let get away? Is it time to renegotiate?

THE COWBOY TAKES A WIFE
by *Joan Johnston*

COMPLIMENTS OF THE GROOM
by *Kasey Michaels*

SUTTER'S WIFE
by *Lee Magner*

Available January 1999
wherever Harlequin and Silhouette books are sold.

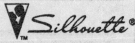

HARLEQUIN®
Makes any time special ™

Silhouette®

Look us up on-line at: http://www.romance.net   PSBR199

MEN at WORK

All work and no play?
Not these men!

January 1999
SOMETHING WORTH KEEPING by Kathleen Eagle
He worked with iron and steel, and was as wild as the mustangs that were his passion. She was a high-class horse trainer from the East. Was her gentle touch enough to tame his unruly heart?

February 1999
HANDSOME DEVIL by Joan Hohl
His roguish good looks and intelligence drew women like magnets, but Luke Branson was having too much fun to marry again. Then Selena McInnes strolled before him and turned his life upside down!

March 1999
STARK LIGHTNING by Elaine Barbieri
The boss's daughter was ornery, stubborn and off-limits for cowboy Branch Walker! But Valentine was also nearly impossible to resist. Could they negotiate a truce...or a surrender?

Available at your favorite retail outlet!

MEN AT WORK™

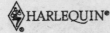 

Look us up on-line at: http://www.romance.net

PMAW4

Bestselling author

LINDSAY McKENNA

continues the drama and adventure of her popular series with an all-new, longer-length single-title romance:

MORGAN'S MERCENARIES

HEART OF THE JAGUAR

Major Mike Houston and Dr. Ann Parsons were in the heat of the jungle, deep in enemy territory. She knew Mike's warrior blood kept him from the life—and the love—he silently craved. And now she had so much more at stake. For the beautiful doctor carried a child. His child...

Available in January 1999, at your favorite retail outlet!

Look for more MORGAN'S MERCENARIES in 1999, as the excitement continues in the Special Edition line!

Silhouette®

PSMORGMERC

Look us up on-line at: http://www.romance.net